RED DOVE
of
MONTEREY

Old California Series
—Book One—

RED DOVE
of
MONTEREY

STEPHEN BLY

CROSSWAY BOOKS • WHEATON, ILLINOIS
A DIVISION OF GOOD NEWS PUBLISHERS

Red Dove of Monterey

Copyright © 1998 by Stephen Bly

Published by Crossway Books
        a division of Good News Publishers
        1300 Crescent Street
        Wheaton, Illinois 60187

Cover illustration: Dick Bobnick

Cover design: Cindy Kiple

First printing 1998

Printed in the United States of America

ISBN 1-58134-004-4

Library of Congress Cataloging-in-Publication Data
Bly, Sephen A., 1944-
   Red Dove of Monterey / Stephen Bly.
      p.   cm. (Old California : bk. 1)
   ISBN 1-58134-004-4 (alk. paper)
   1. California—History—To 1846—Fiction. I. Title. II. Series: Bly,
Stephen A., 1944- Old California: bk. 1.
PS3552.L93R43 1998
813'.54—dc21   98-16580

11	10	09	08	07	06	05	04	03	02	01	00	99	98
15	14	13	12	11	10	9	8	7	6	5	4	3	2	1

For My California Girls
Lois Margaret & Michelle Dawn

To give light to them that sit in darkness
and in the shadow of death. . . .

LUKE 1:79 (*KJV*)

One

The gentle strum of the unseen guitar across the plaza below the veranda kept time with the crashing surf as it broke on the distant shore. Two black-shawled women sat on a worn wooden bench and stared at the moon's gentle reflection on the bay.

"Doña Alena Louisa, would you like to come dance with me tonight?" The words filtered up through the shadows like chords from a favorite melody.

Alena leaned forward but could not see anyone. "Don Fernando? Is that you?"

"Do you have others who pursue you to dance?" he called out.

The older woman next to Alena held a single finger to her smiling lips.

"Perhaps," Alena replied.

"What is your answer?"

"Where is the fandango taking place?"

"In my heart, *conchita!*"

The older woman rolled her soft brown eyes toward the night sky.

"You would have me dance with you to the tunes of Don Ronaldo's guitar?" Alena challenged.

"Yes, there is sweet irony in that, is there not?"

"I'm not sure Don Ronaldo would think so."

"He is young. What can I say? You did promise me a dance before you leave."

Alena thought about walking to the railing. But didn't. "Don Fernando, my promises are true. You will definitely dance with me before I leave."

"With that thought my heart rejoices. I look forward to that time."

"As do I, Don Fernando."

"Perhaps you would like me to come join you on the veranda?" he said.

Señora María Martina Cabrillo called out in a voice a full octave lower than Alena's. "Perhaps that place is already occupied."

"Madre mío! I didn't know you were there!"

"Obviously. Now why don't you find something else to do before you embarrass yourself, Doña Alena, and me."

The sound of leather boots striking the cobblestone courtyard below gradually faded, leaving only the sound of a distant guitar and the ever-present breakers.

This time Señora Cabrillo's voice was soft, gentle. "Doña Alena Louisa, you should be on that sailing ship."

With the only other light filtering from lanterns inside the tile-roofed white adobe house, the younger woman's thick red hair almost glowed. "I've made up my mind, Doña María Martina. I must stay." The night breeze felt pleasantly cool but not cold on Alena's face. The air tasted sweet but not sickening. And the black lace around her neck tickled some but did not torment.

Alena knew without looking that Doña María Martina's brown eyes danced and her wide smile teased. In a voice well trained for only one other person to hear, the gray-haired lady said softly, "You are as stubborn as Doña Joséfa Carrillo!"

"But I thought Doña Joséfa ran away with a sea captain and eloped." Alena tugged on her dangling earrings as she avoided the gaze of the other woman.

The strong, firm hand of Doña María Martina Cabrillo patted Alena's knee. "She did. You see how stubborn she was?"

Both women laughed.

"It is every little California girl's love story and every father's nightmare," Doña María Martina added.

"But I don't want to run away. I want to stay right here." The fragrance of pines and cypress behind the home seemed to tumble down the gradual slope toward the sea and collide with the aroma of the surf and sand right in the middle of the courtyard. That mix of smells was, for Alena, the fragrance of California.

"Ah, but there is a very great difference. Doña Joséfa was a Californian. Her grandmother was no less than Doña María Feliciana Arballo de Gutierrez herself."

Alena reached up in the darkness to unbutton the collar of her black dress and fingered the warm gold cross that dangled against her bare chest. "And me?"

"You are from Boston. You are Alena Louise Tipton, the nineteen-year-old daughter of Capt. Robert Vermont Tipton, formerly of Boston. Lately, a merchant in Monterey in Alta California. For you to leave on a sailing ship would be to go home. It is only natural after the death of your father for you to return."

"I am now a Californio!" Alena declared, then leaned her head on the wool shawl that covered the older woman's shoulder. "Doña María Martina, if I were to leave, who would your sons try to impress with their bravado and cunning?"

The slightly heavy woman slapped her gold-ring-covered hands upon her own knees and laughed. "It is a sad fact but true! Fernando and Ronaldo would rather see your winsome smile than eat."

"But not Don Francisco?"

"Don Francisco is an old man. He has *carne asado* and tortillas *de maiz* in his head."

"He has been totally infatuated with you, Doña María Martina, for nearly forty years."

"You see? It proves my point." Señora María Martina Cabrillo waved her arms at the distant breakers. "Look at the moonlight on the foam of the waves as they break on the sand, *conchita*. They look like ruffled hems on a dark blue dancing dress, do they not?"

"Do you ever get tired of staring at the ocean?"

"Never. But I am only a young woman of fifty-three. Perhaps when I am old, I will tire of it."

"Don Francisco told me you were forty-three."

"Don Francisco is a liar. A gray-haired, handsome, charming liar. I am fifty-three. My bones remind me of it every day. I was born in Monterey. I could never live anywhere else." Doña María Martina brushed her red and black skirt down across her knees. "Fernando said you rode El Blanco a long ways today."

"I needed time to think. I rode to Punta de los Cipres. Each meadow along the way is so beautiful."

"They are majestic, lonely places," Doña María Martina observed. "I do not like traveling alone."

"I had a long talk with the Lord," Alena announced.

"What did you and *El Señor* decide?"

"I am going to stay in California and run my father's business."

Señora María Martina Cabrillo slipped her hand into Alena's. The older woman's palm felt warm and soft, her gold rings cold and hard. "I know," she murmured. "I am glad."

Alena squeezed the woman's hand. "Glad? You've threatened to have me arrested by the *alcalde* if I wasn't on that ship! You as much as told me I could not live with you anymore if I stayed. You had Lupe and Manuela pack my trunks. And now you say you are glad that I decided to stay?"

"I was testing you, *mi dulcita*. I wanted you to have every opportunity to leave. It was a promise I made to your father on his deathbed."

Alena thought about the one small gold ring on her little finger and began to twist it with her thumb. "My brother Robert is busy with his business and family in Boston. Walter is sailing out of the Sandwich Islands. And Henry? Only the Lord in heaven knows where he is! There is no one else to keep this business going."

Señora Cabrillo released her hand and adjusted the shawl on her shoulders. "Yes, well, whoever heard of a beautiful young lady running a hide and tallow business?"

"Yes, and whoever heard of a widow leaving home and towing her little children across a thousand miles of desert to start a new life on the edge of the earth? But Doña María Feliciana did it. California has always been populated with women who are free enough and talented enough to do just about anything they please. I intend to carry on that tradition."

Doña María Martina stood and walked to the wooden rail of the covered veranda. She gazed down into the evening-darkened red-tiled courtyard fountain. "But you have only been in California for three years. Has its enchantment already seeped into your bones?"

Alena stood and felt her right leg tingle where she had had it folded beneath her. She swayed toward the railing. "Some need only to sip the wine to feel its full effect."

"You are beginning to sound like Don Francisco. He thinks of you as his own child."

"You two should have had a daughter."

"We had two, but they both died before they were ten."

"I didn't know that." Alena slipped her arm around the shorter woman's shoulder. "I am so sorry."

"It is a beautiful and lonely land. You are right about that. It is also an unforgiving land. An American ship pulled into the harbor to celebrate the Fourth of July. The *alcalde* refused to quarantine the passengers even though they came from San Blas and had been exposed to the disease. Both of my daughters caught cholera and died within two weeks of each other."

"Are those their graves at Punta Poco?"

"Yes. That is another reason I can never leave Monterey."

Tears welled up in the corners of Alena's eyes. "I buried my father here also." Her voice came out a soft whimper.

"Yes, but you have your life ahead of you. Perhaps California will be too quiet for you."

"There are always mysteries in our wonderful California."

"What are you thinking of, *mi dulcita?*" Senora Cabrillo probed.

Alena patted the older woman's bare arm. "I received an interesting dispatch."

"When did a mail ship arrive?"

"This came from the interior," Alena reported.

"A love note?"

Alena laughed aloud. "No. It was addressed to father. Just a piece of tanned cowhide about the size of a tortilla, with RA branded on one side next to "four dollars and fifty cents—San Juan Bautista—June"

"A hide rancher, no doubt." Señora Cabrillo waved a ring-clad hand. "What is the mystery in that?"

"Perfect penmanship."

"What?"

"This man writes like a schoolteacher," Alena said.

"An American schoolteacher," Señora Cabrillo observed.

"How do you know he's American?"

"He wrote June instead of *Junio.*"

Alena folded her hands in her lap and leaned against the back of the bench. "Have you ever known a hide rancher with perfect penmanship?"

"I have known very few who could write at all."

Alena's voice sparkled. "You see, it *is* a mystery!"

Alena watched one of the Cabrillos' dark-skinned Indian servant girls sprint across the darkened courtyard below. *I wonder if I will ever feel at ease wearing a short-sleeved blouse with a scooped neck and running barefoot across the tile? It looks comfortable. Clothes are supposed to be comfortable, aren't they?*

Alena fiddled with the gold cross around her neck. For several moments neither woman spoke.

"What are you dreaming of, *conchita?*" Señora Cabrillo probed.

"I was thinking of a day years ago when I received this gold cross as a gift." She held out the necklace. "I was given a promise from Scripture that day, too."

"What kind of promise?"

"A secret one that I cannot share."

"A personal mystery? That is good. All women should retain an element of mystery!"

Alena let the smooth cross slip out of her fingers and rest on her chest. *I cannot tell her that I am to "give light to them that sit in darkness and in the shadow of death." She would not think it applies to this land.*

Nor do I.

Doña María Martina leaned over and tugged Alena's head

lower. "Is Ronaldo going to play the guitar all night? Let us hope that he doesn't begin to sing."

"He is a fine singer."

"He will never sing as sweetly as Don Francisco."

"Doña María Martina, how long does it take for a woman to know she's in love?"

"In love? Oh, my! La Paloma Roja has a lover? Now that would be news indeed. Doña Alena Louisa, are you in love?"

"Perhaps. But you didn't answer my question. How long does it take?"

"Well, if you love someone, no wonder you do not want to leave California. It took me one dance with Don Francisco to know that I loved him."

"All right. One dance would mean about one hour then. You knew you were in love within one hour?"

"Sí."

"Well, I am in love with . . ."

Señora Cabrillo held her breath and leaned closer.

"In love with . . . California! I have been here three whole years, and my affection for it has not waned. These have been the most stimulating, adventuresome, yet peaceful years of my life. I have learned the language, the culture . . . and the dance. I love it all."

"I am greatly relieved. I thought you were going to tell me about a man."

"I would not have been able to hide that from you."

"I was frightened that I was losing my skill of knowing all the gossip. I am glad you love California. Yes, it is a wonderful land. But you are quite young. The peace will not last. Don Francisco says the Americanos are coming. Last year Señor Bartleson led over thirty people here from the United States. Ronaldo reports that twice that many have come this year. If that continues, you Americanos will have us Californians outnumbered in ten years. Then the troops will come. Not phony survey parties like Captain Fremont's but regular troops. Troops ready for war."

"I know there is much talk in the East of annexing Texas and all the land to the sea. But what does it matter whether the government is in Washington or in Mexico City? This is California. It

is like no other land on earth. It will always be California," Alena
triumphed.

"You are right. I can see it in your eyes even in the dark and
hear it in your voice. You are in love."

"With California?"

"Yes, with our precious California. I am glad you stayed, *conchita*. Very glad you stayed."

Both women watched a carriage with dull lanterns rumble up
the stone street. It was one of only half a dozen carriages in all of
Alta California. Following the carriage were several mounted
horsemen. "The *alcalde* is leaving late tonight?" Alena asked.

"Don Francisco said he was going to the *presidio* at Yerba
Buena to bid farewell to the Russians."

"They are all leaving Fort Ross?"

"Don Juan Sutter has bought them out."

Alena walked back to the bench. The hard leather heels of her
lace-up boots kept time with the guitar that now seemed to be
moving closer. "I will go to San Juan Bautista Friday," she
announced. "It is time to buy hides and tallow."

Doña María Martina retreated to her side. "We will go with
you."

"That is not necessary. I feel quite safe on the road. I can take
Don Manuel with me."

"And who will oversee your warehouse? You must leave
Manuel here. Don Francisco needs to talk with Don José Castro,
and we can attend worship at the mission. It is Padre Estában's seventy-fifth birthday. We will go with you. It does not hurt for a
young lady to have someone to look after her."

"You mother me, Doña María Martina. I will be spoiled by your
kindness."

"You are the only one left. I have already spoiled all the others. Besides, you are almost the only friend I have who is not a rel-
ative . . . yet!" she laughed and tugged her black wool shawl off her
head and onto her shoulders. Her voice was always kind, soft,
encouraging. "If you insist on staying in California, I will have to
find you a husband."

"Oh no, I will do my own looking, thank you. He must be devout, bold, and handsome, yet tender and compassionate."

"Perhaps you have not heard, *mi dulcita*—San Francisco Assisi has died," Señora Cabrillo laughed.

"He does not have to be Saint Francis. Yet that would be nice, wouldn't it?"

"It will not be easy to find such a perfect young man in California."

Alena glanced down at her thin hands. *I wonder if my fingers will ever be fat and covered with gold rings?* "Then I will just have to search many years. I am in no hurry."

Señora Cabrillo sat with her back straight like a young woman waiting to be asked to dance. "And you will end up like Doña María Concepción Argüello."

Alena gave a shallow, hesitant laugh. "I do not intend to become a nun."

"Neither did Doña María Concepción Argüello. But when Count Rezanov did not come back, what choice did she have? How was she to know he died on his way to Rome to get permission from the Holy Father?"

"That is a point well taken. If I am not married by the time I am twenty-five, I will enlist your assistance," Alena agreed with a smile.

With the air of a queen, Señora Cabrillo pronounced, "Twenty."

With the confidence of a pirate, Alena demanded, "Twenty-seven!"

"Twenty-seven? *Conchita*, what kind of compromise is that? You are going the wrong way."

"I know!" Alena raised her narrow nose in a teasing smirk. "I do not barter well."

"Twenty-five then," Doña María Martina conceded.

"I accept your proposal."

"My proposal? It was *your* proposal! Do you know what I believe, Doña Alena Louisa?"

"What?"

"I believe you will do very well in the hide and tallow business. You know how to get your way."

"Thank you."

"You have worn me out, *mi dulcita*. I believe I will go to bed and listen to the old man snore." The older woman stood but put her hand on Alena's shoulder and motioned for her to remain seated.

"Sometimes I can hear Don Francisco even at the other end of the house," Alena reported.

"Yes, it is terrible. But there is one thing worse than having a snoring man in your bed."

"What is that?"

"Having no man in your bed."

"Doña María! A woman of your age!"

"It is the climate. It makes old women feel young. California is a land for lovers, *conchita*." Doña María Martina leaned over to Alena and kissed her right cheek, then her left. "The fog will roll in soon. Don't get chilled, *mi niña*."

"Yes, Mama. It is true, isn't it? You could never leave Monterey . . . or California, could you?"

"Never. When a woman's heart is in the land, she can never leave. I will stay. You will also stay."

"I know. We are hopeless, aren't we?"

"Hopeless and happy. I could do worse. Very much worse. Now please go stand by the edge of the veranda so Ronaldo can see your silhouette. I am sure he is waiting for me to leave so he can sing you a song."

"Don't you want to stay and listen?"

"Oh, please. Spare me. I have had to listen to him practice this song for months. I could not stand to hear it again."

"Ronaldo is very courteous and sweet. He is like a brother."

"I assure you, his thoughts of you are not brotherly. Good night, *mi corazón*."

"Good night, Doña María Martina."

By the time the fog rolled up from Monterey Bay and blocked the view of the distant moonlit ship in the harbor, Don Ronaldo had finished his song three times, and Alena Louise Tipton was in her room, sitting at the rustic oak dresser combing her wavy red hair that hung a few inches below her shoulders. She had lost count of the strokes.

So La Paloma Roja . . . the Red Dove of Monterey has decided to stay. Is that because you are treated like a princess? Or is it some divine calling? Perhaps I have a divine calling to be treated like a princess.

Forgive me, Lord. I know that is not true. Life is more than parties, dances, and celebrations.

At least, my life should be.

Alena closed the shutters on her windows and then blew out the tallow lantern. With only a thin wool blanket over her flannel gown, she lay on her back and folded her hands across her stomach.

In the distance Don Francisco stopped snoring.

Either Doña María Martina rolled him over . . . or she woke him up.

Lord, I do not know if it is Yankee stubbornness or Your leading that keeps me in California. But without Your constant care, I will surely fail. Have mercy on me.

Again.

This must surely be some of the most beautiful land You ever created. Yet it's wild . . . almost unoccupied.

I know the hide business will not last forever. They are right. Someday people will find out about this land, and it will fill up quickly.

But until then, I will listen to the pound of the surf, I will feel the rush of wind in my hair, and I shall feel the powerful gallop of a stallion beneath me.

May it last a good, long time.

That is all I ask.

That . . . and the companionship of a strong man with a gentle touch and a heart that loves You.

Really loves You.

The long-legged, gangly pilgrim with big feet and large hands who tramped down the steep boulder-strewn Río de las Plumas Cañón was only the second traveler Wilson Merced had seen come over the Sierra Nevadas since last September.

For Merced, it was two men too many.

From the safe cover of the pine trees, he and Echo Jack sat on their horses and watched the stranger's approach through the lens of the cherrywood and brass spyglass. The hatless man's hair was wild, uncombed, pine-needle-infested. It framed a hawkish nose and dirt-caked forehead. The bushy, dark beard looked tobacco-stained and greasy. A clay pipe was lodged in his teeth but showed no signs of being lit.

The man carried a worn canvas knapsack over his left shoulder and a leather powder pouch under his right. He toted a muzzle-loading rifle. Merced noticed that the man's boots were merely rawhide pieces pulled up and tied around his knees.

The hiker's countenance looked permanently locked in melancholy. His clumsy, ambling gait revealed that he would probably look awkward no matter how scrubbed up, no matter what outfit he wore.

Merced moved the spyglass up the canyon behind the man, searching every boulder, tree, and thicket for signs of other hikers. Nothing moved. Just ridge after ridge of mountains stretched up to the east, each more distant and taller than the previous until they stood—granite-faced, treeless, and snowcapped—touching the heavens.

Merced handed the telescope to his companion.

Echo Jack, with buckskin pants and white muslin shirt unbuttoned halfway down his hairless chest, chewed on a grass stem. "El Padrón, you want me to chase off this skunk?"

Merced rubbed the neck of his sorrel stallion, settling him down. "I reckon he'll be rather aromatic, won't he?"

"Have you ever met a pilgrim who wasn't?"

"Nope. Just where do you aim to chase him?"

The black-haired Echo Jack swung his right leg over his horse's neck and rested it near the saddle horn. He pulled a long-bladed buckhorn knife from the stiff tooled-leather leggings that stretched from his ankles to just below his knees. "I'll chase him back to Missouri."

Merced, sitting straight in the saddle, tugged at the dusty black silk cravat double-tied around his neck but never took his eyes off the hiker. "This one's from Arkansas."

"How can you tell?"

"The rope belt, the knife in his homemade boots, the bags under his eyes, and the rounded, drooping chin."

"You can see that from here?"

"Yep." Merced rubbed the back of his neck. It felt very dirty. *Actually, he doesn't look a whole lot different from me, the last time I crossed the Sierras.*

"You want me to kill him?"

Even in the shade of the trees, the hot summer sun made the air feel stuffy and stale. "Nope." Merced breathed deeply and pulled out the .40-caliber, octagon-barreled Paterson Colt revolver from his wide leather belt. He cocked the hammer back and pointed it at the approaching stranger.

Echo Jack slipped his right foot back into the tapadera-covered stirrup and pulled a carbine from his fringed deerskin sheath. "You going to shoot him?"

Merced turned in the saddle with a slow, sly smile. "Of course not."

"Then Piedra will have another mouth to feed."

"I reckon he will. I just don't want to startle him into taking a potshot at us." Merced tugged the brim of his flat-crowned black felt hat a little lower in the front. "Maybe if he sees my gun, he'll be slow to use his."

"That's what you said about the Frenchman on the delta."

"That bullet wound gave him character."

"It gave him a stiff shoulder for the rest of his life and a massive case of vengeance."

Wilson Merced lightly touched the points of his two-inch rowels to the tall horse's flanks, and the horse loped out of the trees toward the man. Echo Jack followed on his buckskin stallion.

The hiker lifted a rifle to his shoulder and then quickly lowered it. He trotted toward the horsemen along a narrow deer trail through foot-tall dry brown grass.

"Mister! Mister! Glory be to the heavens!" The man's voice was cracked and hoarse. "In God's name, I can't tell you how glad I am to see you!"

Merced kept his revolver steady and stared at the man's dirt-caked eyes. The stranger's buckskin shirt hung outside his trousers, belted with a frayed rope. Dirty skin showed at several rips and tears. The hiker glanced over at Echo Jack and back at Merced. "Either of you speak American?"

"Do you speak Spanish?" Merced asked, standing in his stirrups, towering over the man on the ground.

"No."

"That's too bad. You're in Mexico now."

The man pulled the unlit pipe from his mouth and dropped it into the tattered pocket of what was once a heavy wool coat. "Mexico? I thought this was California."

"It is," Merced informed him. "And that makes it Mexico."

The man, who looked a worn-out forty, brushed his chapped lips with dirty bare fingers that poked through worn leather gloves. "Yeah, yeah, I know that. You really are from the States?"

A covey of quail scurried toward the trunk of an oak tree to the right of the evergreen, but Merced kept his eyes and his gun on the man. "I'm from Tennessee."

"Well, I'll be. Ain't that grand? I made it to California, and the first person I meet is a fella from Tennessee!" He spied out Echo Jack.

"I'm not from Tennessee," the brown-complected man declared.

Merced waved his five-shot revolver like a pointing stick. "This is Echo Jack, my ranch foreman."

The man brushed a pine needle from his tattered jacket as if it would improve his appearance. "Is he Mexican?"

Merced didn't smile. "Mexican, Indian, and part grizzly."

"You don't say!"

"Yeah, but he's a hundred percent Californio."

The man shifted the weight of the canvas pack, then looped his right thumb in his rope belt. "You say you got a ranch? How far away is it? I ain't seen a building since I left Fort Hall."

Wilson Merced released the hammer on his gun and shoved it back into his belt. "You've been on the ranch for two days."

"No foolin'. The cattle around here belong to you?"

"Most of them."

The man looked down at the rawhide wrapped around his feet.

"Look, mister, I want to be square with you straight up. I killed one of your cows two days ago and jerked some meat."

"And made some boots?" Echo Jack chimed in.

"Yeah, I wore the last ones out on these blasted boulders. Anyway, I want to pay you off for that cow."

"No man goes hungry around here. There's no charge," Merced replied.

"Thanks, mister. You can't imagine how good it feels to have someone to talk to . . . even if one of 'em is . . ." He stared over at Echo Jack.

"Even if one is quite handsome?" The half-breed flashed his large white teeth but rested his right hand on the buckhorn handle of his sheathed hunting knife.

"Eh, yeah . . . that's sort of what I meant." The man addressed Merced. "I'm Carty Parkins from Arkansas. And who might you be, mister?"

"He's *El Patrón*," Echo Jack replied.

"I don't speak Mexican. What does that L'Pardon mean?"

"It means he's the boss."

"You speak purdy good American for a . . ."

"For a handsome man?" Again a wide grin and a hand resting on the handle of the knife.

"Yeah . . . something like that."

"My name's Wilson Merced. You're on Rancho Alázan property. Have you got a passport or some kind of papers?"

"A passport? What do I need a passport for?"

"Mr. Parkins, if you intend to live permanent in California, you will need to go to Monterey and file papers with the governor. Of course, if you're just passing through, say on your way to Oregon, well, Mr. Sutter can take care of that down at his fort at New Helvetia." The words flowed out of Merced's mouth like an often-used speech.

Carty Parkins rubbed his rawhide-covered toe in the dry, loose brown topsoil. "We aim to settle down and farm, that's for sure."

Merced stood in the tapadera-covered stirrups and stared up the Río de las Plumas Cañón. "*We*? There's more of you coming down?"

Parkins peered at the mountains to the distant west. "There's eighteen of us. Well, fifteen, I reckon. Eighteen of us made it to the mountains. Some wanted to go north until they found a better route across. But me, Charley, Frank, and Sinclair reckoned we would cross right up there." He pointed up the river canyon to the crest of the Sierras. "So they went north, and we came west."

Echo Jack pulled his felt hat on top of his thick black hair. "What happened to the other three?"

"Sinclair got killed by a bear. Frank was shot by Indians." The man carefully studied Echo Jack.

The half-breed glared down at the dirty, tattered, foul-smelling man. "Were they handsome Indians?" Echo Jack asked.

"They were ugly as sin."

"Obviously no relation to me."

"And the third man?" Merced quizzed.

"Charley took a fall and landed on his head three days ago." He glanced back up the canyon. "But I made it. Yes sir, I told 'em we had a good chance of passin' through right here."

Echo Jack frowned. "Three out of four died. That's not exactly a good chance."

Merced waved his arm toward the valley to the west. "Mr. Parkins, you're welcome to come to my hacienda and rest and recuperate before you head on down to Sutter's Fort or Monterey. But I'd suggest you stay away from General Vallejo at Solano. He's liable to shoot you as a spy."

"A spy? I ain't no spy."

"Well, that's up to the authorities to figure out. There's a number of Americans movin' in over at the coast, and they all seem to be talkin' like this is U.S. soil. That don't sit well with the general."

"Say, where is that haysindo of yours?"

Merced pointed down the mountain. "See that cluster of oak trees down on that knoll to the west?"

"Yep."

"When you get there, wait in the shade. I'll send someone back with a horse for you."

"You jist going to ride off and leave me?"

"We could kill you," Echo Jack offered.

"He's jokin', right?"

"Never can tell about—handsome men," Merced replied.

"How do I know you won't ride off and just leave me up here?" Parkins scratched his shoulder and followed the itch all the way down his arm and across his chest.

"You got my word on it," Merced replied. "Besides, what choice do you have? You're a foreigner who has illegally entered the country."

"That ain't the way I see it."

"I assure you, that's the way the governor will see it. So just wait by the oak."

"You got an extree pair of boots in them saddlebags? My feet is hurting something terrible."

"I'll send some back."

"Thanks. Don't get me wrong. I am grateful. Mister, seeing you was like havin' the angel Gabriel himself come and rescue me."

"Whether you've ended up in heaven or hell is yet to be determined." Merced touched his spurs to the horse's flanks, and with a rumble of unshod horse hooves, he and Echo Jack loped down the hill.

Cerro Robles was not much more than a rounded dry, grass-covered butte rising up 800 feet higher than Río Plumas del Norte. To the east, the foothills stretched gradually upward to the crest of the Sierra Nevadas. Across the river to the west, the Plano Sacramento stretched to the Montana de Costa and the Russian settlements.

The recently vacated Russian settlements.

As its name implied, Cerro Robles displayed a scattered collection of oak trees, and on its crown the adobe hacienda headquarters of Rancho Alázan.

In a land of not more than a dozen houses north of Sutter's Fort, the hacienda was majestic, even massive, when caught in the reflection of a sinking summer sun. Closer examination revealed the simplicity of the structure—a rectangular building twenty-five feet by seventy-five feet, divided into three identical-sized rooms, each with a door out to the covered veranda on the west. The only windows faced west, and the courtyard was surrounded by a five-foot high, three-foot thick adobe wall.

The north, east, and south sides of the house had narrow gun slots instead of windows. The roof was made of hand-split cedar shakes, the floor of tightly packed and tamped dirt.

The outdoor kitchen consisted of two adobe ovens in the large courtyard and a thirty-foot table with benches whose legs were buried in the soil like fence posts. North of the wall stood the adobe corrals. On the south side of the walls grew an orchard of small trees and young vines. They were irrigated by a spring that bubbled up in a square trough in the middle of the courtyard.

At the front of the courtyard stood the one gate into the hacienda. It was made of the floors of two wagon carts, attached by leather hinges. Neither side swung closed without the strenuous effort of several strong men.

They had not been closed for two years.

Several oak trees provided shade for the courtyard, and other trees clustered just outside the adobe walls. A dozen chickens roamed in and out of the courtyard.

Wilson Merced climbed the oak-limb ladder to the top of the wide adobe wall and strolled on it, gazing down off Cerro Robles at the rolling grasslands.

It must be a little of the creation joy still left in us from the garden of Eden—to be able to look in every direction and see only what God has made. To know that at this moment in history, I am allowed to supervise everything within sight.

Lord, I am grateful.

Grateful for Rancho Alázan.

Grateful for Echo Jack, Piedra, and José.

He ambled along the wall and glanced at the man washing his hands and face in the courtyard below.

I'm not particularly grateful for Carty Parkins . . . but I'll work on that.

He glanced up at the snow-frosted Sierras.

Even those peaks can't keep out the pilgrims, can they?

Lord, this is the perfect place for me. I can't live in a city. I don't do good around people.

But out here it takes hard work to survive day by day.
You know I like to work hard.
Help me to forget my failures.
I know You've forgiven me.
But I haven't forgiven me.
And, I reckon, neither has my brother.

The sun was low in the west, and the heat rose up from the valley floor like a draft from a furnace. The yellow sun tinged orange, and the blue sky purpled as Wilson Merced set a stack of neatly folded clothes next to Carty Parkins.

"How much do I owe you for outfitting me?"

"Nothing."

"What? I can pay."

"It's California hospitality. It would be an insult for you to pay. All I ask is that when a destitute pilgrim wanders into your place, you treat him the same."

"I like this California already."

"Mr. Parkins, you're in time for a little California supper. I'm afraid it's mainly beef and tortillas. But we have a few dried pears, and I had the cook bake us some peach cobbler to celebrate having company. The fruit trees are just coming into production. This year will be our first real crop."

Parkins stared at the long, massive outdoor table. "How many is eatin' here tonight?"

"The usual, plus you." Merced tried to keep upwind from Parkins, who smelled like three months' worth of traveling sweat and dirt.

"How many does that make?"

"Five."

"A table the size of St. Louis, and only five is eating?"

"I never know who might wander by."

Two men wearing tall boots to just below their knees stomped across the courtyard from the direction of the ovens, carrying bowls of food. Both wore baggy pantaloons, muslin long-sleeved shirts, and wide red sashes for belts. Their felt hats were round with short, flat crowns. The younger one had a wide but thin mustache. The graying one had thick, bushy sideburns.

Merced swept his hand toward the approaching men. "Mr. Parkins, you've met Echo Jack. This is José Fuerte, who also works for me. And my cook's name is Piedra Muerto, but don't ask him to explain what his name means unless you have three months to listen. We just call him Piedra."

"*Hombres*, this is Carty Parkins from Arkansas, which has been a state for about six years now, though not many of 'em know it."

Several heads nodded as the men bunched down at the north end of the table. Merced pulled off his hat, revealing a forehead almost white at the top. The others yanked off hats and dropped their heads.

"Lord," Merced began, "we thank You once again for supper. We got a pilgrim with us tonight, and we'd appreciate it if You'd share our blessing with him, too. In Jesus' name, amen."

Parkins stared at Merced.

"You didn't expect to hear grace in California?"

"I ain't heard a prayer since I left Arkansas. I reckon it startled me, that's all."

"Well, partner, this is a big country out here. Some days . . . some weeks, it's just you and the Lord. A man gets friendly with the Almighty."

"How long you been in California?"

"This time?" Merced fished out a chunk of broiled beef with his hunting knife and plopped it down on a huge flour tortilla.

Parkins watched the others and then imitated them with his chunk of meat. "You come more than once?"

"I was sixteen when I first came in with Joseph Walker. We hiked across the Plano Tulare and into Monterey. Then I trapped my way back to Missouri with Ol' Gabe himself, Jim Bridger. After that I went down and fought at San Jacinto with Sam Houston." Using a wooden spoon, he scooped a helping of salsa out of a pottery crock.

"You might want to watch this stuff. We call it Piedra's *veneno*. That means poison. It takes some gettin' used to." Merced punctuated the sentence with a cheek stuffed with tortilla, beef, and salsa.

Parkins scooped salsa all over his meat. "You got folks in Texas?"

"No, but Houston was a second cousin of my mother's, and she wanted me to go help him out. Then I went back to St. Louis, took a wagon of goods to Santa Fe, and went back for another load, but things took a bad turn so I left in a hurry. I trapped my way out here again. Built this rancho three years ago."

"I figure to get me a place like this, too." Parkins gnawed at his food like a man too long starved.

Merced dipped his tortilla into the crock of salsa and scooped a large bite into his mouth. "You'll have to talk to the governor about that. He's the one that grants land. Mainly to relatives and friends, of course."

Parkins's cheeks reddened, and his eyes began to water. "I cain't jist settle where I want?" he coughed.

"Afraid not." Merced waited for Piedra Muerto to take a turn and then scooped another huge wad of thick, red salsa onto his tortilla.

Parkins suddenly grabbed the red pottery mug of water and poured it into his mouth so fast that half of the contents dribbled down his beard and splashed across his greasy shirt.

"Are you all right, señor?" José asked with a wily grin.

Tears streaming down his eyes, Parkins gasped for breath. "That stuff will take the hide off your tongue and melt your teeth," he puffed. "That will shorten a man's life span by a good thirty years."

"*Gracias*, señor." Piedra's dark eyes twinkled, and his two lower gold teeth glistened. "I consider that a very fine compliment. Something I seldom receive from others around here."

After three more cups of water, the last one poured directly on his face, Parkins asked Merced, "How'd you get this place?"

Fuerte ripped off a piece of tortilla with his teeth, swallowed hard, then waved his finger. "He's the only one dumb enough to take it."

"Don Loco Americano. That's what they call him," Piedra added. "Many said he would be dead in six weeks."

Carty Parkins cautiously plucked up a plain tortilla and slowly took a bite. "Why'd they think you'd be dead?"

Merced rubbed his unshaven face. "Ever since secularization of the missions in '33, the Indians have been on the prowl. They don't exactly like settlers moving up in this country. Sutter's got his fort, but all we have is this adobe hacienda."

Parkins looked at the other men. "It's a wonder you could get anyone to come work for you if it's that dangerous."

"Work?" Merced laughed. "Have you seen any one of them actually do a day's work?"

Piedra Muerto leaned close to Parkins. "*El Patrón* is teasing. He loves us dearly. We are like children to him!"

Echo Jack and José Fuerte slapped each other on the back and almost fell off the bench laughing. It was several minutes before anyone regained composure to speak.

"Mr. Parkins, did you ever hear about Australia?" Merced quizzed.

"Ain't that some godforsaken land where the English send their prisoners?"

"Prisoners, misfits, and hard cases," Merced concurred. "Well, just think of Rancho Alázan as the Australia of California."

Parkins studied the four sitting at one end of the huge table. "You don't say!" Then he glanced up at the mountains stretching to the east. "I only saw one bunch of Indians coming down that canyon."

"There are plenty more." Piedra Muerto waved his hunting knife, which was also his only eating utensil, to the north. "Señor, there is nothing in that direction for 500 miles except Indians."

"If any of them decided it's time to loot, steal, and attack a rancho, guess which place they'd come to first?" Fuerte challenged.

Merced fished in the pot with his buckhorn knife for another chunk of meat. "The only reason Sutter and the governor agreed to let me settle up here is to act as a buffer against attack."

"He figures we'll slow 'em down or at least get word to the Fort that they're on the prowl," Echo Jack sputtered as he filled his tortilla with peach cobbler and a scoop of salsa.

Parkins rubbed the back of his hand across his nose as he studied the northern horizon, as if searching for marauding Indians. "Maybe I'll find me a place further south."

Merced picked his teeth with his fingernails, then turned to Parkins. "What about the rest of your party that turned north? When do you reckon they'll be here?"

"I think maybe they might keep on goin' up to Orygone Territory. The women didn't want to come to California in the first place."

"Women?" Echo Jack wiped his mouth with the back of his hand, leaving a slight trail of cobbler.

"Two married women."

"Were they handsome women?" Echo Jack quizzed.

José Fuerte slapped him on the back so hard he dropped his tortilla. "Since when does it matter to you if they are handsome?" he whooped.

"Like I said," Parkins repeated, "I think they might go north to Orygone."

"That's probably a good idea," Merced agreed. "The Californians don't want too many foreigners moving in."

"Of course, there is another reason *El Patrón* is up here," Echo Jack mumbled as peach cobbler dribbled down his clean-shaven cheek.

Parkins tried to scrape the salsa off the meat on his tin plate. "Why's he keep callin' you *El Patrón?*"

"'Cause he's the Old Father," Piedra hooted.

"You ain't that old, are ya?"

Merced glanced at the cook and pointed at the salsa bowl. "You got anything besides this mild stuff?"

"That's all we got left. Bring me home some hot peppers from Rio Salinas." He turned back to Parkins. "You aren't hungry?"

"I reckon I got to let my mouth heal."

"To answer your question, I'm thirty-two. But around this part of the world, the boss is always called *El Patrón*. This is my ranch, so that makes me the Old Father."

His left hand on a mug of water, Parkins stabbed a small bite of meat with the point of his knife and popped it into his mouth. "What's the other reason you're up here?"

Echo Jack licked peach cobbler from his mostly clean fingers. "To stop pilgrims like you from coming into California."

Parkins slammed down the now empty water mug and waved his large knife at the others. "You ain't going to stop me!"

The characteristic smile dropped off Echo Jack's face. "Señor, if we'd wanted to, we could have easily shot you when you were up on the Río Plumas."

"You cain't shoot a man just for wanting to come to California."

With a lightning move, Echo Jack lunged across the table and grabbed Parkins's wrist, twisting it so tight the knife dropped and stuck, point-down, in the wood table. "Señor, up here we can shoot anyone we want. Nobody will know . . . and nobody cares." The usual wide, easy smile eased again across Echo Jack's face as he released his grip on the startled man.

"Relax, Mr. Parkins. We aren't going to kill you, that's for sure. But if you'd been leading a party of thirty, I would have tried mighty hard to get you to turn north."

Echo Jack wiped his hands on the sleeve of his shirt. "At least, we'd turn the *men* north!"

Parkins chewed a while on a bare tortilla. "I don't figure. You got yourself a place. Now you don't want others to have the same?"

Merced sipped on a tin cup of now-cold coffee and gazed out the open front gates. "Mr. Parkins, all I want is to be left alone. Completely alone. I've got an adobe house built like a fort. No neighbors for fifty miles, and no one to talk to but these three—"

"Handsome men!" Echo Jack piped up.

"Fifty miles to the next ranch?"

"And you have to cross three rivers to get there," José put in.

Parkins cautiously tried a knifeful of peach cobbler. "How far to a town?"

"What do you mean by town?" Merced pushed up from the table and wandered over to a coffeepot that hung on an iron hook next to the open fire. "We buy supplies at Sutter's Fort."

"How about a real town—stores, houses, people, saloons?"

Merced brought the tin pot over and made the rounds pouring coffee. "If that's what you're lookin' for, I'd suggest St. Louis or maybe New Orleans."

"You're just joshin' me, right?"

"Why would I do that? Mr. Parkins, this is the frontier. A person chooses to live here because he wants to get away from the cities."

Echo Jack pointed the scraps of his peach taco at Wilson Merced. "Or at least because he can't go back."

"Take our fine cook," Merced explained. "If General Vallejo knew he's here, he'd march troops in this direction at once. And José? He'd be shot on sight in Monterey or at the *presidio* at Yerba Buena."

"Merely a case of mistaken identity," José snorted.

"Yes," Piedra laughed, "it was a mistake for you to let the *alcalde* identify you!"

Merced sipped from the steaming coffee cup. "Echo Jack is not allowed in many villages. He cannot come within five miles of New Helvetia. Don Juan Sutter has personally threatened to shoot him on sight."

Echo Jack grinned. "He is jealous of my good looks. How did I know she was his mistress? But I can go to San Juan. Padre Estában likes me."

"Padre Estában does not have a daughter or a wife!" José ribbed.

"And you, Merced?" Parkins insisted. "Are you under banishment also?"

"Not yet. I can go anywhere I want in California. But they prefer I stay up here and act as a doormat."

"But you got run out of Missouri?"

"It's my decision to stay out of Missouri. I will never go back. So here we are."

"Three nice fellows and one old grouch," Echo Jack mocked.

"Why's ever'body lookin' at me?" Piedra challenged. "I am not a *malhumorado*, señor. Discriminating, *sí*. And clean, most certainly. About that, some here could learn a lesson."

Carty Parkins glanced around. "I ain't exactly been around a bath house for three months."

"You're in luck, partner," Merced announced. "It's bath time."

Parkins scratched at the back of his knees. "I ain't exactly sure I want a bath."

"Well, here's the choice. If you want to spend the night inside these walls, dress in these clean clothes, buy a horse, and ride along with us south, then you have to kill the lice and fleas first."

"I cain't stay here unless I take me a bath?"

Piedra nodded his curly gray head. "That's the rules."

"I ain't never heard of no rules like that before in my life."

"That's what I like about this country," Merced added. "We get to make our own rules."

"Where do we take a bath?" Parkins asked. Then he pointed to the adobe trough in the middle of the courtyard. "Over in them springs?"

"Not hardly. We don't aim to foul up our drinking water." Merced pointed toward the south. "There's a sulfur springs about half a mile in that direction. Next to it is a granite sink. We use that sink like a big tub. The sulfur water and a little kerosene kills most all the body varmints."

"I ain't used to bein' told to take a bath."

"That's obvious. José will go with you."

"I don't need no help."

"But you will need someone to stand guard. Wouldn't want someone stealin' your clothes or plugging you with an arrow while you're in the water."

"Havin' someone stand guard at the bathtub don't even sound civilized," Parkins complained.

"Mister," Echo Jack hooted, "what in the world ever made you think this land was civilized?"

Five clean men sat on rough-hewn log benches in front of the house under a clear summer night sky. From the top of Cerro Robles, stars could be seen straight out the front gates, as well as overhead. Piedra Muerto's clay pipe glowed in the dark as the sweet smell of tobacco floated across the yard. Wilson Merced wiggled his toes in clean socks beneath worn boots.

Carty Parkins sat with his back against the house, wearing fresh clothes, his face shaved, and his hair washed, combed back, and greased down. "So you all are goin' to this here Seeyoudad San Juan?"

"Just Echo Jack and me," Merced explained. José and Piedra will stay and look after things here."

"I don't figure. You said you could make it to Sutter's Fort in two days, right?"

"Yep."

"But it takes a week to go to this here San Juan? So why make such a long trip?"

"There's a hide trader from Monterey by the name of Tipton that doesn't come inland any farther than the old mission at San Juan. I always get a lot better price from him. I don't mind selling the tallow to Sutter, but not the hides. Besides, Echo Jack is not welcome at the fort."

"I cain't believe you raise cattle for jist the hides and tallow."

Merced crossed his long legs out in front of him. He closed his eyes. The night air was mild and sweet-tasting. "Aren't enough people for sellin' meat. Everyone in California has all the beef they can eat for a hundred years. Besides, there's a couple of bulls at the mission that I aim to buy. I've got to keep this herd strong. I wouldn't mind the Indians taking a cow or a steer once in a while, but when they shoot one of my bulls, it can put me in a tough strait."

"But that is not the real reason we are going to San Juan," Echo Jack insisted.

"What other reason is there?" Parkins's question drifted like smoke in the darkness of the moonless night.

"We heard a rumor that General Castro is giving a big fandango."

"A dance?" Parkins questioned. "You'd drive a cart for a week jist to go to a dance?"

"I'd drive a cart for a month to go to a dance," Echo Jack insisted. "And the women of Bautista—they are the most beautiful in all of California."

"Echo Jack never met a woman he didn't like," José chided in his lyric tenor voice. He retrieved his guitar from the rafters of the porch and began his nightly ritual of tuning.

"That's a lie. I do not like Doña María Damiséla Félix."

"You liked her until she stabbed you six times," Piedra derided.

"*Cinco*," he corrected. "She stabbed me five times. Then her mother stabbed me once. Now I ask you, is that any way to treat a handsome man?"

The men were silent for so long that Wilson Merced began to drift off to sleep. The only sound was José Fuerte's softly plucked guitar.

Parkins's voice sounded gravelly and insistent. "When are you leaving for San Juan?"

"In a couple days. Echo Jack and I will ride north tomorrow. José and Piedra can load the hides."

"You goin' north to look for them others who was travelin' with me?"

"Thought we might look around." Merced's voice was a low, powerful rumble, like a mountain stream during the June runoff.

"I reckon it will take them a few more weeks even if they do decide to come this way," Parkins suggested.

"Not necessarily," Merced corrected. "There's a nice pass up this side of old Mt. Tehema. If they find it, they could be on their way down in the next day or two. It's a lot smoother than the Río Plumas Cañón that you came down."

"You don't say. Well, in that case . . . I think maybe I'll be pullin' out tomorrow."

"What's the hurry?"

"I want to see if I can git my land before a crowd arrives. Figure I'll go see that there German, Mr. Sutter, right off."

"Sutter's Swiss."

"Same difference."

"You don't want to go off by yourself. It would be safer for you to ride part of the way with me and Echo Jack, although we aren't going right up to the fort."

"I ain't afraid."

"There are a lot of dead men who weren't afraid. That's not the issue," Merced warned.

"I thought you said all the trouble's up there in the north," Parkins contended.

"Who said that?" Echo Jack questioned.

"Well, I kin make it on my own. Will you sell me a horse?"

"You got money?"

"I've got a little. What's a good horse cost?"

"Exactly fourteen dollars in gold," Merced declared.

"I ain't picked one out yet."

"Doesn't matter. They all sell for fourteen dollars. That's what an ounce of gold is worth in California."

"Gold?" Carty Parkins gasped. "There's gold in California?"

"Why, there's gold, silver, diamonds, rubies—and piles of buried Spanish treasure," Echo Jack boasted.

"Where?"

"Oh, don't worry. Someone will be glad to sell you a map."

"I have several treasure maps myself," Piedra offered. "Perhaps for the right price, I could sell you one."

"Say, are you tryin' to swindle me?"

"*¿Quién sabe?*" Piedra sighed. "Maybe there is gold!"

"The fact remains, no matter if you have Spanish, Mexican, British, French, Russian, or American coins," José lectured, "it takes one ounce of gold to buy a pony."

"Then I want to buy a horse and ride out of here in the mornin'," Parkins announced.

"Some of them are not for sale, señor," Piedra declared.

"I ain't too particular."

"Then sell him Siete Diablos," Echo Jack counseled.

"Only a Californio can ride that bronc," Piedra cautioned.

Parkins cleared his throat. "I ain't never met a pony I couldn't fork."

"Now you sound like a Texican," Wilson Merced declared. "Mr. Parkins, there's one thing you ought to know about California horses. Most of 'em are only three-gaited."

"Oh?"

"They lope, gallop, and fly. Nobody in California rides slow," Merced explained.

"Not even the women?"

Echo Jack slapped his knee. "Especially the señoritas."

"This place is startin' to feel like a foreign country," Parkins groused.

Merced folded his hands on his lap, dropped his chin to his chest, and shut his eyes. "It is a foreign country."

Two

It was El Blanco's gait that Alena liked best. She called it his royal strut. Standing at over sixteen and a half hands, he towered above the other horses both in height and attitude. He belonged to Don Francisco Cabrillo, who always insisted that Alena ride him.

As the party of Don Francisco Madera Aguella y Cabrillo left Monterey for the journey inland, Alena rode just behind the scouts and ahead of the carts and wagons. On her right flank was Don Ronaldo, on her left Don Fernando.

The Mexican sidesaddle was much more comfortable than any she had ever used in New England, and it was impossible to slide off. It allowed Alena to spread her full black velvet skirt across the horse's withers and flanks, displaying the fringed gold lace trim at the hem. Her white cotton Spanish blouse came only halfway down her arm, but her beaded bleached deerskin gloves stretched almost to her elbows, leaving only a tease of alabaster skin showing. Alena had amended the scooped neckline with gold lace. A black velvet ribbon lightly choked her neck and held a small heart-shaped ivory locket. Inside were pictures of her mother and father. Below the locket, the ever-present gold cross warmed in the June sun on her chest.

Alena had never felt comfortable with the wide-brimmed California hats, but she did have one red and one yellow flower pinned in her hair. The yellow was a gift from Don Ronaldo and the red from Don Fernando. Above her head she held a small yellow lace-trimmed conical parasol and in her right hand the braided rawhide reins.

The big white horse seemed disgusted that she should even have reins. When she did tug on them, he would turn back and look at her with an I-know-where-I-am-going look and then promptly ignore her command.

Don Francisco, like most Californios, refused to geld any of his horses. That made for a remuda of prancing, self-centered, aggressively competitive males.

Not completely unlike the Cabrillo brothers.

"It is such a shame that Fernando has never learned to play the guitar," Don Ronaldo declared as he rode his black stallion next to Alena. He was two years younger and two inches shorter than his brother. Both men were bronzed, more from years in the sun than from natural complexion. His wide-brimmed, flat-crowned hat was tilted in the same swagger as his thin lips. His dark eyes and white, straight teeth were framed by the long, thick black sideburns on an otherwise clean-shaven face.

Don Ronaldo looked past Alena at his older brother. "Doña Alena Louisa was quite enamored with my song, Fernando."

"It was very enchanting," she concurred.

"You see!" Ronaldo exclaimed. "It was enchanting."

"One can be enchanted by a frog on a hollow log at midnight," Don Fernando replied.

"He is jealous, of course, that he plays the guitar so poorly."

"I never had much time to learn. Always the young ladies want me to dance. They never let me have a moment to myself. If I had been like Ronaldo, well . . ." He threw his hands in the air. "I would have had time to learn the guitar . . . the violin . . . and perhaps knit a shawl."

Alena thought that Don Fernando looked like his mother. Kind eyes, easy smile, and a twinkle in his voice. Yet his thick mustache was the image of his father's. The scar on his neck was usually covered with a red silk bandanna, and another bandanna was tied around his waist like a wide belt. She knew its flowing folds covered two *pistolas* and a knife that were at his side.

Don Fernando's square chin seemed always to be held exactly parallel to the ground. "It is fortunate that your brothers are older than you, Doña Alena Louisa. It is annoying to have a younger one."

"I want to know one thing," Alena announced. "What did you two argue over before I came to California?"

"Doña María Juanna," Ronaldo reported.

"And before her, it was Doña María Tomása." Fernando shrugged.

"Of course, when we were young, we fought over Doña María Ramóna," Ronaldo added. "But every boy in California was in love with Doña Ramóna."

The wide dirt road climbed up to the top of the tree-covered hills, then dropped down into a broad valley. To the north of the river was a prominent hill called El Toro. The thick wheat fields were beginning to turn brown. They would supply all of Monterey and the central coast with flour. But Alena thought the real treat of the Rio Salinas Valley was the fruits and vegetables plotted next to the haciendas.

"Is it plum season yet, Don Fernando?" she asked.

"It's early, yet I will scour the orchard to find you a ripe one."

"And if there are no ripe ones," Don Ronaldo boasted, "I will curse until it blushes ripe."

Alena chuckled.

"You doubt my sincerity?"

"Oh no. I was just thinking what it would look like for you to ride up to a tree, lean over to a green plum, and begin to curse."

The pace of the procession would have been considered reckless in the States. But in California it was merely a fast trot. Alena was continually amazed at the speed with which all Californians traveled. She marveled that they hadn't long ago all broken their necks.

Above the dirt-pounding hoofbeats and the squeal of wooden-wheeled carts and wagons, Alena heard a hawk cry. She looked up. The brown bird swooped to the tall grass by the road, then soared heavenward with a rodent lunch in its talons.

That evening they stayed at the hacienda of Don Leandro Timotea Gomez. He showed the grandiloquent politeness possessed by all Californians, even though he could only offer them a dirt floor and blankets to sleep on in his one-story home.

Supper consisted of hare stew with potatoes and a chili colorado sauce that blistered Alena's tongue. She was reduced to eating tortillas and drinking water.

That evening everyone in the Cabrillo party and the Gomez Rancho gathered in the open courtyard around flickering lanterns. They listened to Don Ronaldo and others play their guitars and sing.

There were songs about beautiful, fast horses.

And there were songs about beautiful, fast women.

But most of the songs centered around the land, the mountains, and the lifestyle of Californios.

Alena sat on a small barrel with her back against an adobe pillar to the side of the others. In one way she felt a part of the proceedings. In another, she felt like an observer. With arms folded across her stomach, she hugged herself and rested her chin on her chest.

Lord, this is almost like a fantasy. Like a dream. Since Father's death all my days have flowed together. When we lived in Boston, life was hectic. Every Sunday, when the weather was mild, we would rent a carriage and ride out into the country after worship.

Mother was happy then. Father would joke and laugh. My brothers would shout and tease. And I would fall blissfully asleep on the way home. How I wanted those moments to last forever.

Now I am alone in a foreign land that in no way seems foreign. I am in a land of a different culture, yet I have never felt so at home. It is like a peaceful family drive in the country every day. California is what we wished every other place could be.

Father . . . I don't know whether to bless You for bringing me here or question You for leaving me alone.

Lord, for the first fourteen years of my life, mother made every decision for me. During the past five years, my father has guided me.

Now I am nineteen.

I am on my own.

Lord, it is just You and me. I no longer have anyone to interpret Your
will for my life.

It scares me to think about it.

It excites me to think about it.

A woman alone.

She stared out at the shadowed courtyard crammed full of
happy, laughing, singing, teasing people.

Well, not completely alone.

Rolling golden brown hills and oak trees greeted them on every
side as they left Rancho Gomez on the road east to San Juan and
the mission. Alena had lain awake on the dirt floor most of the
night, listening to Doña María Martina talk in her sleep and waiting for the fleas to find her under the thin wool blanket.

She was grateful there had been no insect attack. But the night
left her tired and sore. She fought the urge to slump her shoulders
as she rode along on El Blanco. She held her small black leather-
bound Bible at her breast and tried to read as the procession
ambled its way into the hills.

Lord, these Californians are the most hospitable people I've ever been
around. The Gomez family had nothing more than rabbit stew, tortillas,
and a clean-swept dirt floor to sleep on, but they offered it without hesita-
tion. They would have been highly offended if we had tried to pay them.
It's such a natural, gracious giving of one's self and one's possessions.

I want to be like that.

I am too selfish.

It is so difficult, Lord.

All my life there have been those who want to do things for me.

I like that.

I liked being served.

But it has robbed me of a servant's heart.

I need someone to teach me how to serve.

She reined up on El Blanco at the sound of horsemen galloping up beside her. In a cloud of fine yellow dust, she was flanked on
each side by a Cabrillo brother.

"There is a rumor that General Castro will give a fandango in your honor Sunday night," Don Ronaldo offered. "We want to know. Who will you dance with, Doña Alena Louisa?"

She tucked the Bible back into a small leather *mochila* sewn on the back of her saddle. Alena reached up and fingered the gold cross resting high on her chest. "Why, I'll dance with the handsome one."

"Sorry, Ronaldo, you heard her. She has chosen me," Don Fernando crowed.

"You? Handsome? Only if she likes someone with large feet and a crooked nose."

"You want a crooked nose? I will give you a crooked nose."

Don Ronaldo dismissed his brother's comment with a flip of the hand. "Just which handsome man will you dance with?"

Her deep blue eyes sparkled, and white teeth peeked out from teasing scarlet lips as she spun the parasol in her hand. "Why, all of them, of course."

"There will be a long line," Don Fernando declared.

"You are both unashamed flatterers. Doña María Martina warned me about you. Besides, there are many women more beautiful than I am," she demurred.

"I will run a sword through anyone who says so," Don Fernando boasted.

"He could not run a sword through a *piñata*," Ronaldo insisted.

Fernando drew his glistening steel saber. "You challenge my bravery?"

Don Ronaldo's reins dropped over his saddle horn, and he waved both hands as he talked. Like the other two, his horse continued at a brisk trot. "I challenge your willingness to run a man through with the sword."

"It was I who stopped Antoine Boudreaux and his pirates from attacking the *padres* at San Carlos Barromeo del Rio Carmelo," Don Fernando shouted.

"Oh yes, it was you. And a well-placed lead ball from the musket of Doña Alena's father, Don Roberto!"

"Don Ronaldo . . ." Alena waved her parasol at the younger Cabrillo. "Don Fernando stood beside my father in a very tense time with the French pirates. I, for one, will never question his bravery."

Don Fernando held his head high as he wiped his brow. His

stern, narrow face reminded Alena of a sea captain's or general's face. *The sons of Cortez! They are the type to burn their boats and conquer new worlds.*

"Yes, but it was I who stood with the *alcalde*, Don Ramon Estrada, when we banished Governor Don Marino Chico and Señora Cruz," Don Ronaldo vaunted.

"I think you are both very brave men," Alena asserted.

Don Fernando's hands were even less patient than his words. "Yes, yes, but which of us gets the first dance tomorrow night at the fandango?"

Alena enjoyed the rhythm of the worn leather saddle bouncing beneath her. "I'm afraid that dance has already been promised."

"*¿Quién es el hombre?*" Don Ronaldo quizzed.

She brushed her wavy red hair off her ear and exposed the onyx and silver dangling earrings. "Don Francisco, of course."

Don Fernando tossed his hands high above his hat. "What? You are to dance with an old married man?"

"Your father is a very good dancer. Since my own father's death, he has treated me as his daughter. I owe him the dance."

"Well, the old man is an *hombre de mucho encanto!*" Don Fernando brushed his thick mustache with his fingers. "But since I am the better dancer of the two, you will undoubtedly want to reserve the final dance for me."

In the distance Alena saw a thin gray coyote slink through the brown grass between two oak trees. *Why do I get the feeling that it is not only coyotes that are busy stalking their prey?* "The final dance? At the last fandango, the final dance was around noon the following day. I cannot dance all night. I am from Boston, not Santa Barbara."

"Well, I ask for the second dance then," Ronaldo insisted.

She turned to the other Cabrillo brother. "Don Fernando, you are the eldest. What is your wish?"

"Let Don Francisco have the first dance and Don Ronaldo the second."

"That's very generous of you." Alena nodded. "But I would like to have a dance with you as well."

"Oh yes, I will have all the others with you."

"What?" Don Ronaldo cried out. "You think you can selfishly

take La Paloma Roja de Monterey for your very own? No one man can dominate her time. It would cause a rebellion."

"And I still say you two are full of romantic flattery."

"We cannot help ourselves. We are Californios! It is in our blood," Don Ronaldo insisted.

"If I cannot have all the other dances, then I choose the second dance," Don Fernando proposed.

"You must choose, Doña Alena Louisa," Don Ronaldo pressured. "Who will you dance with second?"

"One can sing well, and one can dance well. Both are gallant and handsome. How will a girl decide? I guess . . ." She held her finger to her chin and twirled the parasol. "I guess I will dance with the one who is the best horseman."

"A very smart choice," Don Fernando insisted. "In that case, I am sure my little brother will concede defeat."

"I will what? I have been the best horseman since I was four and you were six."

"That, like many of Ronaldo's fantasies, is simply a lie."

"Ask anyone," Don Ronaldo blustered. "Ask Doña María Martina."

"Ask your mother which of her sons is the best horseman? I refuse to demand such information from her. Why not . . . why not a little contest?" Alena proposed.

"When?" Don Fernando probed.

Don Ronaldo swept his jacket-covered arm across the dry-grass horizon. "Where?"

Not looking at either brother, Alena stared straight ahead. "Now. Here."

Don Fernando stood in his stirrups and glanced up and down the road. "Along the trail?"

Don Ronaldo brightened. "It would pass the time, would it not?"

"The challenge has been made," Don Fernando boasted. "Are you up to it, Don Ronaldocito?"

"It would not be a pretty sight for me to defeat my elder brother in such a contest." Don Ronaldo took off his round, flat-crowned hat and bowed his head to his brother. "I will allow you to withdraw now before the humiliation."

"Withdraw? I will do no such thing. Put on your hat, little brother. A heat stroke has already affected your thinking."

Like watching a lawn tennis match in Boston, Alena found herself straining to look in one direction and then the other as she followed the Cabrillo brothers' conversation.

"Who goes first?" Ronaldo demanded.

Don Fernando rode with both hands resting on top of the silver saddle horn. "The younger, of course."

"Very well." Ronaldo bowed his head to Alena. "Señorita La Paloma Roja de Monterey, may I borrow a silk handkerchief from you?"

Alena tugged a one-foot-square yellow silk scarf from the folds of her sash and handed it with gloved hand to Don Ronaldo. He plucked it from her hand, then galloped up the trail far ahead of them. He dropped the scarf on the short brown grass alongside the dirt roadway.

With her hand above her eyes, she strained to watch him. "What is he doing?"

Don Fernando leaned back, his right hand on the rump of his high-stepping black horse. "It is nothing, Doña Alena. Every *niño* in California can do it before he turns ten."

Don Ronaldo rode fifty yards on up the gradual slope of the mountain. The three-inch rowels of his silver spurs reflected in the bright summer sun. He dangled his hat on his saddle horn. Suddenly, the spurs were kicked into the horse's flanks, and the horse bolted down the mountain toward Alena at a precarious gallop. Without slowing down in the least, Don Ronaldo leaned far out of the saddle to the right. His left tapadera and boot seemed to be hung up on the huge silver-plated saddle horn. His arms were tucked along his side; his head bounced only inches from the ground. His black hair swept the dirt roadway.

Alena's hand went over her mouth. "He will kill himself," she gasped. "What is he doing?"

"It is nothing." Don Fernando shrugged it off with the wave of a hand. "But I know of no *vaquero* in California who can duplicate the feat."

As natural looking as if biting an orange, Don Ronaldo

plucked up Alena's yellow silk scarf in his teeth, then smoothly pulled himself back into the saddle while the horse continued its wild gallop.

With his hat now held to his back by a braided rawhide stampede string, Don Ronaldo spurred the horse even faster. His shoulder-length black hair flew out behind him just as the identical-colored horse's mane flagged in front of him.

As he approached Alena and Fernando, he spun the big horse to the right in a quick, tight circle and halted beside them.

"I believe you dropped this, Doña Alena Louisa!"

Alena clapped her gloved hands enthusiastically. "Bravo! Bravo! Don Ronaldo, I am impressed. That was wonderful. But so dangerous. I have never seen anything like it."

She held out her arm. Don Ronaldo leaned forward and took her hand as they continued to walk the horses. He leaned over and kissed it, then draped the scarf in her palm.

"Don Ronaldo, you are quite the gentleman," she cooed.

"Yes, he always did like to kiss leather gloves." Don Fernando scowled.

Alena hesitated, then tugged at the deerskin gloves. Working the fingers loose, she pulled off the long glove. "Don Fernando's right." She held her soft white hand out to Don Ronaldo. "A man shouldn't have to kiss a glove. Not in California."

Don Ronaldo enthusiastically kissed the back of her bare hand, then looked up. "This means I get the second dance, no?"

"Well," she grinned, "that depends on Don Fernando's horsemanship, doesn't it?" She retrieved her hand and pulled the glove back on. *I have never exposed my arm to a man before. Yet it doesn't feel shameful. It is this California climate.*

"If that is the case, it is no contest," Don Fernando insisted.

"Go ahead, big brother. Let's see if your skill is as great as your boast."

"If the señorita doesn't mind," Don Fernando tipped his hat to her, "I would like to wait. This particular skill needs a little level ground."

"Oh, level ground?" Don Ronaldo chided. "No rocks, I suppose? Perhaps you would like for Doña María Martina to bring some of her feather pillows out so that you will have a soft place to fall?"

The sound of a sword drawn on her right side caused Alena to jump in the saddle and accidentally kick the flank of the big white horse. El Blanco looked back at her with a sit-still-and-behave-yourself look.

"Now wait," she insisted. "Put away your sword, Don Fernando. You are brothers. It is not the fault of either of you that you two happen to be the most talented and handsome men in all of Alta California. I blame it on Doña María Martina and Don Francisco. Such a handsome woman and courageous man were bound to have attractive children."

Don Fernando slipped his polished silver sword back into its sheath. "Perhaps Doña Alena is correct."

She turned to Don Ronaldo. "We will wait until level ground."

"Yes," he agreed. "There is a small valley just over this next ridge."

Huge, sturdy oak trees grew in clumps on the hillsides as far as the eye could see. And beneath the oaks in the shade, horned cattle lay passively rechewing their breakfasts. There was absolutely no breeze, yet the air did not feel stuffy or taste stale.

"It is a very pleasant day," Alena announced as they continued their ride.

"And the weather is nice also," Don Ronaldo teased.

"It is the weather of heaven," Don Fernando added.

"Oh?" Alena said.

"Our mother always told us when we were little that heaven would have perfect weather all the time. So whenever there was a beautiful, mild day like this, she would tell us this is the weather of heaven."

"I believe she is right." Alena suddenly tugged the reins to the right and turned El Blanco around.

"Where are you going, Doña Alena?" Don Fernando asked.

"Back to the wagon for a drink of water."

"I will get it for you," Don Ronaldo insisted.

"No, I am quite capable of getting my own drink."

"Yes, Don Ronaldo, you do not have to treat her like a child."

"A child? I was treating her like a lady."

"A lady? You should treat her like a *reina*, of course!"

"That's what I meant!"

Their arguing voices faded as she rode back toward the slowly moving wagon of Señor and Señora Cabrillo.

Doña María Martina sat with her ruffled navy blue dress stretched out over the front of the wagon. The deeply scooped neckline would have caused discussion in Boston, but in California it looked natural and attractive even on a woman in her fifties.

Don Francisco wore a light gray wool suit, black vest, long coat, black bow tie, and a wide-brimmed straw hat. His full gray beard was neatly trimmed. There was an ever-present sparkle in his dark brown eyes.

With the wagon still moving, Alena tugged the top off the ten-gallon wooden water barrel attached to the side of the wagon and dipped a wooden ladle into the clear spring water. After taking several sips, she replaced the lid, and then rode alongside Don Francisco and Doña María Martina.

"*Conchita*, I trust my sons have not been too annoying," Don Francisco offered.

"Of course they are annoying. We raised them that way," Doña María Martina moaned. "May God have mercy on us for the way they turned out."

"They are very handsome and chivalrous sons. You two should be proud."

"I will be proud when they get married, have families, and go off to the Plano Tulare on their own ranchos," Don Fernando insisted.

"Plano Tulare?"

"In the interior. It is unexplored, unsettled . . . wonderful land for cattle. They could both have their own grants if they so choose."

Doña María Martina waved her slightly thick arm at her sons. "And what are my *niños* trying to impress you with this morning?"

"Horsemanship."

"They are neither one as good as Don Francisco in his prime."

Don Francisco sat straight up and sucked in his stomach. "In my prime? Señora, I am still in my prime!"

"Oh yes," Doña María Martina blushed, "perhaps in some things, but not in your horsemanship."

Don Francisco's shoulders resumed their slight sag. "Why are they so intent on making fools of themselves today?"

"They both asked for the second dance at the fandango. It is very nice of General Castro to stage such an event for me."

"They argue over the second dance? Just who gets the first dance?" he asked.

"Why, you, of course, Don Francisco. With Doña María Martina's permission."

"Yes, yes. Of course you have my permission." Señora Cabrillo chuckled. "A father should be the first to dance with his daughter."

"You are right. You two treat me like a daughter. I don't deserve your benevolence."

"Doña Alena Louisa, if we lived this life on only what we deserved, we would all be paupers, wouldn't we?" Doña María Martina lectured. "It is by eternal design that Californians are gracious and kind. It was the extreme tenderness of *El Dios* that allowed us, of all people, to live in this land. How can we be otherwise?"

The land was flat and covered with short grass when they crossed the six-inch deep water of Cala Natividad. Don Fernando rode up closer to Alena. "Now is the time to demonstrate how men ride horses. Ronaldo has shown the skill of a young boy. Would you be so kind as to ride out in that clearing? We will make believe it is a large corral."

Alena, with Don Ronaldo at her side, rode a hundred feet through the short dry grass and parked in a small clearing.

"What is he going to do?" she asked.

· "I have no idea. Fernando is a secretive fellow."

The older Cabrillo brother circled the pair on horseback. He cut a hundred-foot-diameter circle in the brown grass. Then he brought the horse to a full gallop. Alena found it necessary to keep El Blanco in a steady, slow turn so she could watch Don Fernando.

He draped the reins over the saddle horn and slid to the side of the horse. His feet were out of the tapadera-covered stirrups as he swung his chest and head under the horse's stomach.

She twirled the parasol above her head and held her gloved hand to her mouth. *He will be trampled to death! He'll kill himself!*

Clutching the *cincha* under the stallion's belly, Don Fernando seemed to falter, about to tumble beneath the thundering hooves.

"He's falling. Stop him! Stop him!" she shouted.

"He does that on purpose," Don Ronaldo said. "It always impresses the ladies."

"He's done this before?"

"Our father showed us how to do that before we were twelve."

"Don Francisco can do that?"

"Not anymore. Our mother can be very persuasive if she chooses."

With one final thrust of seeming desperation, Don Fernando pulled himself back up into the far side of the saddle, completing the journey under the galloping horse's stomach. He sailed his round black hat high in the air to the shout and applause of those in the caravan that now had caught up with them.

He trotted the horse toward Alena, scooping his hat off the thick brown grass of the valley floor.

"Bravo, Don Fernando," Alena shouted. "That was magnificent! When you slipped, I just about died from heart failure."

"Heart failure? I know exactly how you feel, Doña Alena Louisa," Don Fernando concurred. "I feel the same when I look into your stunning dark blue eyes."

She quickly tugged her right glove off and held out her hand. Don Fernando took it in his rough callused hand and kissed it.

And kissed it.

"Doña Alena does not need to be licked clean like by a dog, big brother," Don Ronaldo insisted.

Don Fernando raised back up and released her hand. The Cabrillo brothers continued to trot along, one on each side of her.

"I have often wondered what it would have been like if mother had sent Ronaldo to the Franciscan monastery as she once proposed. It would have changed life immensely, I suppose," Don Fernando pondered.

"Changed life here or at the monastery?" Alena teased.

"Oh yes, you are right. St. Francis himself must rejoice in her decision to keep him at home."

"Very funny," Ronaldo pouted. "But Doña Alena Louisa has not yet selected the man who will be the *segundo* at the dance."

"You have made it much too difficult to choose. It is too bad I can't dance with both of you at the same time."

"That, Señorita Tipton, sounds absolutely boring," Don Ronaldo huffed.

"For once I agree with my little brother. You must choose."

She pondered the dilemma for several minutes. "Perhaps there is another test."

"What would that be?" Don Ronaldo questioned.

"How about a contest with a *reata?*" she declared. "After we reach San Juan, of course."

"Yes, the *reata!*" Don Ronaldo stared off across the brown hills. "I accept."

"As do I," Fernando boasted. "Meanwhile, I think I will take a shortcut to San Juan Bautista."

"You stay on the right, and I will stay on the left," Don Ronaldo insisted.

The Cabrillo brothers spurred their horses and galloped into the oak trees on both sides of the road.

Alena rode back to the cart and walked El Blanco next to Doña María Martina.

"Your suitors have left you, *conchita?*"

"They talked of a roping contest and then suddenly rode off."

"Roping? Ai yai, I suppose you know what that means, Don Francisco."

"It means a wild time in the plaza."

"Why? What will happen?" Alena prodded.

"Wait and see, *conchita* . . . wait and see," Señora Cabrillo said.

"Don Francisco, your sons are excellent horsemen. I don't know of any in the States who ride like they do."

"There are none in the world that ride like Californios," he boasted.

"And there are none that can brag like a Californian," Doña María Martina insisted. "But it is true. They can all ride like the wind. It is in their blood. From the time they are little boys, they have nothing better to do than to ride and to rope."

"And to dance and chase the girls," Don Francisco laughed. "Mama is right. It is a good land. There are workers to plant the garden and grow the wheat and cook the meals. There are cattle from one end of California to the other, so many that if you are hungry, you merely butcher one and enjoy a feast. There is no work, except to gather some cattle for hides and tallow. Or rope and brand the calves in the spring." He stared across the brown hills. "It will not last this way forever, Doña Alena Louisa. But it is a very good life."

"What will happen here in California, Don Francisco?"

"You have heard that there is talk in the states that the next president will annex Texas. If that happens, the *generales* in *Ciudad Mexico* will want to go to war."

"But that's thousands of miles away from here," she protested.

"Yes, that is the point. We are too remote to protect. The Spanish are gone. The Mexicans are still trying to bring order out of chaos. We will be on our own. General Vallejo has told me that himself."

"But who would attack California?"

"Who would not? It is a paradise. The French pirates know that. . . . The English of the Hudson Bay Company know that. . . . Even the czar in St. Petersburg knows that. But it will probably be the Americanos who will want it most. You Americanos seem to always get your way. You are more stubborn than even the Cabrillo brothers."

"I don't want California to ever change," Alena insisted.

"That is something we all agree on, *conchita*," Doña María Martina remarked.

When Wilson Judd Merced rode out of Rancho Alázan the following morning, he knew he was not the first to follow the Río de Sacramento north. Old-timers in Monterey told of a time thirty-seven years earlier when Spanish sea captain Gabriel Moraga led his party horseback up the big river and declared, "*¡Es como el sagrado Sacramento!*" With oak and cottonwoods clutching its banks, big fish darting through the river's depths, and wild grapevines housing an aviary of chattering birds, Moraga had gulped in a sweet draught of air and pronounced that it was "like the holy sacrament!" When the sea captain reached the fork of the Río Plumas, he mistook it for the main course of the river and promptly misnamed the northern Sacramento, Río Jesús María.

The mistake was not quickly corrected. No one else ventured inland away from the security of the coastal missions and ranchos.

Thirteen years later Luis Arguëllo left his post as captain of the *presidio* at Yerba Buena and followed the great river north. With him was Father Blas Ordaz to evangelize the pagans, and Scotsman-turned-Californio John Gilroy to act as interpreter if they found Englishmen or Americans infiltrating Spanish territory. When he reached the fork in the river and noticed thousands of band-tail pigeon feathers floating down from the mountain stream, he promptly named the branch Río de las Plumas.

After that, no one came.

Revolution was brewing in Mexico, and Spanish control would soon be overthrown. In 1833 the missions of Alta California were secularized and the land sold or given to residents. Following this, raids by the Miwok-Yokut Indians, led often by former mission neophytes, or converts, kept the settlers pinned to the coast.

It was a daring move when Swiss adventurer Johann Augustus Sutter and his Sandwich Islanders offered to settle land far inland on the Río de Sacramento in 1839.

Only a few months after that Wilson Judd Merced rode up to Sutter's fledgling settlement on a sorrel stallion he called Alázan and presented, in flawless Spanish, an even more reckless plan for an outpost in the north.

Today, looking straight ahead as he rode along, Merced knew that the only thing that had changed in the three years since then was the ever-increasing herd of cattle running free.

That and the changes in his heart.

"*El Patrón*, what are we looking for?" Echo Jack called out as they crossed Río Osolíto and spurred their horses up the dry bank on the north side.

Merced stood in the stirrups and stared north. His freshly

washed brown hair curled out from under the brim of his hat. "We're looking for any sign of activity other than animal and Indian."

"Do you think Señor Stinky was telling the truth about the others?"

"Yes, because four men couldn't make it across La Tierra Misteriosa del Norte on their own. I've been through there three times, and I wouldn't begin to try it with less than a dozen men."

"Did you know the reason *Dios Todopoderoso* created California so inaccessible?" Echo Jack asked.

"Why is that?"

"So He could have it all to Himself."

"Where did you hear that bit of wisdom?"

"I made it up myself."

"Not bad for a—"

Echo Jack showed his twin dimples when he grinned. "For a handsome man?"

Merced shook his head. "Being the best looking in an ugly litter does not necessarily make one handsome."

"Where did you hear that bit of wisdom?"

"I made it up myself," Merced admitted.

"It is what I would expect from a jealous man."

"Well, Señor Shadow-Rider, do you want the high road or the low road?" Merced waved at the oak-covered foothills.

Echo Jack pushed his hat until it slipped to his back, held in place by the stampede string around his neck. He brushed his thick dark hair off his eyes and wiped the sweat off his forehead with the sleeve of his shirt. "If there are pilgrims, they will be coming down along the banks of the river." His bushy black sweeping eyebrows rose and fell with each word.

Merced rubbed the dust out of his eyes. "And if there are Indians on the prowl, they will be in the foothills."

"I will take the foothills." Echo Jack unfastened the top button of his collarless shirt. "If the pilgrims see me, they might shoot me before they know who I am."

Merced's sorrel horse pranced and tugged at the reins. "The Indian fathers will shoot you because they do recognize you."

"Yes, but perhaps I will get to talk to them before they kill me. *¿Quién sabe?* Maybe a headman who doesn't know me has a beautiful daughter."

"I thought you had personal contact with all the beautiful daughters for a hundred miles."

Black eyes flashed. "I do . . . but maybe one has grown up."

"You think about women too much."

"You think about women too little, *El Patrón*. If I find a beautiful woman, I'll ask if she has a fairly handsome, needy older sister."

Wilson Merced waved him off with a toss of the hand. "Thank you, but I'll pick out my own woman."

"When?"

"When the timing is right."

"You didn't have an accident when you were young, did you?" Echo Jack teased.

"An accident?"

"I knew a man who had an accident as a child. We called him Don Poco Cosa. He was attacked by a grizzly in Ojai and was not able to—well, not able to father children."

Wilson Merced glared at Echo Jack. Finally the half-breed spoke up. "No, that is not your problem. Of course not."

"I do not have a problem."

"*Sí.*" Echo Jack waved to the north. "Where will we meet?"

"Río Paraíso at noon. Wait awhile. If I don't show, come look for me. If you don't show, I'll come look for you."

"What if neither of us shows up?"

"Then José and Piedra get to keep all the hide and tallow money."

Echo Jack spurred his black horse toward the foothills and shouted, "At least *they* will spend it on women."

The oak chaparral led Echo Jack north, and Wilson Merced followed the cottonwoods straight up the Sacramento Plain. Except for the riverbanks and spring floodplain, the grass was golden brown. As the sun rose higher, the heat rolled up off the land and caused the horizon to vibrate like a mirage on the desert. In the distance Merced could spot a few cows grazing but didn't bother to investigate.

They are either RA cows or wild ones. Either way, they will wind up someday as a stack of hides on a wagon to Monterey. It is a different kind of land where there is no problem growing beef and crops. The only problem is what to do with them once they're grown. I imagine this valley could support 10,000 people . . . and there aren't even a hundred.

Parkins is right. There is plenty of room for others. But I like the isolation.

I'd hate for others to move in.

Farmers.

Families.

Women and children.

A man should not live here with a wife and children. When it becomes that settled, I will have to move on.

Merced tugged at the dusty black silk cravat double-wrapped around his neck and tied in the front. He wiped the corners of his eyes.

Riding along untrodden ground about half a mile from the river, he crested a knoll and again saw several brindled short-horned cows grazing near a stand of cottonwoods. The cows suddenly bolted away from the trees and out into the grasslands.

He saw a very young boy, completely naked, run after the bovines and throw a four-foot spear well short of the cows. When the boy saw Merced riding toward him, he screamed, snatched up his sharpened stick, and ran back into the trees.

As Merced approached the trees, he discovered a small, smokeless fire and a loosely woven stick hut. Several naked children ran back into the brush. The young hunter stood in a wide stance with his feet braced against the dirt. His arm was cocked back behind his ear, spear in hand. Beside him, squatting near the fire was a short, emaciated-looking Indian woman. She didn't move when Merced rode up.

So you're ready to defend your mama? Your daddy should be proud of you, little warrior. I wonder where your daddy is?

Merced studied the brush near the camp but could only see tiny brown eyes peering back at him.

When the woman looked up, he saw the exhausted eyes of a worried woman. *She is too tired to run.* He pointed at her, then held his index finger up, with his fingers folded toward his body. Then he held his two index fingers side by side, touching each other and pointing straight away from himself. *Where's your husband?*

The woman, wearing a short buckskin apron for a skirt and a deerskin shawl buttoned only at the neck for a shirt, fingered the shell necklace that rested on her chest. She held her left hand straight out in front of her, thumb up, and drew her index finger of her right hand under the left. Then she tilted her head to the right and cradled it on top of her hands.

He is dead? No wonder you have cut your hair short.

Merced held his right index finger shoulder high, back of the hand facing his right, and then moved the hand up and to the right several times. *And your people?*

She pointed to the mountains.

He pointed to her, the brave little warrior, and the peering eyes in the brush. The he held the little finger edge of his right hand against the center of his body, moving it to the right and left as if cutting his stomach in two. *Are you hungry?*

The woman held her right hand, back to the right, in front of her right breast. Her index finger was extended and pointing upwards, the other fingers clenched loosely under her thumb. Then she moved her hand slightly to the left and a little downwards, at the same time closing her index finger over her thumb.

That's what I thought. "Starved is more like it, I reckon," he mumbled as he turned his horse back out toward the dry-grass field. He rode straight at the cattle, which had stopped to graze not more than fifty feet from where the boy had tossed his spear.

Pulling his .40-caliber Paterson Colt percussion cap revolver out of his belt, he aimed it at the heifer.

The explosion broke the summer silence.

The acrid smell of gunpowder drifted across the grass.

The animal dropped dead to the dirt.

Merced rode back to the wickiup and found four naked children huddled behind their standing mother. He reached into the square leather pouch sewn to the back of his saddle and pulled out a tattered piece of buckskin. Unrolling it, he lifted out a small turquoise-handled hunting knife. He motioned toward the boy still holding the pointed stick and then handed him the knife.

The woman reached up with soiled and sticky hands and gripped Merced's wrist as if to question the transaction. He nodded his head. Her eyes widened and noticeably relaxed.

He pointed toward her, then at the dead animal, and finally pinching his fingers together, he touched them against his mouth. *It's for you to eat.*

With a yip and a wide smile, she jabbered to her children. They raced to the animal, led by the boy with the knife.

The woman looked Merced in the eyes. She extended both hands flat, backs up, then moved them out and down toward Merced in a sweeping fashion.

He tipped his hat. "You're welcome, ma'am. *¡Vaya con Dios!*"

When Wilson Merced turned his horse to ride away from the river, one of the naked children raced back toward her mother carrying a slice of meat the size of a small loaf of bread, blood dripping from her dirty hands.

Lord, have mercy on their souls.

No mother and children on earth should have to go through life without a daddy.

And no daddy should have to go through life without his wife and children . . . whether they live in California or St. Louis.

Lord, have mercy on us all.

Echo Jack and Wilson Merced rode into Rancho Alázan about sundown. Two heavy carts were stacked high with hides tied down with rawhide ropes.

"Oh, yes . . . now you show up," Piedra complained. "We worked all day to load the carts, and *El Patrón* and *Segundo* show up when the work is done."

"You worked all day on those?" Merced pressed.

Even Piedra's thick gray sideburns couldn't contain his grin. "At least until noon."

"Almost noon." José shrugged with a smile. "Then we were so tired we needed a long *siesta*."

"Not to mention picking peaches," Piedra added.

Merced glanced over at the sliced yellow peaches drying on wooden trays. "You did save a few for fresh?"

"There is a cobbler in the oven. Is that what you were whining about?"

"I wasn't whining. It's just that a couple weeks of trail food is going to get *muy aburrido*."

"Yes, Piedra's cooking will probably even taste good after that," Echo Jack said as he climbed down off the black horse.

Piedra Muerto waved a clenched fist. "Hah! You will miss me!"

José toted Merced's saddle to the covered porch. "This time you will be gone for two weeks?"

"If we buy a bull or two, we'll return only as fast as they can travel," Merced explained.

"You could load them in the carts. It would be faster."

"You might be right, José. But you'd better count on us being gone for a couple weeks anyway."

"Longer if I find a woman," Echo Jack added.

"Yes, if you find a woman, it will be two weeks and ten minutes," Piedra whooped.

Merced began brushing down his horse. "We'll turn it around as soon as the hides are sold."

Echo Jack tossed his dusty black hat on the ground and danced around it, snapping his fingers over his head. "And when the fandango is over!"

Merced glanced at Muerto and Fuerte, the oldest and youngest of the quartet. "You two won't get lonesome, will you?"

José tied a lead rope around the sorrel horse's neck. "Us? We plan to have a fiesta every night. Señoritas are even now waiting for our signal to come and celebrate." When the smile faded from his lips, he turned to Merced. "Bring us plenty of chocolate, *El Patrón*."

"It's on the list. Now stick close to home. Don't wander too far from the hacienda unless it's an emergency. I heard there's a band of Miwoks just north of here."

"*Sí*, Papá," José mimicked.

Piedra brushed his mustache with his fingers and adjusted his unlit clay pipe. "Miwoks this far north? How do you know that?"

"*El Patrón* visited with a young *viuda*." Echo Jack grinned.

"You aren't the cause of her being a widow, are you?" Piedra challenged.

Merced shook his head. "Nope, but she said her band was up above Little Bear Creek. If the Maidu find them, there might be a squabble."

"Or they could join together and attack Rancho Alázan?" Piedra proposed.

"Yeah. You two take care of yourselves. And listen, if a short little Indian woman with four or five kids shows up, give them something to eat. Her husband died, and for some reason the band went off and left her."

"How will we know her?" Piedra queried.

"I gave the oldest boy my old turquoise-handled hunting knife."

"He finds a widow lady, and all I come across is an angry mountain lion." Echo Jack turned to Merced. "What time are we leaving in the morning?"

"As soon as it's light enough to look down and see our boots."

Wilson Merced had a gold engraved pocket watch that was given to him by Sam Houston. It was wrapped in a burgundy velvet bag and tucked in the bottom of an oak box that sat on the three-foot adobe ledge that served as a windowsill in his room. He hadn't looked at the watch for nearly three years.

California time wasn't told by minutes and hours.

Months, years, and seasons were all that mattered.

Yet Merced did operate on a fairly disciplined schedule. He woke up one hour before daylight, built a fire, washed up, and made a pot of coffee or chocolate if they had any. Then he pulled out round gold-framed glasses, perched them on his nose, and read two chapters in a small Bible so worn that most of the pages were loose. When he was through reading, he tied it together with rawhide strings.

It was the same routine every month, year, and season.

When Piedra Muerto summoned them to breakfast, Echo Jack and José had the two teams of horses hitched to the hide carts and parked by the front gates of the courtyard.

They ate by lantern light. By the time they gathered their bedrolls and firearms, they could almost see the river at the foot of Cerro Robles.

Echo Jack drove the lead team.

Merced followed close behind.

Both men carried pistols in their belts and cap-lock breech-loading Hall carbines in their laps.

For six days Merced heard little more than the squeak of wooden cart wheels and the off-key singing of Echo Jack. They bypassed Sutter's Fort at New Helvetia and kept pushing across the great valley until they reached the coast mountains near Paso Pacheco.

The next morning Merced and Echo Jack were freshly scrubbed and wearing their best clothes. That meant single-breasted wool frock coats over once-white linen shirts and silk cravats tied at the neck. Both had undyed linen trousers held up by suspenders and decorated by wide silk sashes around their waists. Echo Jack's sash was bright red. Merced's was black. Both sashes covered up pistols that were tucked behind leather belts.

Echo Jack wore moccasins pulled up on the outside of his trousers. Merced wore tall brown leather boots that almost reached his knees, also with trousers tucked inside.

Echo Jack's hat rested on his back, held to his neck by a braided rawhide stampede string. Thick black hair hung to his shoulders and was parted in the middle and highly greased. Although a few inches shorter than Merced, the half-breed's shoulders were just as broad and strong, making him look the stockier of the two. His naturally smooth face showed only a faint trace of a beard.

Merced wore his round brown, broad-brimmed felt hat low in the front, giving shade to his face, and a month-old beard showed signs of brown, red, and gray whiskers.

Once their teams were hitched, the two men surveyed the gradually descending oak-covered hills in front of them.

"It's getting crowded, *El Patrón*. Nothing but ranchos between here and the old mission."

"Perhaps this is our last trip to San Juan. It is closer to go to Yerba Buena or San José."

"But the girls are not as pretty," Echo Jack complained.

"You never met an ugly woman in your life."

"Yes, but some are more beautiful than others."

"No chasing the girls until we get the hides unloaded and sold," Merced warned.

"I wouldn't think of it."

"Of course you'd think of it."

"Well, I will try not to do it."

"Good. Let's go to town, *compadre*." Merced swung up into the second hide cart.

It was almost dark when the Cabrillo party crossed the hill by the bridle path and caught sight of the old Mission of San Juan Bautista. Like all the twenty-one California missions, it had suffered severely from the secularization edicts of 1833. The mission days were gone. After only nine years, the neglect of the buildings was evident. It was Saturday night, and people had come in from all over the region to attend the worship services the following day in celebration of Padre Estában's birthday.

In the evening shadows the mission building did not look as worn and collapsed as it did during the bright light of noonday. The big square plaza that separated the mission from the town of San Juan was crowded with carts, hides, and people.

Alena looked out across the San Juan Valley.

It is a beautiful land. Cattle and horses as far as the eye can see. Orchards by the mission. Vineyards and rows of vegetables behind every house. It is like a peaceful, quiet spring day on Cape Cod . . . right before a violent storm.

Don Francisco is right. There is change in the air. Perhaps it is only the aroma from the close of the mission. Everything happens so quickly here. Within the span of one generation the missions have faded. The ranchos still spread across the land, but they, too, have their limits.

I wonder if any besides the Franciscans mourned the death of the missions? I hope they are repaired and preserved. They will remind those who follow that they aren't the first to come to this golden land. And perhaps they can remind the faithful they aren't the first to spill their blood for the faith. The missioners truly were the ones who gave "light to them that sit in darkness" . . . but now that time seems past.

Lantern lights flickered out into the crowded street next to General José Tiburcio Castro's large two-story home facing the plaza. Several women on the covered balcony surveyed the throng camped in the plaza. Don Francisco helped Alena and Doña María Martina into the house and then took the horses across to the livery stables and corrals.

Within a few minutes Alena had been introduced to most of the female members of the Castro household. She was even greeted by Don José himself.

While Doña María Martina scurried with the others around the ovens in the backyard, Alena perched on the second-story veranda in front of her room and tried to get the feel of what was going on in the plaza. She stared into campfires and shadows. She had pulled a black lace shawl over her shoulders, but her red hair was left uncovered.

Of the 500 residents of the San Juan Valley, nearly 200 were concentrated in the town of San Juan, located just southwest of El Camino Reál, next to the Mission San Juan Bautista.

Half the population were of Indian heritage; the other half were Californians. Because it was Saturday when Merced and Echo Jack rolled up Calle Segunda toward the plaza next to the mission, the town was crowded with visitors.

Some came for barter.

Some for the next day's worship.

And all came to attend the fandango of Don José Castro.

Heavily loaded carts of cowhides drew little attention in a crowded town. As they passed by the west side of the decaying mission, Merced spotted the two-story house of Castro. Even though the sun had set behind the house, there was still enough twilight to see señoritas in brightly colored dresses standing on the veranda and gazing out at the crowded plaza.

Their lace-covered black hair framed coy smiles.

Even from a hundred feet away, one woman caught Merced's attention.

The head was uncovered.

The hair was very red.

The skin fair.
The nose slightly upturned.
The gaze regal.
Not Andalusian.
Nor Castilian.
Maybe Scottish.
Or American.
I'll never get Echo Jack past the veranda.
He's like a kid in a candy store.
Too many choices.

The squeaking wheels of two wooden-wheeled carts piled with cowhides caught her attention.

Perhaps I will buy those hides tomorrow.

Her eyes followed the first cart pulled by a strong pair of matched buckskin horses with light-colored manes. The second cart had almost identical horses pulling it, but the manes were dark, almost black in the twilight. The first cart stopped right in front of the veranda, and its driver stood and shouted up at her, "¡*Señorita Roja, usted es una mujer muy hermosa!*"

Wilson Merced brought his cart to a halt and stood up. "Keep moving, Romeo!" he shouted.

Echo Jack stood, removed his hat, and bowed toward the veranda. "You are Americano, no? Or English perhaps? You are the most beautiful woman in San Juan. Will you save me a dance at the fandango?"

Merced watched the redheaded woman step back into the shadows of the veranda. *Obviously he means her, although I reckon he doesn't care all that much which one answers him. She looks too young. Too skinny. Too out of place. What's she doing here anyway? A girl shouldn't be allowed to stand on the veranda and flirt with cart drivers.*

Not that it matters to me.

From the shadows Alena could no longer see the cart driver. "Señorita?" he called again.

"You have me at a disadvantage, señor. You claimed to have seen me. But in the dark, I have not seen you."

"That is to your advantage," a strong voice shouted from the second cart.

"My name is Echo Jack," the first driver called back.

"Echo?"

"You see, wherever I go, people repeat my name like an echo. Will you dance with me tomorrow?"

"That remains to be seen, Echo Jack. I do not dance with men I have never been introduced to in the light of day."

"I will come see you tomorrow and introduce myself."

Alena turned to see Doña María Martina walk along the veranda.

"What is your name, señorita?" Echo Jack called out.

"That is for a resourceful man like yourself to find out," Alena replied.

"Yes, you are right. I will find out."

"Echo Jack, move that wagon," the second man shouted. "I don't have time for you to court every lonely señorita in town."

I assure you, mister cart driver, he is not courting me. And I am not a lonesome señorita."

"*¡Hasta mañana, Señorita Roja!*"

"Move it, Echo Jack. We've got to park these carts and go find old man Tipton before he gets too drunk to buy hides," the second driver shouted.

Alena folded her arms across her chest and gently bit her lip. *Old man Tipton is dead. And he did not drink himself drunk . . . very often. I shall not buy hides from men so filthy and disrespectful.*

When the carts were out of sight, she turned to Doña María Martina. Lantern light reflected on the older woman's kind, round face. "Who were those rude men?"

"Echo Jack is part Indian, part Mexican, part gray wolf."

"And the other?"

"That is Don Juan Sutter's El Americano del Norte."

"El Americano del Norte?"

"Sutter has given him land in the north of the Sierras in order to keep the Indians from attacking his fort."

"He didn't even know that Father had died."

"You must forgive him for that, Doña Alena. He only comes to town once a year. He is probably behind in his news."

"Well, I will refuse to buy his hides. He said Father got drunk when he came to buy hides. He didn't get drunk, did he?"

"No more than any man."

"Perhaps he confused Father with another buyer."

"Perhaps. You do what you want. But El Americano del Norte will have the finest cured *cueros* in the plaza. They always are."

"It doesn't matter. I'll have nothing to do with him."

"You two do have one thing in common."

"Don't tell me he's from Boston."

"I don't know that. But you are two of the few people the governor has granted papers to, who have not been required to convert."

"He refused to convert on religious grounds?"

"Yes, he claims to be a Presbyterian."

"A Presbyterian? Then he must be a Scotsman."

"Wasn't your father, Don Roberto, a Scotsman?"

"Half Scot and half English."

"And I wonder which half you are?"

"I am Californio!" Alena asserted.

"Ah, yes, *mi dulcita*. I almost forgot."

Three

Alena Louise Tipton perched on a round oak stool to comb her hair, but the seat was a little too low and much too hard to be comfortable. *Señorita Tipton, you need more padding in your backside if you intend to ride a horse eight hours a day every day.*

She considered the image in the mirror. *And you need more padding all over if you're going to look like a California* mujer *instead of a* joven!

Doña María Martina swept into the room, her full red lips smiling and brown eyes sparkling. "Doña Alena, you have a gentleman caller this morning."

She spun around on the stool. Her bare toes dug into the woven wool rug that covered the rough wooden floor. "It is Sunday. What does he want?"

Señora Cabrillo's thick gray and black hair was braided and wrapped high on the back of her head, her Sabbath day—and fandango—coiffure. "A vision of the beautiful La Paloma Roja de Monterey, I suppose."

Alena glanced down at her pale white toes and wiggled them. "Who is it?"

"The one called Echo Jack. The man who works for El Americano del Norte. He is the one on the cart who spoke to you last night."

"Tell him I do not wish to buy hides from rude men." Alena turned back to the mirror and resumed combing out her blazing red hair.

Doña María Martina stepped over to Alena and tugged the abalone shell comb from her hand and began to comb the younger woman's hair. "*Conchita*, I think his purpose is to introduce himself to you in the daylight so that he may ask you to dance. Remember, you did indicate that you wouldn't answer him unless you could see him in daylight. But you do not need to dance with his kind, of course."

"He didn't waste any time calling on me."

"It has been daylight for over three hours. But anytime earlier would have been inappropriate."

Alena closed her eyes and enjoyed the feel of the short comb weaving its way through the tangles of her thick tresses. "Oh . . . well, tell him I will be right there."

"Take some time, *mi dulcita*. You do not want to seem to be in a hurry."

"What?"

"Timing is important. It does not hurt them to have to wait. He did not have an appointment. You should talk to him at your convenience, not his."

"Yes, well, tell him I will be there as soon as—" Alena surveyed the room, resting her eyes on her Bible. "As soon as I finish my meditations."

"Yes, I will tell him that. That should keep him waiting." Señora Cabrillo handed her back the comb. "Meditations. I like that. That sounds like a very pious diversion. Perhaps I will use that line with Don Francisco someday."

The rough oak door to the veranda was open, as was the window facing the Castros' backyard. This allowed a warm drift of late June air to carry the sounds of the crowded plaza into Alena's room.

She took one last look at herself in the mirror, adjusted the black lace shawl over her hair, and pinned it just below the gold cross on her chest. The words and phrases from the street continued to float on the breeze.

"¡Adorador!"

"Corista buena . . ."

. . . llevar el corazón en la mano . . ."

Spanish is such a pleasing, melodious language. So relaxed and easy-going. It is a language for lovers. English is harsh, like German. Blunt. To the point. No nonsense. A language for businessmen . . . or generals.

She stood up straight and threw her shoulders back.

Snap out of it, Alena Tipton! You are not Spanish, Mexican, or Californian. You are a New England girl with a silly romantic mind. You should have stayed in Boston. Look at you. Look at the way you are dressed. It is shameful.

She stole over to the window and glanced down at the women at the ovens in the backyard of the Castro home.

Shameful in Boston perhaps.

But not here.

I am treated with honor and respect.

More respect than I ever received in Boston.

That's why I love it here, Lord. My heart is Californian, even though my skin, as Doña María Martina once said, looks like milk from a vaca enferm.

She watched an old woman shovel hot coals out of one of the ovens. Her companion inserted several round loaves of unbaked bread.

I should have her teach me to cook. Of course, she would only tell me to marry a man who can hire a cook.

She and I think a lot alike.

Alena plucked up her Bible and opened it to the red silk ribbon bookmark. *Well, if I'm to be fashionably late, I should really read something.*

" . . . *while they behold your chaste conversation coupled with fear. Whose adorning, let it not be that outward adorning of plaiting the hair, and of wearing of gold, or of putting on of apparel; but let it be the hidden man of the heart, in that which is not corruptible, even the ornament of a meek and quiet spirit, which is in the sight of God of great price.*"

Lord, that is not the passage I wanted to meditate on today. If You're going to nag at me like that, I might as well go to greet and dismiss this Echo Jack fellow.

She repinned her lace shawl tight under her neck.

Walk slowly, Doña Alena Louise, just like la reina *entering her court.*

The hallway from the second story of the Castro house led to a narrow interior staircase that opened into the sitting room. Instead of finding a nervous suitor, Alena spied only Señora Cabrillo standing at the open front door, staring out at the street. "He is gone, *conchita.*"

Alena peeked over the señora's shoulder. "It is just as well. I don't think I wanted to dance with him at all. He and the other one were so forward and discourteous."

Doña María Martina patted Alena's thin hands. "I am glad it did not break your heart."

"Break my heart?" Alena glanced down at the turned-up toes of her crimson and black velvet shoes. "Because some hide skinner didn't ask me to dance? It saved me from trying not to lie."

Señora Cabrillo brushed her bangs back to each side of her round face. "I am glad to see you take it so well."

"You make a big concern of this matter?" Alena stepped past Doña María Martina and leaned toward a large red rose that blossomed near the doorway.

Señora Cabrillo scooted after her and gazed down the packed dirt street toward the livery stable. "Echo Jack is a handsome man. In a wild sort of way. All the señoritas agree about that. But he is, of course, far below your station."

Alena tilted her head and raised her nose at the same time. "He didn't look that handsome last night."

Doña María Martina waved a gold-ring-laden finger at her as she spoke. "Was he wearing a velvet *chaqueta* trimmed with gold braid and lined with red silk?"

"Of course not."

"He is today. It was a very fine *chaqueta.*"

"It takes more than a fine jacket to make a man." Alena tugged at a bare earlobe. *I can't believe I came down here without earrings. It's like I'm only half-dressed.*

"That's exactly what I told María Alejandra. But does she listen to me? Her *madre*, rest her soul, was a very good woman. But her father has no refinement."

Alena scanned the house as someone scurried through the sitting room. "María Alejandra? You mean, Señora Castro's *sobrina?*"

"Yes, she just ran off with that mestizo, Echo Jack."

"She did what?" Alena's thin arms dropped to her sides.

"Echo Jack is not a patient man, *mi querida.* When you delayed in coming down, he chatted with María Alejandra. The next moment he handed me this note and told me to tell you he will dance with you next year when he comes to San Juan." Her voice was musical, like a melody with an I-told-you-so chorus.

"Next year? I didn't even want to dance with him this year! I just wanted a chance to tell him so."

"Perhaps you waited too long."

"You told me not to hurry."

"I did not know that you would spend such a long time meditating."

"The impertinence! A man does not call on a lady and then leave with another woman before she reaches the parlor. This kind of thing just isn't done!"

"Perhaps not in Boston. But this is California, *conchita.* It is a land for lovers—not waiters."

"I don't believe this." Alena took a deep breath, held it, and felt her neck muscles tighten. "You just let him go off like that with María Alejandra?"

"She is not my *sobrina.* What could I say? It is well you did not want to dance with him."

"Yes, it is a great relief to have him busy with someone else. I do not need any more pursuers."

"That is a very wise attitude."

The rising sun, still low on the eastern horizon, cast long shadows across the plaza from the alamo trees. "Yes, I am taking it well!" Alena snapped, shading her eyes with her hand. "And I never want to see that disgusting Echo Jack again."

Doña María Martina's voice was soft, teasing. "Did you, eh, finish your meditations?"

"Yes!" Alena fumed as she locked her arms and puckered her lips in a frown.

"I believe I will not use that tactic with Don Francisco," Señora Cabrillo demurred. "Its success has not yet been proven."

Alena spun on her heels toward the house. "This day is certainly starting out disappointingly!"

Doña María Martina waved a small folded piece of paper. "Do you want this disappointing note Echo Jack handed me, or shall I return it unopened?"

Alena raised her narrow, sweeping dark red eyebrows in an arrogant burst of superiority. "I am highly surprised that he can write Spanish."

Señora Cabrillo plucked a flaming yellow rose petal from a vine that climbed the wall by the front door and held it to her nose. "It is not from Echo Jack. Nor is it in Spanish. It is in English and written by El Americano del Norte. Not that I've read it, mind you."

Alena yanked the note from Señora Cabrillo and plopped down on a worn, unpainted wooden bench that faced the plaza.

This is absolutely silly. I was mad when this rude man asked me to dance. Now I am mad because he jilted me before I ever got a chance to reject him. It's just that María Alejandra is younger . . . and thinner . . . than I am.

At least, she is younger.

Well, Mr. Rude Americano del Norte, what do you have to say to me? Are you going to insult the memory of my father again?

She unfolded the stiff paper and studied the sweeping cursive India-ink letters that had been carefully quilled on the paper.

It's him! The mysterious hide with the RA.

Did he write this? Perhaps he had to pay someone to write it. The penmanship is too perfect.

Surely such a rude man is illiterate.

She turned the paper toward the rising sun.

Señorita Tipton:

   Please accept my regrets and sympathy concerning the death of your father, Robert Tipton. I have just learned of his death. He always treated me fair, as I did him. I understand you are going to continue Señor

Tipton's business. I would like to give you first option at my hides. If you'd send your business manager over to my wagons, I will be more than happy to show him the quality of hides. As your records will show, your father usually paid $4.50. I will expect the same from your rep.

However, I will not do business on Sunday. It is the Sabbath. But I would like to conclude this business before noon on Monday. It is a long trip back to Rancho Alázan.

Please forgive me for not speaking to you last evening when we came to town. At the time I did not know that you were Robert's daughter.

Sincerely,
Wilson Judd Merced

Alena stared across at the busy plaza.

My business manager?

You will "expect" the same?

That's presumptuous, Mr. Merced.

I might not want to buy your RA hides at all!

I will not give you fifty cents above the top price unless you can prove to me they are worth it.

And I do not do business on Sunday either. So don't try calling on feigned religious convictions to get yourself a better price.

You're not dealing with a little girl.

I happen to be nineteen.

A very mature nineteen.

A flash of red silk and gold braid caught her eye. Two riders bolted out of the livery stable on one yellow-maned buckskin. As they loped past her, Echo Jack tipped his hat. María Alejandra, sitting sidesaddle in front of him with long, thick black hair blowing in the wind, held her nose high and refused to look at Alena.

Alena felt her teeth grind. *If she had looked my way, I'd have stuck out my tongue. May they fall off a cliff and both have a painful, slow death!*

She stood with stoic expression until the riders were completely out of sight.

All right, Lord. So I'm not a real mature nineteen.

I still miss my father.

Sometimes California seems as if it's one big family. And sometimes I feel completely alone.

I think I'm going to cry.

By the time the sun stood a quarter of the way above the Sierra Diablo mountains in the east, the entire tone of San Juan had changed. Alena Louise Tipton leaned on the balcony railing of the Castro home, gold dangling earrings in place, a deserted 400-foot-square packed-dirt plaza before her.

No longer was it a busy market village on the verge of a fandango. It was instead a town at worship.

The huge mission sanctuary was filled with 300 worshipers. Another fifty crowded at the front door, in silent reverence for what was happening inside. Filtering out across the plaza came the strains of the crank-operated English barrel organ.

Almost sixty other worshipers knelt inside the covered arcade that stretched on the plaza side of the long monastery wing of the mission. Running at a right angle to the front door of the church was a 230-foot-long cloister with nineteen arches averaging nine feet high.

The red tile roof and white adobe walls of the church showed heavy wear, upon close inspection, but with a bright summer sun beaming in Alena's eyes, the mission was as dramatic a sight to her as the Spanish Franciscans had envisioned it forty-five years earlier.

Slanting down off the hill to the northeast was a cemetery, and beyond that, Alena could see fruit-laden trees in the orchard. Somewhere back in town dogs barked. A rooster crowed. Below her tiny finches darted among the rosebushes.

Everyone in town goes to church.

Especially when it's Padre Estában's seventy-fifth birthday mass.

Alena thought of Echo Jack and María Alejandra.

Except for those who rode out into the country on one horse with their arms wrapped around each other.

Movement to the right of the plaza caught her eye. She watched a tall figure that could only be El Americano del Norte amble slowly from the livery stable toward the Castro home.

And the Presbyterian. He, of course, did not go to the mission.

Alena casually gazed at him from behind a rough wooden post.

He looks about six feet tall. Wide shoulders. Kind of thin. Doesn't eat well, I'd guess. Probably eats nothing but meat. He needs some fruit and vegetables. I wonder if there is a Señora Americano del Norte? Dark brown hair, stubborn square jaw. Pointed, dimpled chin. His ears stick out through his hair.

He needs a shave.

And a haircut.

Probably a bath.

So do I.

That's a nice single-breasted wool frock coat. Dark brown looks nice on him.

If he weren't so rude.

But why the black silk cravat? It should be brown. I am sure there is no Señora del Norte. She would insist he dress better. He dresses like an Americano. If he's in California for good, he should dress like the others. Father did.

Even though he's walking, he has on stiff leather leggings, long-roweled spurs, and tall heavy botas. Obviously he'd rather ride a horse than walk.

His eyes are too narrow. He looks like he's inspecting the world.

Relax, Mr. Americano del Norte! You are too intense.

He continued to walk straight toward the Castro home and focused his view upon her. She stepped to the rail of the balcony but glanced off at the fruit orchard, as if ignoring him completely.

Wilson Judd Merced felt the dirt crunch beneath his boot heels. The plaza had been cleared of wagons and people. A fiesta was being planned. He knew that by nightfall, the sounds of dancing and singing would bounce throughout the San Juan Valley.

Everyone is gone.

All of them in church.

I don't even know where Echo Jack went.

Obviously he didn't go off with the red-haired one.

He stared up at the woman on the balcony.

So this is Robert Tipton's daughter? I thought Castro told me she was just a little girl. She does look young and a bit pale. Compared to the Californio women.

I suppose she has blue or green eyes. What else would a red-haired woman have? The eyebrows tease a man from a distance. Her smile can be seen for miles. As can her frown, I reckon. Full cheeks, pointed chin. Upturned nose.

She's a little tall and thin.

She must not eat well. Probably nothing but fruit and vegetables. She needs some meat.

A crepe print dress but with long sleeves, lace shawl, dangling earrings . . . Señorita, you dress like you're from Monterey and look like you're from Boston.

One thing's for sure.

You are not a hide and tallow buyer.

That's a man's job.

Some things will never change.

He strolled over to front of the Castro house, removed his wide-brimmed brown felt hat and clutched it in his hand.

"Excuse me, señorita. May I have a word with you?"

Her response came with raised eyebrows. "Yes?"

"I'm Wilson Merced. I've got a rancho over at—"

"You are Sutter's El Americano del Norte."

"I guess I have a reputation."

"And I am Alena Tipton."

"La Paloma Roja de Monterey."

"I can see I, too, have a reputation. What can I do for you, Mr. Merced?"

"I needed to ask you a couple things. First, did you get my note?"

"Yes, I did."

"I hope you understand why I don't do business on Sunday."

"I understand perfectly. I have similar spiritual convictions." Alena rubbed the gold cross dangling at her neck.

"Then we can do our business in the mornin'. Four-fifty per hide?" He brushed off his whiskered upper lip and chin as if they contained unseen biscuit crumbs. "Send your business manager over first thing. I'll need to head back to Rancho Alázan as quickly as possible, so I'll need the silver by then."

"Mr. Merced, I will be happy to look at your hides in the morning, but I am not guaranteeing that I will purchase them. Nor am I guaranteeing that I will pay that price. And, furthermore, I inspect my own hides. I have been actively supervising our warehouse operations for several years."

Merced shuffled his feet. His spurs rang out like a muffled supper bell. "Your daddy always—"

She laced her fingers together and rested them on the railing of the balcony. "Perhaps my father operated the business differently than I."

Merced ran his hand through his neatly combed hair and stared back across the plaza. "Miss Tipton, there are other hide buyers here. Maybe I should look around."

"And there are other hides to be purchased. Please, by all means, check out the others. I have a feeling you would be much happier dealing with someone besides a woman."

"You do have a business manager, don't you?"

"I said, I buy my own hides!"

Merced said nothing but kept looking at her. Alena considered stalking back into the house but decided that would be a retreat from battle. Finally Merced jammed his hat back on his head.

"Señorita, am I imagining it, or do we have a tendency to rile each other?"

It seemed like a good time for him to smile.

He didn't.

But Alena thought she caught a twinkle in his eyes.

She found her anger difficult to maintain, and her shoulders slightly relaxed. "Mr. Merced, you come across as arrogant and overbearing."

"You are probably right. And you strike me as being condescending and manipulative."

"How dare you judge me so quickly!" Then she dropped her eyes to the balcony railing. "And so correctly."

"Now that we have the insults out of the way, I presume our

relationship will improve." He hung his thumbs in the outside pockets of his coat.

Alena raised her eyes to his. *His face is old, but his eyes are young.* "Why would you assume that?"

"Because anything else we might say has to be more complimentary. Miss Tipton, I'm a little rusty at talkin' to pretty girls."

Woman, Mr. Merced. Pretty woman. "Yes, it shows." *Are you just trying to flatter me now?* "I will look at your hides tomorrow."

"Thank you."

She walked along the balcony until she was straight above him. "What else did you want to ask me?"

Merced stared off down the vacant street. "Have you seen my *segundo*, Echo Jack? I thought he was heading this way to pay you a social call. I can't imagine him being in church if you're standing here."

Alena folded her arms across her chest. "He became enamored with a girl named María Alejandra, a *sobrina*, a niece of Señora Castro. They were last seen entangled arm in arm riding out into the country."

Merced shook his head. "I should have known! Do you know if this girl has a father or brothers living here in San Juan? If she does, they will soon be looking for his head."

"She is staying here. I have heard that her mother has died. I presume her father and siblings live elsewhere, but I'm not sure."

"Well, don't take it too personal. For Echo Jack, there is no woman as beautiful as the one standing closest to him at the moment."

"Personal? Actually, Mr. Merced, it simplifies my day. Or at least the dance tonight."

Wilson Merced jammed his hat on tighter and glanced across the empty plaza, then back at Alena. *It's like a vacant stage after the audience has gone home. Two actors just practicing lines, waiting for the real performance.* "If you are not visiting with Echo Jack, then I wonder why you, too, are not in church?"

Alena's neck stiffened. *Are you questioning my faith?* "I could ask you the same thing. I was told you are a Presbyterian."

"Cumberland Presbyterian."

"Yes, that explains things."

"Explains what things?"

"Your innate stubbornness."

There was a slow warming sensation at the back of Merced's neck. He knew it was not caused by the sun. "How do you know I'm stubborn?"

"I was being presumptuous." *My oh my, Mr. Merced, you do gall easily.* "I have heard others tell me so."

"And do you believe what they say?"

"They have not lied to me before."

"That is a good answer. Now we know why I am not at the mission. I am a very stubborn Presbyterian."

"Cumberland Presbyterian," she corrected with a throat-tickling chuckle.

"How about you, Señorita Tipton? You are staying at the Castro home and dressed as a Californio; yet you look as though you come from Boston. Your Spanish is flawless. You run a business in Monterey. Obviously you have the approval of the governor. Have you not converted? Why are you not in church?"

"Because, Mr. Merced, I am a stubborn Congregationalist."

"That is another good answer." Merced's round brown hat slipped off his tilted head and tumbled to the dirt street. He swooped down to retrieve it. "Señorita Tipton, I wonder if we might continue this conversation on level ground? I seem to be getting a sore neck."

She brushed her thick hair off her neck and fingered the gold earrings. "I'm not sure we have much more to talk about, Mr. Merced."

"But I have a question I'd like to ask you. I'd feel more comfortable if we were a little more . . . private."

Alena tried to study his eyes. *Private? There is no one within screaming distance now. How much more private does he want to be? What on earth does such a man want to talk to me about in private?* "Since I am the only one left here, it would not be proper for me to ask you in."

"Even if the house were full of people, I would not accept such an invitation."

"Oh? Is entering a Californian's home beneath your station, Mr. Merced?"

He rubbed his bearded chin. *Exactly why do you always think the worst of me, Señorita Tipton?* "Hardly. I am the only one in my hacienda who is not native born. I have personal reasons for not entering such structures. I assure you it has to do with the building, not the people."

"Well, I'm glad to know that. But it sounds mysterious. I'd like to hear more."

Merced pointed his hat across the abandoned plaza. "Now we have two things to talk about. I was thinking of strolling over to the orchard to examine the fruit. Would you care to join me?"

"The plums are not ripe yet."

"I have some early peaches that are coming off at my ranch. I thought perhaps there would be some here as well, since this is where I bought my seedlings."

"You have peaches at your rancho?"

"Twelve different kinds of fruit trees and four types of grapes. Of course, they aren't all in production yet."

"Your ranch sounds quite lovely."

"The orchard is next to the hacienda. Everything else is grazing land. It's very isolated. But that's what I like best about it. Some men should live in cities and towns." He shook his head and looked away. "I don't know why I'm tellin' you all of this."

"I will be down in a moment, Mr. Merced. I will enjoy a stroll over to the orchard, although I might need to walk slowly. I've spent two days horseback, and I'm afraid I'm quite stiff."

Wilson Merced ambled to the front door of the Castro home and sat on a faded wooden bench parallel to the front of the house. He held his hat in his hand as he ran his fingers along his face.

I probably should have shaved.

I didn't intend to have a discussion with a young lady.

A very young lady.

A very pretty lady.

Lord, I am not at all sure why I'm talking to Señorita Tipton. It just seemed natural to visit. Which is shocking, since I haven't said more than a dozen words to a woman in more than three years.

San Juan is too far to travel to sell hides. Next year I will sell them to Sutter. Echo Jack was right. It's getting crowded here.

I don't like crowds.

Never did.

I wonder how old she really is?

Not that it matters.

Alena entered the room and glanced at the mirror. *I dress like a Californio but look like I come from Boston? I like dressing this way. It is not insincere. It is not immoral. It is very practical for life here.*

Perhaps I should braid my hair, at least before the fandango. Of course my hair is not as long as some. Yet.

I wish I had black hair. Mine is such a bizarre color. Red hair in California? That's the way you look, Alena Louise. Besides, you would not be called La Paloma Roja with black hair. Still they are all so . . . so robust.

She glanced down at her chest. *Really robust.*

She held back her long, full yellow skirt with red print flowers and gazed at her shoes. She stared at the distinctive upturned toes and lace on the shoes. The ornaments included embroidery, beads, and brass sequins, with braided silk laces.

I can't wear zapatos del berruchi to hike in the orchard.

Wilson Merced stood, his hat still in his hand, when she opened the heavy oak door of the Castro home and stepped out next to him. "I'm afraid I'll need to change shoes to walk to the orchard. I left my *zapatones* here at the doorway."

She retrieved a pair of brown leather "turned-shoe" fashioned shoes from a collection of footwear that waited at the door, like kittens for a saucer of milk. Alena sat down on the bench next to Merced.

"I hope you won't think it inappropriate of me to change shoes in your presence, Mr. Merced. It's strange how California seems to give us the freedom to do things we wouldn't otherwise do."

Merced turned and stared across at the vacant plaza. "It is a different country, isn't it?"

"Yes. Have you been here long?"

"Several years. How about yourself?"

"I came to live with my father when I finished school three years ago, but he never brought me with him when he came inland to San Juan. He said it was too wild and dangerous."

"This is hardly what you'd call inland."

"Well, for those of us who spend our days next to the ocean, this certainly is inland."

"Inland a little—but wild and dangerous? Not hardly."

She finished slipping on her walking shoes. When they both stood, she noticed that Merced was several inches taller than either of the Cabrillo brothers. "I need to keep the *berruchis* clean for the fandango. Are you going to General Castro's dance tonight?"

They sauntered across Calle Segunda and into the plaza, which was packed dirt and scattered dry grass. "Actually I did want to talk to you about the dance," Merced mumbled.

"I'm sorry, I didn't quite hear you." She cocked her head and leaned closer to him.

"I, eh, said I wanted to ask you a question about the dance tonight."

She noticed beads of sweat spring up on his forehead. "I am going to the dance with the Cabrillo family," she informed him. "If that's what you wanted to know."

"Oh, no, I wasn't going to ask you to go to the dance with me." He blushed. "I hope you didn't think I wanted to ask you to the dance."

And just why not, Mr. Merced? Are you too proper to dance with a woman who dresses like this? Are you so cavalier? Or are you that bashful? Perhaps there is another reason for your haughtiness. "Are you married, Mr. Merced?"

Wilson Merced shoved his hands into his coat pockets and looked straight ahead as they walked. *Why does she ask me if I'm married? Can't a man talk to a woman without her asking if you're married? What does marriage have to do with anything? I'm not married. I don't intend to get married. I'm certainly not thinking of marrying you.* "No, are you?"

A sudden teeth-flashing smile popped out on her face. "Me? No, I'm not married. I have a feeling it will take a good long time to find the one I'm looking for. But I'm nineteen. I'm in no hurry to marry." *This would be a very good time to tell me how old you are, Mr. Merced. Perhaps he is old but well preserved.*

Wilson Merced tried to slow down his stroll so he wouldn't keep walking ahead of her. *Nineteen? I can hardly remember when I was nineteen. I was trappin' beavers in the Rockies when I was nineteen. This is absurd. What am I doing talking to this young girl? I should have stayed at the ranch and sent Piedra to sell the hides.*

They reached the northeast edge of the plaza and surveyed the orchards that stretched alongside El Camino Reál. Alena noticed that Merced was staring down at his brown boots.

"Mr. Merced, I believe you had a question about the dance tonight."

"Well," he stammered, "it seems like a rather silly thing to ask. Perhaps even inappropriate."

"Mr. Merced, are you always this obscure when you talk to women?"

"I don't usually talk to women."

I can certainly see why. "Did we walk all the way to the orchard so that you could refuse to talk to me?"

Merced folded his arms across his chest. "Okay, I'll get right to the point. But don't get angry with me. The more I talk to you, the sillier this seems. I don't mean this in any way improper. Well, tonight is the big dance . . . and Echo Jack whom you've met . . . he's my ranch foreman—"

"Yes, I know all of that." *Somehow Mr. Merced does not seem like the type to do something silly. Don Ricardo, sí. Don Fernando, sí. Wilson Merced, no.*

"Echo Jack has insisted I should have someone to dance with tonight. He believes my life can't be fulfilling unless there's female companionship. He has threatened to line me up with someone. I don't aim to let that happen. First, if I wanted to dance, I would certainly be capable of selecting someone myself. And, second, if he lines me up with someone, she might be expectin' more than I want to give."

Alena felt a slight bounce in her step. *Just because you dance with her, you think she will make demands on you? Where have you been living? In a cave? Did you ever consider that perhaps she only wants to dance? That is all. What a charmer you are, Mr. Wilson Merced.* "Where exactly is this leading? I've explained to you I'm going to the fandango with the Cabrillo family."

"Okay, here's what I wanted to ask. If you think it's proper, would you . . . consider . . . dancing one dance with me tonight? Just one dance. A short dance. Then I can refuse Echo Jack's offer and escape another fandango without complications."

"The only reason you want to dance with me is to get you off the hook with your *segundo?*"

"Yes."

Alena chuckled. "That's the most strictly functional request I've ever received."

"Well, it's . . . I mean, it's nothing personal."

That's for sure. "Tell me, Mr. Merced, just how did I get the great honor of being selected to be the winner of your one dance?"

"You were the only one I saw when I walked out of the livery just now."

Alena gazed at his blue-gray eyes. *Is he teasing me? He's not serious . . . is he? I feel like I've won a footrace when I'm the only one running.* "What a charming way to select someone with whom to dance."

"Actually if you want to know the truth, I was hoping I'd find you this morning to ask you about the dance. You have quite a fetching smile, and you being so young and handsome and everything."

Just exactly what do you mean by "everything"? "Oh?"

"What I mean is, no one is going to think it's anything serious, a young gal like you dancing with a dusty older hide rancher. You dancing with me wouldn't make any complications for you, would it?"

"Certainly none whatsoever that I can think of."

Merced scratched his neck. *You were mighty quick to say "none whatsoever." You might have given it a little more thought.* "What do you think?"

"I believe I could arrange one dance, just for the sake of our joint interest in the hide business."

"That would be mighty fine."

"It's strictly a favor."

"Exactly."

"But you have to answer a question first."

Merced glanced up and down El Camino Reál as if expecting a stagecoach to roll along.

"What's that?"

"A few moments ago you said you would not enter the Castro home even if they were there. Why not?"

As if ashamed to speak up, Merced mumbled, "I only go into one-story buildings, that's all."

"What?"

Alena thought she detected sadness in his blue-gray eyes. "I had a bad experience in a tall building in St. Louis. I don't go into anything but single-story houses."

"Never?"

"Not even at Fort Sutter. I eat out in the plaza with the Indians, but I don't go into his big dining hall in the second story."

Alena looked away as she mused on his revelation. "It sounds like you are a superstitious man, Mr. Merced."

"I assure you it's not superstition. It's caution."

Straight-lipped. Never revealing his heart. You do have a heart, don't you, Mr. Merced? "Where is your faith in the Almighty to protect you?"

Merced felt rigid all over. *Relax, W.J.M.—she's young. She blurts things out.* He spoke softly, with what he hoped was patient indulgence. "You don't know me. You don't know anything about me, and you question my faith in the Lord?"

She raised her hand to her mouth, then lowered it slowly. *He's right . . . but at least it brought fire to his eyes.* "That was not my intent, Mr. Merced. But it must have sounded that way. I apologize. Your anger was justified."

"I was not angry."

"You most certainly were. And I withdraw the question."

Merced looked down at his boots and rocked back on his heels.

"I made a vow to the Lord, and part of it was that I would not enter again into buildings over one story tall."

A vow to the Lord keeps him out of certain buildings? That is strange. He is one of the most difficult men to figure out that I've ever met. Most men are so obvious. "That is an . . . interesting vow."

"Well, Miss Tipton, I keep all my vows. But that's all I have to say about that."

They promenaded through the shade of the orchard. The trees, now about fifteen feet tall, had been carefully planted in twenty-foot rows, each tree winter-pruned, symmetrical. Scattered throughout the orchard, small re-plant trees allowed in the sunlight, like a small meadow in a forest. Although it was well past blossom stage for all the different varieties, a sweet perfume-like aroma surrounded them.

The floor of the orchard was leaf-scattered packed dirt that still showed signs of irrigation. Alena walked a step ahead of Merced. She knew he was watching her.

Finally he spoke. "Would it be proper to inform Echo Jack that I indeed have secured a dance with La Paloma Roja de Monterey?"

Her stunning dark blue eyes sparkled. "Yes, and let's hope the dance is not held in a two-story building."

His light blue-gray eyes panicked. "The fandango is in the plaza, isn't it?"

"Yes. You may relax. I was teasing, Mr. Merced. I wanted to see if you ever smiled."

He halted next to a heavily laden peach tree. "I believe these peaches are ripe. Shall I pick you one?"

I presume we're changing the subject. "Yes. That would be lovely."

Merced bent low, pulled a knife out of his tooled-leather leggings, and then cut the peach stem just above the fruit.

"Would you like me to peel it for you?" he asked.

"Thank you."

"I just eat 'em skin and all."

"You do what? Doesn't the fuzz get caught in your throat?"

"I don't reckon so. But I never heard of a man dyin' of peach fuzz."

"Mr. Merced, I believe you almost smiled."

"I won't let it happen again."

"Well, I should say not. It made you look ten years younger. *He would look ten years younger without a beard also. But ten years younger than what?* "I believe it had the beginnings of a quite pleasant smile."

"You probably say that to all the *vaqueros.*"

Alena started to laugh. "Wilson Merced, control yourself. I swear, you smiled at me. Why, the next thing you know, you'll be laughing and having a good time. What then will happen to the somber reputation of El Americano del Norte?"

His dark brown eyes narrowed. "Can you cook a peach pie, Señorita Tipton?"

Why on earth would he ask me that? What difference does it make to him what I can or can't do? I don't think he was listening to me at all. It's like two separate conversations are going on at once. "I never tried. Can you cook a peach pie, Mr. Merced?"

"Me?" *That is a strange question to ask! What difference does it make to her what I can or can't do?* "No. But my cook, Piedra Muerto, makes a very good pie." He handed her a thick orange slice of very juicy peeled peach.

She leaned forward. The peach juice dripped to the dirt as she took a bite. "Your cook is named Stone Dead?"

"Yes, but don't ask him to explain." Wilson Merced chomped on a peach like it was an apple. A little peach juice dripped down his beard, which he quickly wiped on his shirt.

"Did he travel here with you?" Alena retrieved a linen handkerchief from the folds of her sash and carefully wiped the corner of her mouth.

"No. Piedra's back at Rancho Alázan."

"Since I don't intend to ever travel inland beyond San Juan, I will never have the pleasure of not asking him about his name."

"Yes, I reckon you're right about that."

They strolled side by side. The broad plains of the San Juan Valley could be seen beyond the orchard—miles of brown dry grass broken by distant haciendas and groves of oak trees.

"Just how far is your rancho from here?"

"About a week by cart. With good horses only four long days."

"No offense intended, but it sounds like the end of the earth."

Merced tipped his hat without showing any emotion. "Thank you. That was my reason for selecting that location."

They meandered across the orchard to a very worn bench on the northern side of the plantings. They sat at opposite ends of the bench in the shade of a large tree heavy with green plums. With a hunting knife cleaned on his pant leg, Merced peeled another peach and handed it to Alena.

Music from the church crank organ rolled out the door, past the worshipers, and down into the orchard.

"I can't tell the melody, but it sounds lively," Merced offered.

The second peach had an even deeper sweet flavor than the first. *I must always live near fruit trees.* Alena waited until she swallowed the bite. "The Cabrillos told me that the mission Indians always liked fast music."

"I kind of fancy slower guitar music myself. But that's because that's all I hear around the ranch."

"You play the guitar?"

"No, but one of my men, José Fuerte, plays well and often. Almost every night."

I wonder how many men he has on his rancho? "Even on a remote ranch there is music. This is California."

The light filtered through the leaves, leaving a sparkling reflection on her face. Merced tried not to stare. *She looks sort of like an angel when the light hits her right.*

She licked her fingers and then dabbed her handkerchief to her mouth. "There is a special story about this organ at San Juan Bautista."

Merced sheathed his knife. "Oh?"

"There is a legend of how the Tulares came through the pass to attack the mission one time. When they reached the plaza, the *padre* didn't know how to repel them, so he ran into the church and began playing that organ."

"What happened then?"

"They all laid down their weapons and began to sing and dance. The next day they went home happy."

"Perhaps I should buy an organ for the ranch. It might be a more effective weapon than our guns."

"It would certainly be better than shooting people."

He stared at her for several moments. "I only shoot the ones that are tryin' to kill me."

"How noble."

"What are you insinuating?"

"Nothing, Mr. Merced. You seem to be defensive."

"I guess you bring that out in me."

"Why do you think that is?"

"I have no idea on earth."

She glanced back at the mission, then up through the plum leaves at the sunlight. "When do you suppose they will finish worship today?"

"I have no idea about that either. Miss Tipton, would you like me to walk you back to the Castros' house now?"

"Are you getting bored with my company?"

"No, ma'am. I just figured if we sit here long enough, I'll say something that will make you so mad you will not want to save that dance for me tonight. Figured I better let the wolf sleep."

"Very well." Alena stood and brushed down her colorful skirt. "Mr. Merced, would you mind walking me around the outside of the mission grounds? I'm curious to see what it looks like on all sides."

With almost the entire population of San Juan at the mission, Tipton and Merced wandered through empty grounds and by deserted homes. They stopped and drank at a crystal-clear spring that irrigated a freshly hoed vineyard. They dawdled by a corral of anxious horses and debated the merits of each. They circled through the village and perused the windows of the closed shops.

By the time they reached the plaza, several worshipers who had been standing or kneeling in the sun near the door of the church began to trudge across the plaza toward their homes.

Merced nodded his head toward the people. "I reckon church is over."

Alena tried to brush her crimson hair back over her ears, but it broke free and dangled across her earrings. "Either that or they're getting tired of the sun's glare. The crowd overflowed out into the plaza."

They loitered at the street corner next to a clump of ambitious barrel cacti. "Do you miss having your own church to go to?" he asked.

"Yes, I do. It's the one thing I haven't really gotten used to in California. How about you, Mr. Merced? Do you miss your Cumberland Presbyterians?"

"Some of them." His thick lips parted in a sly grin.

"Wilson, you smiled at me. You can't deny it!"

His face broke into a wide grin.

"Oh, be still, my heart." She giggled. "What a handsome man you are when you smile!"

"And you, Miss Alena, are just about the most disarming woman I've ever met."

"Thank you, Mr. Merced. I take that as a compliment."

"I meant it as such."

"This has been a nice morning."

"Miss Tipton, your presence has made it so . . . well, *he pasado las vacas gordas.*"

"I take that, too, as a compliment, although I've never understood why a phrase about fat cows is a compliment."

"I reckon it's like saying I had a whale of a time, a large time, a good time."

"Well, El Americano del Norte, I have had a fat cow of a time also." She made a deep skirt-holding curtsy as if in the court of a queen.

He pulled off his hat and responded with a sweeping bow.

Then they both laughed.

Real laughs.

Alena recognized the older woman who approached them as one of Señora Castro's cooks. "Emilia, is church over now?"

The gray-haired, black-shawled woman shrugged her shoulders. "¿Quién sabe?"

"What do you mean?"

"I got there late because I had much bread to bake this morning. I have been standing in the sun for several hours. Perhaps I do not understand."

"Understand what?" Alena pressed.

"I thought we were concluding the service. Padre Estában went to the altar and knelt for prayer. When the prayer is over, he will stand and give us his birthday blessing."

"When the prayer is over? You mean he is still praying?" Merced interrupted.

The older woman pursed her lips and studied him from head to toe. "He has been in prayer for quite some time. My knees are sore. The sun is hot. I decided to come home. *Padre Santo*, have mercy on my soul. Sometimes my faith is so weak."

Alena laced her fingers together as she glanced back across the plaza at the church. "Does he normally pray this long?"

"He never prays this long. He must be praying for the entire human race—by name." Emilia crossed herself and bowed her head. "*Padre Santo*, have mercy on my soul."

Merced pulled off his hat and wiped his sweaty forehead on his shirt sleeve. "There are some days when I feel like prayin' from dawn to dusk, too."

Alena's throat tightened. "Yes, but not while hundreds of people wait for your benediction."

Merced nodded. "That's true enough. The Lord must be dealin' with him on some matters. I imagine *padres* have plenty to be concerned with."

"For several hours?" Alena pressed.

"Haven't you ever wrestled with the Lord over somethin' day and night?"

"I don't believe so."

"You will. You're young still."

"Are you saying I'm young and immature, and when I grow up to be wise like you, I'll have a deeper spiritual commitment?" she fumed.

"No, I'm just sayin' the longer you live, the more chances you'll have to do some dumb things."

Mr. Merced, does this dumb thing that drove you to days of prayer have anything to do with why you refuse to enter two-story buildings?

Alena relaxed as she fingered the gold cross at her neck. "You might be right about that."

Wilson Merced's attention was solely on the mission. "I think I'll mosey over to the livery and see if Echo Jack has come back to town yet. Again, Miss Alena, it was a beautiful mission mornin'. One of the most pleasant I've had in years. Thank you for the walk."

"And thank you, Wilson, for your companionship. I enjoyed both walking and arguing with you." She smiled. "In the morning we will do business on the *cueros*, the cowhides."

"You mean, those $4.50 *cueros?*"

She shook her head. "I believe this is where we began the day. But now I honestly look forward to bartering with you. Until then."

"Yes, ma'am. And we'll see each other tonight at the fandango. You did say we could dance, right?"

"Oh, yes, certainly. I forgot." She flashed a full-toothed smile.

His face was once again expressionless. "I didn't."

Alena Louise Tipton scooted a straight-backed oak chair out to the veranda of the second-story Castro home to watch the plaza. In her right hand was a small woven bamboo leaf fan with an orange butterfly painted on one side and a green parrot on the other. She cooled herself as she gazed across at the largest mission sanctuary in California.

Padre Estában must hate to see his vast congregation dissipate.

She glanced to the right at the livery stable. Wilson Merced crouched on a saddle on the ground, his back propped up by unpainted, weathered gray barn boards, his round broad-brimmed hat pulled over his eyes.

You are not asleep, Mr. Merced. I saw you peek up here a few times. Not as many times as I've peeked at you, but several times nonetheless.

The plaza looks so deserted. By tonight there will be music, dancing, lanterns, laughter. And this afternoon? Don Ronaldo and Don Fernando have promised me a surprise.

What will it be?

Some demonstration of their roping.

I will have to decide which one I will dance with first.

They are both very gentlemanly.

Don Fernando is taller.

Not as tall as Mr. Merced.

I do not have any idea why I thought that.

Perhaps I should dance with Mr. Merced second and get it over with. Somehow I do not envision him as much of a dancer.

From her view 400 feet across the open plaza, Alena thought she saw Doña María Martina Cabrillo leave the front of the mission church and trek toward the Castro home. Scattered worshipers quietly filtered out of the church in ones and twos, returning to their homes or campsites without talking.

At 200 feet Alena could tell for sure that the well-dressed, gray-haired woman was indeed Doña María Martina.

At 100 feet she could tell that Señora Cabrillo wore a worried frown, but she didn't come straight to the Castro home. She veered off toward the livery stable. Alena watched with wonder as the driving force of the Cabrillo family spoke to Mr. Wilson Merced.

What does she want with him? What is going on? Where's Don Francisco? Is the worship service over?

Alena slipped downstairs in time to greet Doña María Martina and Mr. Wilson Merced.

"*Conchita!* We need your help, *conchita!*" Señora Cabrillo said, extreme concern on her face.

"What's wrong? What has happened?"

Wilson Merced stood behind Doña María Martina. Even with hat in hand, he was a foot taller.

Alena watched the normally soft and comforting eyes of the Californian grow tense with anxiety. "Doña Alena Louisa, we fear something is wrong!"

Alena spied out the plaza. "At the church?"

"With Padre Estában." Señora Cabrillo looked old, her brown eyes lined and tired.

"What happened?"

"Nothing. That's the problem." She let out a deep sigh of resignation.

When Alena laid her hands on Doña María Martina's, she could feel them quiver. "I don't understand."

"At the end of the mass, Padre Estában always kneels at the altar for prayer. Then he stands and blesses us. Padre Estában *es muy santo*. He often prays for quite a while. *El Diablo* squirms when Padre Estában prays."

Alena's eyes were briefly diverted by a large, skinny dog that loped down the dirt street as if it were the only creature on earth.

"Well, we have been waiting for him to finish his prayers and bless us for almost two hours. Don Francisco thinks perhaps the *padre* is sick. He is very old, you know."

"Did someone go up and check on him?" Merced asked.

"*Por el amor de Dios*, no! It would be a sin for us to interrupt the *padre* in his prayers."

Merced stepped closer. His shoulder brushed against Alena's. She didn't move away. Neither did he.

"You could all just quietly leave and let him continue his prayers."

"But we haven't received the blessing yet. That is why we have come—to receive the birthday blessing."

"Then you will need to wait it out longer?" Alena gave the señora a hug, then stepped back. "Do you want me to go ahead and prepare some of the food for dinner?"

"No, no. Don Francisco asked me to talk to you and to El Americano del Norte." Doña María Martina glanced up at Merced. "How shall I put this? He thought it would be good if you two came to the church and went up to Padre Estában to examine him."

Alena wrinkled her smooth brow and glanced at Wilson. "You want us to do that? But we're both Protestants."

"*Sí*. That is the point."

Alena waved her hands. "I don't understand."

Wilson Merced reached over and held Alena's arm. It was a strong, confident grip that was not overlooked by Doña María Martina's piercing brown eyes. "I think what Señora Cabrillo means is that since we're outside the church—and because of that, technically under sin anyway—it wouldn't hurt us all that much more if we were to interrupt the good *padre*."

"*El Señor* would forgive you. You don't know any better," Señora Cabrillo explained.

"Let me see if I understand. The church is full of worshipers," Merced began.

"On their knees for almost two hours."

"And the *padre* is still kneeling at the altar?" he questioned.

"Yes, yes."

"So Mr. Merced and I should walk up and check on his health?" Alena pressed.

"Tell him we are all worried about him."

Merced pulled his hand off Alena's arm and jammed his sweat-soaked felt hat on the back of his head. "It's a mighty unusual request."

"There are times that it is nice to have a Protestant or two around." Señora Cabrillo held each of their hands with her ring-covered fingers.

"What if Padre Estában becomes angry with us?" Alena cautioned.

"I'll be leaving for the north land tomorrow, not to be back for a year . . . or longer," Merced announced. "I'll do it on my own. That way Doña Alena Louisa won't garner the *padre's* and the people's disdain."

"No," Señora Cabrillo cautioned. "Don Francisco said the Indians would not understand if you interrupted by yourself. They would think you are trying to break up the worship. There could be trouble. But if La Paloma Roja de Monterey is with you, they will see it is a peaceful visit."

"Perhaps then," Alena suggested, "I should go on my own."

"No, no, *conchita!* If you go together, the curse would be halved. That would be best."

"Exactly how should this be done?" Merced quizzed.

"Don Francisco said I should get all the people to return. Then we will all kneel again. After that, you two will come in, walk up to the altar, and talk to the *padre*."

Alena's heart raced. *Lord, being a light in a dark place doesn't mean inside a mission church, does it? I am very, very glad I don't have to do this by myself. Thank You for sending Mr. Merced here today.* "What do we say?"

"Ask him about his health. Tell him you would like to study

the faith. . . . Ask him if . . . if you can pick peaches. . . . I don't know, *dulcita. El Señor* will provide you the words. Will you do this for us?"

Alena looked over at Wilson Merced, who nodded agreement. *Yes, he is a man to go through tough times with. There is something in the countenance. Just like my father.* "Yes, of course, if that is what you want," she conceded. "We'll do it."

"It is with humble gratitude we thank you. Give me a few minutes to talk to the others and return to the church," Señora Cabrillo instructed. "When you see me enter the church, then start across the plaza, but proceed slowly. I don't want anyone to suspect I put you up to this. They must think it is all your idea."

Doña María Martina scurried to tell the stragglers to return to the service as Merced and Tipton stood side by side and gazed across the plaza.

"There is a woman who is playing it safe. It's like raising the pot only a nickel when you have four aces," Merced concluded.

"For the first time in a long time, I feel like an outsider again," Alena admitted. "Sometimes I get so caught up with California, I am just sure that I'm a native. But right now, it all came back. I am a visitor to the land and to this church."

"That makes both of us," Merced admitted. *Only nineteen? Perhaps on the outside. But she has a heart much older and wiser. She is the type who will march through tough times. Especially if you rile her a tad. It is to your advantage, Wilson Merced, that she is too young for you.* "We will be, of course, the only ones with blue eyes in the building."

"Do you think the Lord will be displeased with us for doing this? It's not just a matter of violating their faith. We must be obedient to our faith as well."

"I reckon we can serve these people best by checking on their beloved *padre.* That's what the Lord wants us to do, right? To be servants."

Alena turned from the plaza to glance at Merced. "I have a difficult time with servanthood. I confess I love having others do things for me and often overlook opportunities to help. Do you know what I mean?"

"Yeah. It used to be more of a problem for me, too."

"What happened? How did you overcome it?"

Merced's normal relaxed baritone slipped down to bass. "I failed so bad that it caused a horrible tragedy that I carry before my eyes every day of my life."

"Oh, dear! Is that connected with the reason you left Missouri?"

"Yes, but I refuse to talk about it."

"Well, I am certainly sorry for your pain . . . and sorry for my self-centeredness. . . . There is Doña María Martina. She is going back inside the church. Shall we proceed?"

"Slowly."

"Do you know what we are going to do, once inside?"

"Follow the Lord's leading, I suppose."

The two meandered side by side across the plaza. Alena was once again wearing her *zapatos del berruchi*. *I have been in California for three years, and I don't think I've done one thing that really mattered. Perhaps this will be the first. To help a people, a padre, a congregation.* She could feel the palms of her hands begin to sweat.

Merced strolled with hat in hand. "If I would have known I was going to church," he mumbled, "I would have shaved."

"You look fine. Your beard looks nice, for an older . . ."

"An older man?"

"Yes, well. That sounds quite rude. Please forgive me, Mr. Merced."

"You're forgiven, *young lady*."

"Let's hope the *padre* is as gracious."

When they reached the crowded doorway, they waited until kneeling worshipers finally scooted aside and provided them a path down the center aisle. Questioning eyes surrounded them. They huddled together as their eyes adjusted to the candlelit room.

"What a huge sanctuary!" Alena whispered. "How tall is the ceiling?"

"Forty or fifty feet," Merced whispered back.

"There is no second story?"

"No, I already checked that out." Merced leaned down, and she could feel his whispered words tickle her ear.

"How many candles in those iron chandeliers?"

"Maybe twenty-five in each."

"Who are the statues of in the *reredos*?"

"I don't know, but I reckon the one in the lower middle is St. John the Baptist," Merced surmised, "since this is San Juan Bautista."

"The carved wooden altar is beautiful."

"The *padre* looks like he's meditating." Merced stared down at his feet. "Look at that red tile." He pointed to the flooring that had been placed on packed sand. "That's a bear print . . . and that one's a coyote. The night they made these tiles they had some visitors. Shall we proceed?"

"Yes, but to tell you the truth, Mr. Merced, when I dreamed about going down the aisle of a crowded church with a handsome man—"

"Handsome older man."

"—a handsome older man at my side, I thought it would be for some other purpose than this."

"Think of it as practice for your wedding."

"Yes, Father. Thank you for giving me away. Try not to cry."

"Straighten up," Merced challenged in such a way that Alena did not know if he was serious or teasing.

"Now what shall we do?" she asked.

"Do you kneel when you pray, Miss Tipton?"

"Sometimes."

"Well, let's walk slowly and quietly to the front. I'll kneel on the *padre's* right and you on the left."

"One step lower than he is," she advised.

"Yes, that will show respect. Then we'll ask him if he is ill or needs our help."

"And tell him the people are worried about him," she added.

"Right."

"Who does the asking?"

"I will," Merced volunteered. "I do live a long ways away. Perhaps I will carry any curse away with me."

Tipton and Merced promenaded up the center aisle past hundreds of weary, kneeling worshipers. Whispered conversations rolled as they passed each row.

Stopping on the fourth step, they glanced at each other and then knelt in unison. Alena bowed her head and folded her hands in front of her. *Lord, be with Mr. Merced. May he say the right things. May we not offend this padre nor these people nor You.*

Holding his hat in front of him with both hands, Wilson Merced cleared his throat and whispered, "*¿Padre?*"

All they could see was the dark brown robe that covered the *padre* and the soles of his worn sandals.

"*¿Padre? ¿Cómo está usted?*"

There was no answer.

Alena leaned over to Merced. "I believe the *padre* speaks English."

"Padre Estában? This is Wilson Merced. I bought some fruit trees from you a few years ago. I don't want to interrupt, but your people are worried about your health. Can we be of some help to you?"

Alena scooted on her knees closer to Merced. "Is he ignoring us?" she whispered.

Wilson Merced scratched his head behind his right ear. "Well, here goes. If the people don't stone me, I will at least get his attention."

Still on his knees, Merced scooted up the final step alongside the aged *padre*, who knelt with hands clasped in front of him, his bare forehead resting on the carved oak altar.

Alena watched Merced take a big, deep breath, then reach up and touch the *padre's* shoulder. After that, he touched the *padre's* hands, then slid his fingers along the *padre's* cowled neck.

He glanced back at Alena.

Padre Estában!

Merced, still kneeling, scooted back down beside her. The whispers of the congregation surged to a low roar.

Alena's lips brushed against Merced's ear. "He's dead, isn't he? I read it in your eyes."

"Yes, but I'm not sure how and when to tell his congregation."

"Some have probably guessed it."

"Should we go over to Don Francisco or Don José Castro and tell them first?" he asked.

"I don't know. But what a wonderful way to die," she said.
"Oh?"

She could feel tears trickle down her cheeks. "A *padre* in his own church, among his people, in the midst of worship—while in prayer at the altar. I think it was the Lord's final blessing to Padre Estában."

"You're probably right." He took another big, deep breath. "Well, *conchita*, pray for me." *Why did I call her conchita?*

Alena kept her eyes on the altar. *Why did he call me conchita?*

Wilson Merced stood up and turned to face the great congregation. He cleared his throat. Every eye focused on him.

"May *El Señor* be praised," Merced began. "Padre Estában has completed his work here on this earth and has gone home to be with his Jesus. I am sure the *padre* would want you to rejoice in his good fortune, just as you mourn over your loss. Señorita Doña Alena Louisa Tipton and myself wish you our deepest sympathy and prayers over the death of your *padre*."

Wilson Merced held his hands up as if to bless the congregation. "May God have mercy on us all."

For several long minutes there was stunned silence.

"What are they doing?" Alena whispered, still kneeling, her back to the congregation.

Merced held his hat over his mouth so that only she could hear. "Trying to figure out whether to thank us or hang us."

Suddenly Don Francisco Cabrillo stood up. "May God be praised! The servant of the Lord has gone to his Master!"

A wave of worshipers, both Californios and Indians, rose to their feet, each with a shout of praise.

Alena stood up beside Wilson Merced. "What are we supposed to do now?"

"I think we should sneak out that side door toward the cemetery and rejoice that it isn't our final resting place."

She slipped her arm into his. "At least, not yet."

Four

The Indian members of the congregation of the Mission San Juan Bautista seemed to understand, even better than the Californians, the joyous homegoing of Padre Estában. In spontaneous celebration, they grabbed ribbons, flags, tree branches, and scraps of bright-colored cloth and then danced in a serpentine fashion up and down the streets of San Juan with choruses, chants, and cheers.

The Californios, led by Don José Castro and Don Francisco Cabrillo, removed the *padre's* body from the ornate sanctuary to the simple spartan quarters of the rectory and began making preparations for his burial. They sent a rider south to San Luis Obispo where the mission president was thought to be currently residing. The noon meal was abandoned by most, including the Castros and all in their home.

Talk centered around the morning's shocking event and whether to continue with the plans for a fiesta and fandango in the evening. Doña María Martina summed up the feelings of them all. "The *padre* deserves an enthusiastic farewell. He served his people and *El Señor* with sincere devotion during the difficult time of secularization of mission land. We will have months to mourn our loss. The Americano del Norte was right. Today will be a time to rejoice with the *padre*. Today he went home. We are happy for him."

That message floated out of the Castros' home and up and

down the twelve dusty streets of San Juan. Within an hour the plaza was beginning to refill with those planning on celebrating.

Not long after that, the festivities began.

Horse races thundered along the stretch of El Camino Reál between the orchard and the mission. Nearly everyone competed against Señor Livermore's red mare. An instant open market sprang up again around the outskirts of the plaza. Fruit, vegetables, furs, jewelry, trade goods, wine, chocolate, lead, gunpowder, and clothing of various stages of wear could be purchased.

While the local Indians mixed with the Californios, most of the Indians who came in from the Plano Tulare set up their lodging on the far east side of the plaza. The men huddled together and sent the women and children to inspect the goods for sale. From the veranda of the Castro home, Alena could hear the shouts and cheers from the cockfights taking place behind the livery. The large unpainted barn blocked her view of the activities, but she had attended enough such events to visualize the scene.

On the southwest side of the plaza Don José Castro oversaw the installation of packed sand and red floor tiles on the plaza itself, in preparation for serious dancing later in the evening.

The town was filled with noise and color.

Happy noise.

Bright, vibrant colors in every skirt and shirt, hat and sash.

Alena was delighted to sit on the balcony and watch the proceedings. Out in the middle of the plaza, Don Francisco Cabrillo and sons supervised the erection of a fifty-foot circular corral. When she asked the purpose of such a structure, Alena was told it was to be a surprise especially for her.

It's obviously some sort of competition arena. Perhaps to demonstrate Don Fernando's and Don Ronaldo's roping talents. This is quite extravagant. When I mentioned a contest yesterday, I certainly didn't want them to go to all this trouble.

She rocked her upper body back and forth on the bench as she enjoyed the feel of the warm summer air on her bare arms and neck.

You love it, Alena. You're a coquette. You want them to fuss over you. It's like being a medieval lady and having the knights joust over you. How did a skinny red-haired girl from Boston end up in such a position?

Lord, I'm not sure I should like all of this so much.

But I don't think I could go back to long-sleeved dresses with high, tight collars nor to the stuffy conversation and the social-climbing games. I love it right here.

But perhaps that's because I'm already near the top of the social ladder.

Even with all the excitement in the plaza across the street, Alena kept an eye peeled on Calle Segunda. Shortly after she had returned to the Castro house, a frowning Wilson Merced rode a buckskin horse with a blond mane out of town.

He didn't mention needing to go anywhere to me. Where is he going? Isn't he going to stay for the fiesta? Surely he'll be back for the fandango.

I think.

Relax, Doña Alena Louise. You've known the man one morning, and you think he should report to you before going anywhere. What did he call me? Condescending and manipulative? At least he didn't say haughty and egotistical. But he could have.

Lord, I love California.

But I'm not sure it brings the best out in me.

Perhaps in Your wisdom You could change that.

Doña María Martina scooted out to the bench and plopped down beside Alena. Her long black and gray hair was pulled back and braided in a bun on top of her head. The flower-printed long green overskirt was in a reverse design from her bodice. A gold brooch fastened the black lace shawl, and a string of mother-of-pearl beads encircled her neck. "I am tired, *conchita*. It is not good to be exhausted before the fandango. You have the right idea. Park yourself and watch everyone work." Señora Cabrillo kicked off her red and black shoes and wiggled her black-silk-stocking-covered toes.

"I do feel very lazy. But I have no idea how I could be of any help." Alena reached back and lifted her thick red hair, trying to cool off the back of her neck.

Doña María Martina fanned herself with her hand. "It is good for you to sit here and watch. Everyone looks up and sees you and then works all the harder. *La Reina* de Madrid would not generate more fervor than La Paloma Roja de Monterey."

Alena dropped her hair and sat up, straightening her slumping shoulders. "Now I really feel guilty."

"Well, I don't. I'm going to sit here, too. I'll be *La Reina Madre*."
Señora Cabrillo folded her hands and rested them on her lap.

"Well, Queen Mother, I wish my hair were longer so that I
could braid it and roll it up on my head like you and the others."

"That would be a waste!" Doña María Martina reached over
and ran her fingers through Alena's hair. "The *caballeros* and *vaqueros* want to see this beautiful vermilion hair. There would be so
many tears it would look like spring rain if you put your hair up."

Alena began to laugh.

"It is true! It is true," Señora Cabrillo insisted. "I do not lie.
Little girls in Monterey are begging their mothers to dye their hair
red like yours."

"You flatter me so. No wonder I like California. It is delightful.
Everyone says what everyone wants to hear. Except, of course,
Señor Wilson Merced." Alena brushed her hair with her fingers. *If
my hair is always down, I will need to wear larger earrings so that they
will show up at a distance.*

Señora Cabrillo glanced down, then tugged up the neckline of
her bodice. "*Es verdad.* Many have come to San Juan just to see you,
conchita."

On the distant eastern horizon above the plaza, Alena could
see brown grass hills against the summer blue sky. "They have come
for the fandango," she insisted.

"The fandango is because of you."

Alena laughed again. "They would all come if it were given for
a bull."

Doña María Martina joined in with the laughter. "*Sí . . . sí . . .*
you are right. It doesn't take much to entertain a Californian.
Many want a fiesta every day. But I think you are avoiding an
important topic."

"What do you mean?"

"I mean Mr. Wilson Merced. What lies has the Americano del
Norte told you?"

Alena suddenly remembered his strong arm that she held as
they had exited the church. She had been sad to have to let it go.
"He didn't lie. He just sized me up in about two minutes and told
me what he thought of me."

Señora Cabrillo patted Alena's knee. "He has no diplomacy, no refinement, *mi dulcita*. Americanos are a blunt people. They act as if speed in business, in relationships, and in living life were a virtue. Speed is no virtue! It is not merely enough to get to your destination, *conchita*. You must learn to enjoy each moment that leads you there."

Alena reached down and laid her hand on Señora Cabrillo's. "I'm not sure I follow you."

"Well, let's take two different cases." Doña María Martina pulled her arms up and began to wave her hands as she spoke. "On the one hand there are the Cabrillo brothers who will stand on their heads to impress you today. On the other hand is Señor Wilson Merced. He, too, is interested in you."

"He is not."

"*Conchita*, don't be naive. I saw it in his eyes."

Alena felt her face blush. "Besides, he is much older than I."

"Not that much older, I fear. And I saw it in your eyes, too." Señora Cabrillo leaned over with her head close to Alena's.

"Just where is this leading?" Alena turned her eyes away and glanced up Calle Segunda.

"You see? You are in a hurry already! That is my point. Relax. Enjoy my story, *mi dulcita*. Now, as I said, you have several suitors. You do not know where any of these relationships will lead. Some might be failures, some successes. But that doesn't matter for today. Today enjoy the journey. Some can so worry over where something's leading that they lose sight of the joy of the moment. This is a very joyous occasion. The *padre* is in heaven."

Alena sighed and could feel her shoulders relax. "The sky is clear, the air warm, the blossoms fragrant. It is a blessed day, isn't it?"

"Yes," Señora Cabrillo concurred. "It is the weather of heaven. It is a beautiful mission morning!"

Alena looked out across the busy, crowded plaza, the noise from which made their conversation seem private. "I like that. You should be a writer."

"Ha! My only school has been the wisdom of my parents."

"Then I shall be the writer and tell the story of Alta California."

"*Sí . . . sí!* That would be quite nice."

Alena pointed across the plaza. "Are they building some seating at the corral?"

"Yes, it is for you and me."

"Really?"

"Well, it is for you. But I am tired. I will use it, too. And Señora Castro and some of the other ladies. We will all sit there."

"And you aren't going to tell me what will take place?" Alena feigned a pout, puckering her thin yet wide mouth.

"No! Fernando and Ronaldo made me take an oath under threat of eternal damnation not to tell you."

"I don't think I'm worth all this effort," Alena insisted.

"Of course not. What woman is?" Señora Cabrillo chuckled. "But it gives them an excuse to do what they wanted to do anyway."

Before the festivities in the corral began, Alena took an inspection tour of the marketplace. Most vendors were no more than families who laid their produce and goods out on colorful hand-woven blankets on the dirt.

Alena could tell how far some of the Indians had traveled by how primitive their clothing was. Those who lived in San Juan dressed like the Californians but without the splendid accessories. The women from the San Juan Valley wore simple cotton dresses in off-white, with a little color in a sash or ribbon. Some wore worn clothing that was obviously hand-me-downs from the Californio women. The men wore *calzoneras* rolled up to the knees, cotton shirts, rough cloth sashes, straw hats, and *botas*.

Those who came in from the great valley and the Tulare Plains to the east of Paso Pacheco wore clothing that barely covered their essentials. The barefoot women dressed in shifts of unbleached cotton tied with twine at the waist. The men had trousers of cotton or buckskin and well-worn shirts of rough cloth, and many wore buckskin *botas* held up with cloth strips or rawhide strings.

Alena and Señora Cabrillo carried parasols in one hand and baskets in the other. By the time they circled the entire plaza, their baskets were full.

"I hadn't intended to purchase much of anything," Alena groaned as she trudged up the narrow stairs of the Castro home.

Doña María Martina puffed along behind her. "It is always like this. They give you a present . . . act insulted if you refuse it . . . then expect you to pay them for it. They are shrewd traders, no?"

Alena plunked her basket on the striped wool blanket that covered her bed and pawed through the items. "The silver work of that one was incredible. Did you see all those rings he made?"

"Where do you think these came from?" Doña María Martina flashed her hands.

Alena slipped an engraved silver band on the ring finger of her left hand and held it up. She tugged it off and pushed it on the middle finger of her right hand. "Some of the Indian women could dress more discreetly," she suggested. "It is embarrassing when they expose themselves."

"What they wear now is a vast improvement over the old days. When I was your age, not one in ten of them had any clothing at all."

"The children seem so dirty. I'd like to teach them about cleanliness. When I was young, I wanted to grow up to be a teacher. Can you imagine that?"

"You still are young. Perhaps you will get the chance. But remember, *conchita*, when they don't know where their next meal will come from, and they worry about their children living until tomorrow, they have little concern for how clean they are."

"I guess I need to get used to it." Alena pulled out a brown rabbit pelt from her basket. "What am I going to do with this?"

"If you had a hundred more, you could make a quilt."

"I don't know why I bought it."

"Because a dirty-faced little girl wanted to trade with you for it."

"She was a beautiful little girl with those round brown eyes, but half naked. When I gave her my yellow ribbon, she wanted a hug, but I was afraid of getting dirty," Alena admitted.

"The dirt will wash off. But I caution you about hugging the Indian children. Most have lice and fleas."

Alena fought the urge to scratch her arms. "I think I miss our Monterey."

"Yes, it is the fairest of all of California. Of course, those at Santa Barbara and San Buenaventura might argue with us."

Alena repacked the items into her basket. "There is nothing so pleasant as the California coast."

"Concerning that, there is no debate. Now, *mi dulcita*, wash your face and recomb your hair. I believe we are wanted at the arena."

People crowded ten to fifteen deep around the five-foot high heavy board corral. Some stood on boxes, logs, and benches to see over the solid fence, their arms waving, and shouting as Alena, Señora Cabrillo, Señora Castro, and several other ladies approached the hastily built benches stilted high enough for a view into the arena.

Alena shielded her mouth with a gloved hand. "Has the surprise started already?"

There was what Alena called a Californio strut, and Señora Cabrillo was a master at it. She also was very good at smiling and talking under her breath so that only those near her could hear. "No, it is probably a cockfight, just a diversion until we are in place, *conchita*. Now walk slowly and smile. Remember, you are the queen today."

"I am glad the cockfight is not my surprise. Cockfights are so brutal. I don't think I'll ever get used to them."

"Some think the butcher's ax in the chicken's neck is brutal, too, but they all eat the meat. Doña Alena Louise, this is not a tea party in New England. You want to be a Californian? These are our diversions."

Alena, imitating Señora Cabrillo's sashay, hiked up the stairs to the highest bench on the bleachers. *I will never enjoy an event where the purpose is to watch animals peck and gouge each other to death.*

Once all the dozen or so ladies were seated, the festivities formally began. Each woman held a pastel parasol above her head, which made the stands look like a garden of colorful flowers. Each wore a colorful print skirt with ruffled lace and embroidery that stopped well short of her ankles. Each wore pink or white or black silk stockings. The scooped Californio neckline was covered with jewelry, as were the ears. And all had long, deep black hair braided and rolled in a bun on the back of their heads with one lock hanging down on each cheek.

All except one.

Don Francisco Cabrillo entered the arena riding El Blanco. His black velvet *chaqueta* was lined with red silk and embroidered with gold and silver thread. His round, flat-crowned hat was tilted a little, his short gray beard neatly trimmed. His back was straight as he paraded around to the cheers of the crowd. El Blanco had bright red ribbons braided into his tail and mane. He strutted as if to demonstrate that he was well aware of how handsome he looked.

Señor Cabrillo yanked off his hat and held it above his head to quiet the crowd, then shouted, "*¡Bien venidos!* Welcome to all! We have gathered today to celebrate two events. The farewell fiesta for Padre Estában . . . and a welcome fandango for the first visit to San Juan by La Paloma Roja de Monterey." He waved his hat toward Alena, and the crowd enthusiastically applauded.

"Now let the festivities commence!"

Just as Don Francisco Cabrillo rode out of the arena, three horsemen entered. All rode tall black horses with silver-decorated saddles.

"It's the La Guerra brothers from Santa Inez," Señora Cabrillo leaned over and whispered in Alena's ear. "They are such show-offs, just like their mother!"

"I thought their mother was your cousin."

"*Sí . . . sí*. That is why I know all about them."

The young men raced the horses counterclockwise around the arena close to the fence, their black hatless hair blowing in the wind. On the third lap, right on cue in front of the seated ladies, they dropped their reins to the saddle horns, and stood straight up on top of their saddles.

The crowd went wild.

"Oh, my, that was quite dramatic!" Alena gasped.

For three full laps around the arena, they rode standing in their saddles as a fine red dust fogged up from the galloping hooves. Then in unison they bent at the waist, placed their hands on the saddles, and lifted their feet in the air.

"I can't believe this!" Alena squealed.

"I told you they were show-offs!" Señora Cabrillo huffed.

For three more laps the La Guerra brothers rode the black horses, standing on their hands. On the third pass in front of the ladies, they somersaulted to a sitting position. They rode to the far side of the arena, in unison turned back to the ladies, galloped toward them, then came to a sliding, dirt-slinging stop. All three bowed at the waist and raised their hands.

The people standing around the outside of the corral whistled, yelled, and applauded. Alena jumped to her feet and balanced her parasol to applaud, shouting, "Bravo! Bravo!"

Someone tugged at her dress.

It was Doña María Martina. "Don't encourage them too much, conchita. They are from the south. They are not from Monterey."

Alena looked down at her older friend. *There is prejudice even among Californians?*

Don Francisco rode triumphantly back into the arena. Again he removed his hat and shouted, "Next we have La Pájara de San José and the *bailarín mejor* in all of Alta California, Doña María Felícia Cervantes and Don Miquel Rudolfo Ortiz y Tajo."

Six men in silver-trimmed black and red velvet jackets carried in wooden planks that were positioned in the center of the arena. Alena looked over at Señora Cabrillo.

"It is a temporary dance floor, *mi dulcita*," she instructed.

When the men, who wore round black hats and tightly laced *calzoneras*, reentered the arena, they carried guitars. For several minutes they played as the standing crowd jockeyed for positions to see the performers.

When Doña María Felícia and Don Miquel strolled into the arena, the cheers began. They hushed only when Don Miquel started to dance to the fast strumming of six talented guitarists.

Señora Cabrillo leaned over to Alena. "Don Miquel is the best dancer in all of California!" she whispered. "I should know. He is Don Francisco's nephew!"

Doña María Felícia began to clap her hands in time with the

dancing and the music. Soon everyone in the crowd did the same. Then she sang.

Alena thought it sounded like a high soprano shout. But it was an on-tune shout. The song seemed to last an hour, but Alena knew it had not been more than fifteen or twenty minutes. The crowd roared as the performers marched regally out of the dirt arena.

Once again Don Francisco rode in on El Blanco and raised his hat. "Unfortunately, because he is my brother-in-law, I was obligated to invite El Tonto to come and perform."

At this name the crowd burst out with laughter and applause.

Doña María Martina fanned the still, hot summer air with her hand, then leaned over toward Alena and spoke under her smile. "I should have worn short sleeves like you, *conchita*."

"It is rather warm."

"It is hot! But El Tonto is funny. Watch him."

"The Fool? Someone actually goes by that name?"

"He is very good at what he does," Señora Cabrillo insisted.

The man who entered the arena wore a pure white shaggy wig, baggy trousers, and a torn and ripped shirt. It looked like it had been sliced with a knife. He wore a narrow-brimmed English bowler hat that sat high on top of his head, seeming horribly out of place in California, and was tied under his neck with a bright orange ribbon. He carried a rather large basket over his arm. Halfway out to the center of the arena, El Tonto tripped and fell flat on his face.

"Oh, dear!" Alena gasped.

The crowd roared with laughter.

"Relax, *conchita*, it is his act. He is a *payaso* . . . How do you say it? A clown."

El Tonto set the basket near the giant log pole planted in the middle of the arena and then pulled out several peaches. He began to juggle them, first just one peach. Everyone laughed and shouted. Then two peaches, then three, then four, five, and six. The fruit sailed six feet above his head.

Just as they were all flying with perfect timing, Don Francisco yelled out from horseback outside the arena, "El Tonto, hurry up!"

The man in the white wig stopped and stared over at Don

Francisco, seemingly forgetting his peaches. The entire collection of six peaches then slammed down on his head one at time. His feigned grimaces brought roars of laughter from the crowd and tears of joy to Alena's eyes. She leaned over to Señora Cabrillo. "He is very, very funny! He should be in a circus."

"He is."

"Which one?"

"What do you think this is? Is it not a Californio circus?"

"Yes . . . of course," Alena mumbled.

El Tonto sheepishly gathered up his peaches off the dirt one at a time, carefully inspecting each. With the last peach in his hand, he declared with a shout, "This one is damaged!" And then he slung it over his shoulder behind him into the crowd. The children scrambled for the discarded fruit.

El Tonto scanned the audience of seated ladies. "*Por favor*, señoras y señoritas, do any of you have an extra peach to lend me?"

To Alena's surprise the women around her who had been so reserved suddenly laughed and shouted in unison "No, we do not have a peach!"

The crowd is laughing in anticipation, but I don't know what to anticipate. She twirled her parasol, creating air movement about her.

El Tonto waddled over to the edge of the arena and yelled to Señor Cabrillo, who remained mounted outside the corral fence. "Don Francisco, do you have a peach I can borrow?"

"Of course not!" Don Francisco hollered. "Hurry up, El Tonto. We have more entertainment to follow."

"I cannot continue until I have another peach! Perhaps Don Frambueso could ride over to the orchard and secure me another peach."

Once again the crowd exploded with laugher.

Alena leaned over to Señora Cabrillo. "Frambueso?"

"Raspberry."

"Oh, dear."

"Perform with what you have, El Tonto! Hurry, or you'll see the point of my knife!" Señor Cabrillo threatened.

"Your knife? *Sí, sí.* That will work. May I borrow your knife, Señor Cabrillo?" El Tonto asked.

The crowd applauded as he took the foot-long hunting knife from Don Francisco.

"What is he going to do?" Alena asked.

"Just wait and see, *conchita*."

El Tonto scurried to the center of the arena and began to juggle the remaining five peaches. When he had all five sailing into the air, he suddenly tossed the knife up with the fruit.

"Oh, my!" Alena shouted.

With the same flair and showmanship, El Tonto now juggled five peaches and one hunting knife at the same time.

Higher and higher they went.

All eyes, including Alena's, focused on the knife.

Suddenly Don Francisco shouted, "You must finish now, El Tonto. Your time is up."

The *payaso* stopped juggling and stared blankly over at Don Francisco. One by one, the peaches bounced off his head.

"Oh no!" Alena shouted. *The knife! He forgot the knife!*

El Tonto looked straight up at her as the hunting knife descended, point-down, toward the top of his head. The point impaled itself in the top of the bowler and remained sticking straight out of the top of his hat.

Alena turned away and gasped. *He just stabbed himself for a laugh? This is not funny! This is horribly gruesome.*

The rest of the crowd laughed and applauded.

"Look, *conchita* . . . look," Doña María Martina insisted. "It was a trick."

Alena turned back to see El Tonto remove his hat and bow. There was a block of wood underneath the brown bowler.

"The knife sticks in the wood?" Alena laced her taut fingers and wrung them in her lap.

"Yes, you don't think he would stick it in his head, do you?" There was a knowing tingle in Doña María Martina's deep voice.

"Well, I sort of . . . I thought . . . he is very good, isn't he?" *Alena Tipton, you were completely fooled!*

"Yes, but this was nothing! You should see El Tonto when he juggles six small cats."

Alena sat straight up and shouted, "He does what?" All the ladies turned to stare at her.

Señora Cabrillo broke into a laugh. "*Conchita*, you must not believe everything! You are so easy to tease!"

All the ladies in the bleachers giggled.

All except Alena Louise Tipton.

Once again Don Francisco Cabrillo rode into the center of the small arena. This time he pointed to the log planted in the middle of the arena.

"Señors y señoras, it is time for the special event. And it is in honor of La Paloma Roja de Monterey." He waved his hat toward Alena.

The entire audience clapped and cheered.

"Stand up and wave, *mi dulcita*," Doña María Martina urged.

Alena stood, small pastel yellow parasol held high above her head, and waved her beaded-silk-gloved hand at all the crowd.

When she sat back down, Don Francisco rode the big white horse around the perimeter of the arena, shouting his announcement as he went. "We have a special contest here today. And the prize for winning is worth more than the gold in the streams of the Sierra Nevadas. The Cabrillo brothers, Don Fernando and Don Ronaldo, are going to compete for the honor of having the second dance with Doña Alena Louisa Tipton."

"Who has the first dance?" someone in the crowd shouted.

"The most handsome man in all of Alta California!" he declared.

"El Tonto?" came a mocking reply.

"Of course not! It is me!"

The crowd roared with laughter, as did Don Francisco Cabrillo.

"Now the Señorita Tipton has decreed that there should be a roping contest to settle the matter. But, as you know, roping contests can be—well, they can be quite boring. So Don Fernando and Don Ronaldo decided to go a little better. They will bring into this arena the animals they have roped. Then they'll let the animals decide who the winner is."

"What does he mean, let the animals decide?" Alena prodded.

Señora Cabrillo tugged her laced shawl down so that more of

her chest was exposed and fanned herself with her hand. "*Espera y verás, mi corazón.*"

Like a scolded child, Alena turned back to stare in silence at the arena. *Yes, but wait and see what?*

Don Francisco waved his hat back at the corral gate. "First, Don Ronaldo will bring in his captive!"

The crowd waved and shouted as Don Ronaldo Cabrillo rode his black horse at the head of a yoked team of oxen pulling a heavily ladened two-wheeled cart built like a large cage.

Don Ronaldo's handsome face beamed. Dressed in a velvet, silk, and jeweled *chaqueta*, he was clearly one of the most striking young men in California.

But Alena's eyes were on the cart. "It's a bull? A huge bull."

"Not just any bull, Doña Alena. It is El Toro Diablo."

"The devil bull?"

"He has roamed these mountains for years," Doña María Martina explained. "Some say he has killed six men who tried to rope him."

Alena's hands started to sweat. She tugged off her long gloves. "What are the splints on Don Ronaldo's leg?"

Like a mother explaining her young son's skinned elbow, Señora Cabrillo shrugged. "He busted his knee roping the bull. He got off very fortunate, don't you think?"

"But . . . but . . . he shouldn't take such chances!"

"For you he would rope *El Diablo* himself. Don't worry, *conchita*," Doña María Martin comforted her. "Don Ronaldo assured me he could still dance with you."

He injured himself to dance with me? I am not worth it. What am I doing? Did my coquettishness cause Don Ronaldo to be injured? Lord, forgive me. I thought they would rope a calf or a pig or something.

The crowd was growing in size by the moment. Alena could not imagine anyone for fifty miles who was not there. The Indians from the Plano Tulare, on the east side of the arena, lifted children to their shoulders so that they, too, could peer in.

Don Ronaldo tugged on a chain at the back of the cart and pulled it out, threading it through the ring in the post. After fastening the chain securely, he and the cart driver climbed to the top of the cage and lifted the huge tailgate. The giant brown and white brindled, sharp-horned bull lumbered off the back of the wagon to the roar of the crowd.

The cart was driven out of the arena. The bull angrily rattled the chain linking his leg to the post. Don Ronaldo circled in front of the ladies and tipped his hat. "Doña Alena Louisa—La Paloma Roja de Monterey—I present to you, El Toro Diablo! Never before has he been roped."

Alena handed her parasol to Señora Cabrillo, clapped her bare white hands, and blew Don Ronaldo a kiss. A wide, full-toothed smile swept across his face. He sat tall in the saddle. His long rowels jingled like miniature wedding bells. *Why did I do that? This is not a play. I am not following a script. Control yourself, Alena Louise.*

El Toro Diablo charged the massive post. With his head down, he slammed into the log with a noise like the shot of a large-bore rifle. The crowd grew quiet. Don Ronaldo exited the arena, and the gate was closed behind him. The bull backed up, and all held their breath for the second charge at the post.

But instead El Toro Diablo shook his head, then wandered to the limits of the chain, sniffing and nibbling on some of the trampled grass that was trying to survive in the plaza-turned-into-arena.

Movement back across the plaza toward the livery stable caught Alena's attention. She thought someone rode a buckskin horse past the Castros'. But by the time she turned to get a good look, there was no one in sight. *Maybe it is just as well Señor Merced is not here! He wouldn't think much of me for endangering the life of Don Ronaldo just for a dance.*

Of course, I don't think much of it either.

The crowd cheered again as a second cart came into view, creaking its way up the hill from the direction of the orchard, also pulled by a yoked team of oxen. The Indians parted like the Red Sea to allow it to pass. Don Fernando Cabrillo straddled the left ox with an eight-foot whip in his hand. There was no cart driver, and no one but Don Fernando entered the arena.

He, too, was dressed in his California finest. His round black, flat-crowned hat was tilted in *caballero* fashion. His left arm was wrapped in a linen bandage.

"What happened to Don Fernando?" Alena pressed.

Señora Cabrillo pointed to the cart. "El Oso Grande. He does not like being roped."

Alena shaded her face with her parasol and squinted to see inside the cart cage. *Lord, if I had one day to live over, it would be yesterday. I would never have challenged them to a roping contest!* "A bear? He roped a bear?"

Señora Cabrillo wiped her forehead with her embroidered handkerchief. "Not A bear. THE bear. He is the biggest grizzly left in the Coast Range."

"How does someone rope a grizzly bear?"

"Very carefully, *mi dulcita*, very carefully indeed."

"Don Fernando's arm—is it broken?"

"No. The bear ripped through his jacket into his arm—that is all. Don Fernando told me to tell you he could still dance quite well."

Lord, this isn't fun anymore. I have no business teasing them to do such dangerous things. I'm just a skinny, young lady who is very dumb. Lord, forgive me.

Don Fernando drove the cart around inside the arena fence. The crowd cheered, the bear growled, and the bull paced at the end of the chain.

Alena had a sinking feeling in the pit of her stomach. "What is going to happen?"

Doña María Martina waved a finger out at the post. "The bear will be chained to the other side. Then they will fight to see who is the winner."

"How can you tell which won?"

"When the other is dead. See, Doña Alena Louisa, aren't you glad you did not sail back to Boston? This is the most exciting bull-and-bear match in the history of Alta California. Even Don José Castro said so." Señora Cabrillo leaned over and brushed down Alena's yellow flowered skirt.

While the angry bear paced in the cart, Don Fernando circled in front of the ladies' bleachers. He tipped his hat and called out, "This bear is for Doña Alena Louisa—the fairest flower in a garden of magnificent blossoms. From Don Fernando Cabrillo, the best with the *reata* in all of Alta California!"

Alena stood and curtsied. Then she blew Don Fernando a kiss.

In an act of extreme bravery, Don Fernando carefully parked the cart in such a way as to keep the bull and bear separated. Then he fastened the bear chain to the other iron ring on the post.

Alena tapped Señora Cabrillo on the shoulder. "With his injured hand, why doesn't someone help him?"

"Are you joking, *conchita*? No one else will get within fifty feet of that bear. He's a killer."

Alena felt the muscles in her neck tighten. *I certainly hope that is a stout chain!*

With the bear finally out of the cart and tugging on his chain, Don Fernando drove the cart out of the arena and quickly had them shut the gates. As Alena scanned the immense audience, she noticed that all the distant Indians huddled on the eastern side of the arena, the Californio and local Indians on the west.

In the middle of the arena the bear and bull assessed the situation. Both tugged on the chains, their eyes intent on the other animal.

The crowd shouted encouragement and curses at their favorites. Wagering flew all around the arena. *And I thought cockfights were brutal. I can't believe this is all done because of me!*

The bear slowly pursued the bull, who backed away by circling the post.

Alena dropped her parasol to her lap. "Won't they get the chains all tangled? It will be a mess."

"Yes, sometimes both of them get killed. It could end in a tie."

"Will there be much blood? I really don't like to see blood."

"Don't worry, *conchita*. All the blood will be in the arena. You don't have to worry about it getting on your dress."

Alena rubbed her forehead and closed her eyes. *For years I've avoided such events as this. Now they are having one in my honor!*

The bull suddenly turned and charged the growling bear. The crowd roared. Alena's eyes flew open, frozen to the unfolding scene. The bear retreated quickly behind the post. The bull crashed headlong into the buried log. A loud crack silenced the crowd.

"Did he break his head or the post?" Alena asked no one in particular.

No one answered her.

All watched the spectacle in the arena.

The Indians seemed to be rooting for the bear, the Californians for the bull.

The bear lunged at the bull, slashing with five-inch claws and drew blood from the bull's nose. The bull threw a horn into the bear's shoulder. A flash of bright red blood appeared in the yellow-brown fur of the grizzly.

This has got to stop. This is gruesome!

Alena thought she should get up and walk away. She wanted to at least turn her head. Instead, like everyone else present, she held her breath and stared at the battling beasts. At the same time that she felt disgust, there was also a tickle of excitement, a thrill in her throat, a pounding in her heart.

The bull, tasting his own blood as it dripped into his mouth, retreated to the limits of his chain. The bear, incensed by his own wound, followed in frenzied pursuit. When El Toro Diablo reached the end of his chain, he yanked his foot and, to the gasp of the crowd, pulled himself loose from the iron shackle.

"Oh no!" Alena cried out. "What happens now?"

"Better the bull than the bear," Señora Cabrillo counseled. "It is all right, *conchita*. They both smell their own blood. They will fight to the finish. But the bull has some advantage now."

The bull circled around the outer limits of the bear's chains. He snorted and pawed the dirt. The bear growled with such ferocity that the hair on the back of Alena's neck stood up. Unhampered by the confines of the chain, the bull backed up, and then broke into a charge at the bear. The grizzly stood on his back feet and waved his front claws as if challenging the bull to give it his best.

Suddenly, with a seeming change of mind, the bear turned and ran. Alena was surprised that the shackled bear could move so quickly. The bull pursued. The bear darted behind the post at the last minute.

This time when the bull hit the log, the explosion was like a small cannon, and something did crack.

The big log broke off at the ground. The impact stunned the bull, who stood dazed, shaking his head. The huge bear, now only limited by the dragging log still chained to him, lunged at the bull, this time striking the other side of the nose.

The bull turned and ran to the edge of the arena with the log-dragging bear in furious but lumbering pursuit. The two, with the bull in the lead, circled the arena in front of the bleachers, and Alena covered her mouth as she gasped, "Is this the way it always happens?"

Doña María Martina slipped her arm around Alena's shoulder and squeezed. "It never happens this way! May God have mercy on us."

Alena looked over and could see beads of perspiration cover Doña María Martina's forehead. *I'm not sure God wants any part of this spectacle.*

The bull, deciding it was prudent to leave, raced to the closed gate and then took a flying leap to try and clear the log barrier. He was not as athletic as he thought. Instead, he crashed full force into the stout log gate.

The wood held.

But the hinges didn't.

To the gasp of the crowd, the gate slammed to the ground, and the bull, with the bear in pursuit, raced out into the panicked crowd of Indians. All the ladies, including Alena, stood for a better view.

Oh, Lord . . . no . . . they will kill the Indians. Not because of me . . . oh, Lord, do something!

Then a tall man rode a buckskin horse at a gallop right at the fleeing bull. One Indian woman panicked and froze. She huddled down circling her arms around her children, like a hen with her chicks. With the bull no more than twenty feet from the terrified family, a lasso flew from the hands of . . . Wilson Judd Merced.

Catching the animal around the neck, he flipped a wide loop of slack into the rope, then dallied the other end to the horn of his saddle and jerked his horse back. The big bull tripped over the rope and sprawled on the ground only a few feet from the crying Indians. Several *vaqueros* raced with *reatas* to rope the downed bull.

The pause gave the bear, still dragging the log, a chance to catch up. Spectators fled in the direction of the mission. Merced and his horse were between the two animals and unable to flee because of the rope attached to the bull. But the bear suddenly turned away from Merced and his horse and charged at a little naked Indian girl who looked about seven years old.

Even in the commotion, Alena could hear the terrified girl's cry. The child stood frozen in place, wetting the soil beneath her.

Merced leaped off his horse, pistol in hand, and rushed the bear. The first shot, from twenty feet, hardly slowed the animal. The second, from ten feet, hit the bear in the neck. As blood pumped from the animal, it turned and charged right at Merced.

What kind of gun does he have? How many shots without reloading?

Standing on its hind legs, the bear was so close now that Merced had to duck to miss the razor-sharp claws. The third shot hit the bear in the right chest. It backed up one step and then lunged at Merced.

The fourth shot hit the bear in the forehead but didn't drop him. Merced could almost shove the barrel of the pistol into the bear's open, growling mouth. With a loud blast and puff of black powder gun smoke, the fifth bullet went straight into the bear's mouth. The massive animal dropped at Merced's feet.

The grizzly didn't move.

But Merced did.

The little girl, eyes shut tight, held her arms tightly about herself and continued to scream.

Shoving the Colt Paterson revolver back into his belt, Wilson Merced trotted to the girl and scooped her up in his arms, hugging her tight. The grateful crowd reassembled with the loudest cheering and shouting of the day.

Alena stared at Merced holding the girl.

She's dirty. She stinks. She has just wet herself. She has lice. Even fleas. And he cradles her like she was his own.

Tears trickled down Alena's face. Soon they turned to torrents.

Lord, I don't know if I'm crying because I was so scared or because I'm so ashamed. I wouldn't touch a child like that under the best of circumstances.

He didn't hesitate.

He didn't have to think about it.

A child needed a hug.

He hugged.

Filth and all.

Lord, I wish I could be that way. Why am I so self-centered? I am next to worthless to You, aren't I?

"It's all right, *conchita*." Doña María Martina slipped her arm around Alena's shoulders. "All is well now. But I tell you, they will talk about this in the ranchos for a hundred years. I was scared, too. And I have seen dozens of these. There was death in the air. You felt it, didn't you, *conchita*? Well, death was cheated today. Praise God! The only death today will be the one God has divinely chosen."

Alena wiped her face with her linen handkerchief. "It was all so frightening for a moment."

"*Sí*. We were fortunate they broke out toward the Indians rather than for us," Señora Cabrillo declared.

What difference does that make? Alena took a deep breath and sighed. *Lord, may I never see any child as more expendable than another.*

She watched as Wilson Merced handed the girl back to a grateful crying mother and father. The *vaqueros* had the bull securely tied as Merced returned to his horse. Don Francisco rode alongside him and discussed something. Then the two rode back into the corral. But it was Don Francisco who took a position in the center of the arena where the snubbing post had been.

"El Americano del Norte has done us two favors today—one in the mission, one here at the fiesta. I told him if he keeps this up, we will appoint him *alcalde*!"

The crowd cheered and yelled.

"But he said he would refuse. He is needed back at Rancho Alázan. I asked him to address you, but he declined. He said it was only what any man would have done. Well, it is true. Any man would have wanted to do that. But very few could have pulled it off." Don Francisco yanked off his hat, revealing his thick gray hair, and waved it at Merced. "*Gracias*, Señor Merced. We are grateful."

The crowd cheered. The ladies stood and applauded.

Merced lowered his head and stared at his saddle horn.

"Now I have made an important decision," Don Francisco shouted. "La Paloma Roja de Monterey will still have to decide which of the Cabrillo brothers gets the second dance. But I will donate the first dance to El Americano del Norte!"

All eyes turned to Alena.

All eyes except those of Wilson Judd Merced.

Alena nodded her head, like an empress commuting a death sentence. The cheers rang out.

When the crowd settled down, Don Francisco waved his hands to get their attention. "I believe we should award the bull and bear to El Americano del Norte. What is your wish, Señor Merced?"

His head still down, Merced mumbled something that Alena couldn't hear.

Don Francisco held up his hand. "El Americano del Norte says the bear is to be given to the little Indian girl and her family. The bull he will take home to Rancho Alázan, if he can get it back into a cart. I believe this concludes the contest in the arena. But the festivities continue. The fandango will begin at sundown!"

For a while everything was confusing. The women promenaded single file back to the Castro home. Several times Alena tried to catch sight of Wilson Merced, but the crowd of Indians that surrounded him blocked her view.

She heard later that the Indian family promptly skinned the bear on the spot and hung the meat to cool in the orchard. The bull, only slightly wounded, was herded to a corral behind the livery. The arena was disassembled as quickly as it had been erected.

From her perch in the shade of Don José Castro's balcony, Alena watched the plaza return to a marketplace filled with those buying and selling, everyone talking about El Americano del Norte.

Doña María Martina approached carrying two pottery mugs with steaming hot drinks.

"What are you bringing?" Alena asked.

"The official drink of Alta California." Señora Cabrillo grinned as she handed a cup to Alena, then sat down on the bench beside her.

"I have never known any people who drank as much chocolate as Californians," Alena commented.

"Yes. Don Francisco says that the man who learns to grow cocoa beans in California will become a wealthy man indeed."

Alena cradled the cup with both hands and took a sip. "Even on a hot day I love it."

"Yes. It is like the kiss of a handsome man," Señora Cabrillo declared.

Alena took another sip and giggled. "What do you mean by that?"

"Once you've tasted the sweets, you are anxious for more no matter what the weather!"

"Doña María Martina!"

"I saw you scrutinize Señor Merced. He is a chocolate man, no?"

"I wouldn't know," Alena insisted.

"But you'd like to."

"I will not answer that, but he is obviously a very brave man."

Señora Cabrillo took a long, slow sip from the thick chocolate drink. "Brave? No, he is reckless. A brave man tries to herd the bear toward the open ground or the orchard, away from his horse. A reckless man runs up to a bear on foot with nothing but a *pistola*."

Alena perspired from the effects of the hot, steaming drink. "A five-shot *pistola*."

"Yes. That is a good gun. Now every man in San Juan wants such a weapon. But he was foolish to leave his horse."

"He wouldn't have been able to save the child if he had waited and untied the bull's rope from the saddle. He had to run on foot." *And I have no idea why I feel that I must defend him.*

"Perhaps you are right." Doña María Martina rocked back and forth on the bench. "But don't marry a man who will make you a young widow, *mi dulcita*."

"Marry?" Alena sat up straight so quickly that she nearly spilled her hot chocolate. "I have no intention of—"

Señora Cabrillo dismissed her protest with a flip of her hand. "*Conchita*, you have a Californio heart. You told me so. If you do, you have thought about marrying El Americano del Norte. Most of the single women in the crowd today and half the married ones are thinking the very same thing."

"That's preposterous."

"That's California. After he gave the girl back to her mother, he could have ridden to the stands and pointed at any woman there, and she would have ridden off with him faster than María Alejandra rode off with Echo Jack. If you have a California heart, you know that is true. Now tell me, *mi dulcita*, do you have a Boston heart . . . or a California heart?"

I wish sometimes a person would be wrong about me. Everyone seems to be able to figure me out faster than I can figure me out! "Yes," Alena sighed, "I have a California heart."

"I know. Look." She pointed out to the street. "Here come your other suitors, the 'almost-brave' Cabrillo brothers."

Alena stood and walked to the rail as Don Fernando and Don Ronaldo rode their long-legged black horses up near the balcony. Each tipped his hat.

"It looks like Don Francisco gave away the dance," Don Fernando declared.

"What do you mean?"

"We suppose you will want to dance all night with El Americano del Norte," Don Ronaldo offered.

"I'll do no such thing! He gets the first dance, that is all. If you two refuse to dance with me, it will break my heart. And I will retire to my room in tears."

Both Cabrillo brothers sat straight in the saddle.

"Well," Don Ronaldo offered, "we wouldn't want your heart to break."

"Yes, who will you dance with at the second dance?" Don Fernando insisted, his broad shoulders thrown back, his square chin held high.

Alena glanced back at Señora Cabrillo who sat on the bench drinking her chocolate. "You must guess how many rings your mother is wearing right now. The one who comes closest wins the second dance."

"*¡Diez!*" Don Ronaldo shouted. "She has one on every finger."

Don Fernando thought for a moment. "No. It is a fiesta. There is fandango tonight. I say *quince*."

Alena glanced back at Señora Cabrillo. "How many rings, *madre amada?*"

Doña María Martina held up her hands and laughed. "*¡Dieciséis!*"

Alena leaned over the balcony railing but held her shawl at her neck. "So Don Fernando gets the second dance, and Don Ronaldo gets the third."

"It is just as well," Don Ronaldo announced. "After Doña Alena Louisa dances with me, she will certainly not want to dance with anyone else."

"Ha! You will limp around the floor. She will have to carry you," Don Fernando chided his younger brother.

"But I will have two strong arms to hold her tight in case she starts to fall."

Alena shook her head. "You two are the most fun friends I have ever had in my life. I love you both dearly."

"What?" Don Fernando gasped. "You love two men?"

Señora Cabrillo stepped up beside her. "She did not say she loved only two men. Perhaps she loves three."

"El Americano del Norte?" Don Fernando asked.

"He doesn't count," Don Ronaldo insisted. "After this afternoon all the women love him."

"*Hasta el fandango!*" Don Fernando tipped his hat. Both men bolted down the road toward the livery stable.

"I told you so, *conchita*," Doña María Martina added. "They will all love him until tomorrow at least."

Alena turned around and leaned her backside against the railing. "They will forget him by tomorrow?"

"No, but he will go home, and no one will see him for another year. And they will forget him by next year."

"Living so far out in the wilderness sounds like a lonely life." Alena began to stroll along the balcony.

"For a Californian? Yes, it would be worse than prison." Doña María Martina set her cup on the bench and joined Alena in the stroll. "For an Americano with a broken heart, perhaps not."

"What do you mean, a broken heart? What do you know about him?" Alena heard pounding hooves in the street and spun around to see several unknown horsemen gallop by.

"Only that he is usually a sad man. Doesn't that mean a broken heart?" Doña María Martina slipped her arm into Alena's. It felt strong and assuring. "He is trying to forget a lost love."

"Or trying to forget something else," Alena insisted.

"Now you go in there and take a nap. The fandango will begin in two hours, and it will last all night. They will not let you sit out a single dance. You will need your rest." Señora Cabrillo snatched up the two empty chocolate cups.

"*Sí*, Mama. You worry about me too much."

"And who will worry for you if I don't?"

Alena looked into her gray-haired friend's brown eyes. Tears slid down her face.

Señora Cabrillo threw her arms around Alena and hugged her as tight as Wilson Merced had clutched the little naked Indian girl. "*Mi dulcita*, I have made you cry. You miss your papa, don't you?"

"Yes, you are right. It just dawned on me. I don't have anyone left to think about me. Don't you ever stop worrying about me," Alena sniffled.

Señora Cabrillo pulled back. "Then take your nap."

"I will."

"I know you will. *Conchita*, if *El Señor* had let my daughters live, I could only wish they would have been as noble and honest as you."

She followed Doña María Martina back into the room. When Señora Cabrillo traipsed down the stairs, Alena flopped back on the low, narrow bed that was one of three in the room she shared with the Castro daughters.

Noble and honest?

I am haughty and a charlatan. Playing a game. Wanting to be queen. Wilson Merced is noble and honest. Lord, is there any way I can learn those qualities from him . . . besides marrying him and moving to the ends of the earth?

Marry him?

Last night about this time, I saw him for the first time and detested him.

But Doña María Martina is right. It is something in the California air. It makes a girl silly. He gets a dance. That's all. Then he will go home tomorrow.

One dance.

Well . . . perhaps two dances.

But not more.

Not many more.

Alena, you are acting nineteen.

I am nineteen.

But he isn't.
How old is he?

The nap was fitful. There were visions of growling bears, charging bulls, crying children—and gallant horsemen. But everything was so jumbled Alena woke in a sweat of confusion. She sat up and dried off her face on a small muslin towel. The room felt very stuffy at the sunset of a breezeless day. She sauntered out onto the balcony. It was almost dark. Across the street the lanterns around the dancing tiles were already lit, and a few had assembled even though there was no music.

The slow, ambling walk of a tall man strolling toward the Castro home caught her attention. "Good evening, Mr. Merced. I want to thank you for stopping the bull and the bear," she said.

"Evenin', Miss Alena." He tipped his hat. "Might we sit and talk?"

"Certainly. Would you like to come in, or shall I come down there? Oh, I'm sorry. You can't come into two-story buildings. I'll be right down."

"I'd appreciate it."

Wilson Merced was sitting on the bench in front of the Castro home staring across at the festive plaza when she came out the open front door and sat beside him.

"That was the most thrilling display of bravery I've ever seen!" she began.

"Miss Alena . . . I really don't want to talk about this afternoon. Ever'body is making too much of it. Some women and children and a beautiful little girl were going to get seriously hurt or killed if someone didn't do something. I was the one mounted up with rope and gun. I only did what I had to do. Nothin' special."

"Well, I've never seen anything like it. But I will honor your request. What would you like to talk about?"

He tugged at the tight collar of his white cotton shirt. "Have you seen María Alejandra?"

She fidgeted with her fingers, finally laying them in her lap. "No. I presume she is still with your friend Echo Jack."

He pulled his hat off and held it in his hands. "I can't find any trace of them." His tan callused hand rested on his knee only inches from hers.

Don't you dare put your hand on his, Alena Louise! "Is he late for some work?"

"Not really. I'm just worried. The longer he's gone, the more certain I am that he's in trouble. I'm tryin' to keep him from being run out of San Juan. It's about the only town left he can enter without being shot by some girl's father."

Her voice was low but steady. "Perhaps Echo Jack deserves to be shot."

"You might be right, but I've sort of taken it on myself to look after Echo Jack, Piedra, and José."

Alena tried to look at his eyes, but he gazed across at the plaza. "Those are all your workers?"

"More like family than workers. Yeah, they work for me. They're about all I got."

"You don't have family in the States?"

"None that would speak to me."

"That sounds terribly sad."

"It ain't nobody's fault but mine. But I don't want to talk about that. What I want to say is, if Echo Jack isn't going to be at the fandango, you don't have to dance with me."

"Wilson Merced, are you trying to jilt me?"

His mouth dropped open. "No, ma'am!"

"Alena—not ma'am, not Doña Alena, not Miss Tipton. No one has just called me Alena since my father died. Would you just call me Alena?"

"Yep. I'll do that . . . Alena. But I'm not tryin' to jilt you."

"Wilson, I have enjoyed our visits today. I wish you weren't going back to your rancho tomorrow. I hope that doesn't sound too forward."

"Alena, I surely wish I would have met you several years ago."

"Is that because I'm so much younger than you?"

"That, too."

"Just how much younger am I?"

"What month is your birthday?"

"February."

"You are thirteen years and one month younger."

"You're thirty-two?" *Well, at least he's not forty.*

"Yep, but that's not the main reason I wished I had met you earlier." Now he turned toward her, but Alena looked away. "You see, something happened in my life I'm not proud of, and I can't . . . well . . ."

"What do you mean?"

"I mean, I have to go back to the ranch tomorrow. And I'm going to regret terribly saying good-bye to you. Now you must think I'm the one who is quite forward. Perhaps I shouldn't visit with you."

Finally their eyes met. "Just the opposite. I think we should talk all we can."

Three horsemen galloped up in the shadows and reined up at the Castro house.

"Is María Alejandra at the Castros'?" the older man demanded.

"No," Alena replied, "I believe she went for a ride."

The older man rested his hand on his red scarf, which only partially covered a pistol. "How about the one called Echo Jack?"

"He's gone, too," Merced replied.

All three surveyed the plaza. "Is he coming to the fandango?"

"I reckon that's a possibility."

"Then we'll wait." The men dismounted from their horses and headed toward the livery.

Merced stood up and called out, "If I see him, who shall I say is looking for him?"

"I am María Alejandra's father, and these are—"

"Her brothers?"

"Yes."

"I don't suppose you're lookin' for Echo Jack to buy him a drink."

"We'll shoot him on sight if we find him," the man growled, then stalked on across the street.

Five

Wilson Judd Merced spent the first dance of the fandango immersed in the sparkling deep blue eyes of Miss Alena Louise Tipton.

He spent the rest of the evening watching her dance with a procession of Californios.

And trying to spot Echo Jack before a young lady's angry father did.

Merced knew it was well into early morning because around midnight the first band retired, and a second one began their serenading. For several hours before that, Californians and Indians had paraded by the bench on which he sat, wanting to discuss the bear and the bull. But right before the change in guitar orchestra, all the Indians from the Plano Tulare retired as if on cue from a silent summons. That still left several hundred Californians and local Indians to carry on the rest of the night, a task they seemed to relish.

It left Merced sitting alone in the lantern-lit shadows.

His eyes swept along with each step of the red-haired girl in the middle of the red-tile dance floor.

Miss Alena Tipton, what in the world are you doing in California? You are totally different than any woman at this fandango . . . and yet . . . yet it is as if you belong. They love you like you were one of their own.

How would you look in Boston?

Say, the governor was throwing a New Year's ball, and all the dig-
nitaries and officials would be there. With all those fancy French dresses,
lace, and wigs, would you still be the center of attention?

Probably.

But you wouldn't have danced the first dance with a poorly dressed
hide rancher who lives a four-month trek west of the Mississippi River.

But you aren't in Boston. You came around the Horn to be with
your daddy, and you have never returned. So here you are. Determined
to make a life in this land once thought to be a golden island, very near
the terrestrial paradise, populated only by women and ruled by fictional
Queen Calif? Well, tonight, Doña Alena Louise, Queen Calif would
have to sit on a bench and watch. You are the queen. And the dance floor
is filled with courtiers and jesters.

And some of the jesters think they are courtiers.

They fool only themselves.

For the past four years I've succeeded in seldom thinking about
women at all. For the past twenty-four hours, I have thought about lit-
tle else but you, Miss Tipton. You have tested my mental discipline.

I'm not sure if that's a boast or a complaint.

Merced stood, stretched his arms, and strolled to one of the
open campfires on the east side of the plaza. It was fifty or so feet
from the red tiles of the dance floor but still within sight of everything and everyone. He took a black coffeepot off a hook above the
flames and poured his tin cup full of steaming, grounds-laced coffee.

"Señor Merced, do you not like chocolate?" asked one of
Castro's Indian servants who tended the fire.

"It tastes too much like dessert," he said. "Besides, it's mighty
hard to find coffee in California. I enjoy it whenever I can." The
hot liquid trickled down his throat. The coffee grounds lodged
between his less-than-straight teeth.

A hatless man with thick black hair hanging well past his
shoulders stepped over next to Merced. "Did the Los Baños family
talk to you?"

"Who?"

"The family of the little girl you saved from Oso Grande? They
belong to the Los Baños band out on the Plano Tulare."

Wilson peered over the top of his coffee cup as firelight flickered on the man's brown eyes. "I talked to lots of folks tonight. Maybe I did talk to them."

Sweat streaked the dust on the man's brown face. "Did they give you anything?"

Merced glanced back at the darkness of the Indian encampment. "No."

"Then you did not talk to them." The man squatted down next to the fire and poured himself a cup of chocolate.

"They don't need to give me anything." Merced hunched down next to the man as both stared at the dance floor. "You would have done the same thing if you had been on the horse."

"And if I had a gun that shot five shots before reloading. Well, perhaps . . . for my own daughter, yes . . . but I am not a brave man. For another's daughter, I am not so sure. Please don't leave town until they talk to you. It is very important to them."

Merced pushed his hat back and could feel the campfire-produced perspiration begin to bead on his forehead. "If you see them, tell them I'll be around until at least noon tomorrow . . . maybe later if I don't get any sleep tonight."

The man shoved an oak log into the fire. "I'll tell them."

Merced glanced at the blanket rolled out in front of the man. Lit only by the flickering fire, a number of items were lined up in neat rows. "You got a piece of that sugared sweetbread I can buy?"

"I would be highly insulted if you did not take it for free."

"Thanks, *compadre*, but a man has to make a profit on his goods, or he'll starve to death. I'll pay like the others."

"Señor Merced, please. You must take it. You did much more than save a little girl's life today."

"What do you mean?"

"You showed that a little Indian girl is precious in *los ojos de Dios*."

"Sure, she's precious in God's eyes. I didn't think that had to be proved."

"Sometimes people need a reminder."

Merced accepted a four-inch cube of sweetbread with bright red frosting. "I didn't reckon I was makin' a theological statement. Thanks for the cake, *amigo*."

"My wife colored it red in honor of La Paloma Roja. She is very beautiful, no?"

"Your wife?"

A wide smile broke across the man's face. "Oh yes! My wife is very beautiful. But I meant Doña Alena Louisa."

"I agree with you on that." Merced wiped cake crumbs off his chin. "If you see Echo Jack before I do, will you send him my way? I need to warn him about something."

The man leaned close enough that Merced could smell chocolate mixed with garlic on his breath. "Echo Jack is on his way to Monterey," he confided.

"What? How do you know that?"

"Because he went there with María Alejandra, the Castros' *sobrina*."

"How long have you known?"

"Since the first dance. I caught María Alejandra sneaking into the Castros' house to get her things just after the fandango began. She said she was running off to Monterey with Echo Jack and that I should not tell the Californios. But you are not a Californio!"

Merced gulped down a thick bite of red sugar frosting and wiped his mouth on the back of his hand. "Do you see the man out there dancing with the lady in the yellow dress? That is María Alejandra's father. Don't tell him about this until I can go to Monterey to see what's going on."

"I will not tell him at all."

Merced hiked back to his vacant bench near the dancing floor. He plopped down, coffee in one hand and the rest of the cake in the other.

Echo Jack went to Monterey? Why? He knows I need his help here. Why didn't he say something to me? Of course, I was dancing with Doña Alena at the time. He could have left me a note.

If he knew how to write.

He'll be arrested if he goes to Monterey. Jilting the alcalde's youngest daughter is not the only bad memory they have of Echo Jack. Of course, he won't be arrested if María Alejandra's father catches up with him first. I need to get to Monterey. I could leave now. But it is still dark. Perhaps at daylight.

Monterey? Why on earth would anyone want to go to Monterey so bad as to risk his life? I should have left him at the ranch. Next time I will bring José.

No, José is banned from Monterey also.

You will live a short life, Echo Jack.

A short but happy life.

In between dances, he watched Alena Tipton return to a circle of Californio friends that centered around Señor and Señora Cabrillo. Merced had made his station on the Indian side of the dance floor, but with the Indians retired, he sat almost alone in the shadows of flickering lanterns and a half-moon.

He finished his sweetbread and coffee. There was a dull, aching tiredness in every bone in his body. He thought about lying down on the bench, or even the dirt, and going to sleep.

This is not my schedule. I don't like staying up late. Go to bed at dark, get up before daylight. What am I doing hangin' around a dance by myself? I'll need to get some sleep if I'm going to leave at daylight. But I need to sell those hides, too. I should talk to Miss Tipton before I leave. She will sleep late. I will leave very early.

I could just walk over there and talk to her now, I suppose. She is not dancing this dance. But it would be awkward. She is busy with the others. I'll wait until I catch her eye. Perhaps I should ask her to dance. No, I will not make another spectacle of myself.

I'll say, "Excuse me, Miss Tipton, I need to discuss a little hide business with you for a moment in private." And she will say, "Can't it wait until morning, Mr. Merced? I don't do business on Sunday!" Of course, technically it is Monday already.

But why should she do business when she can dance?

I'll just wait for a more opportune time.

He picked coffee grounds out of his teeth with his fingernail, then folded his hands in his lap and stretched out his legs. His chin dropped to his chest.

When the tempo of the music crested, he opened his eyes. Alena stood on the far side of the dance floor with no one beside her except Señora Cabrillo.

He stood, pushed the sleeves of his shirt halfway up his arms, adjusted his hat, and hiked around the edge of the dance floor. By the time he came within twenty feet of Alena Tipton, the music stopped. She was immediately surrounded by several Californio men.

You're too late, Merced. That's the story of your life. You think of everything too late. Go on to the livery and get some sleep. You can leave her a note in the morning.

Instead, he walked straight up to the group of people surrounding her. He stood behind the others, waiting for a break in the conversation.

Don Fernando Cabrillo was speaking. "It is my great misfortune that Padre Estában died today. If he were alive, I would ask him to perform a wedding tonight!"

"La Paloma Roja marry you?" the younger Cabrillo brother chided.

"Yes, little brother, it is *predestinado*. You must learn to be more gracious in defeat. Don't worry, you will find your own señorita when you grow up."

"Grow up? You are the one who babbles like a baby. Doña Alena Louisa does not want to marry you." He turned to Miss Tipton. "Do you?"

"Oh, why do you two talk about marriage? How could I marry one of you and then sneak off and dance with the other? That would not be proper."

Señora Cabrillo stepped between them. "If you two are serious about marriage, you would go down into the Plano Tulare and build yourself a rancho. Doña Alena Louisa deserves a hacienda of her own. So there will be no talk of marriage until you prove you are not lazy."

Don Ronaldo rolled his eyes. "Just whose *madre* are you?"

Señora Cabrillo held her chin high. "Why, I'm Doña Alena's mama, of course!"

All in the circle began to laugh and nod their heads.

Wilson Merced cleared his throat. "Eh, excuse me, Doña María Martina . . . I wonder if I might have a word with your 'daughter'?"

Don Fernando stepped over to Merced. "I am sorry, Americano del Norte, but Señorita Tipton has promised if she dances again, it will be with me."

Merced, standing four inches taller than any of the other men, squeezed between Don Fernando and Alena. "That's all right with me. All of you know I dance sort of like an old dog with a cactus thorn in his paw. This being Monday already, I needed to talk to Miss Tipton for just a moment about some hide business matters."

"You see, *conchita*," Señora Cabrillo added, "Americanos are always in a hurry. Didn't I tell you? They do not know how to relax."

"The señora's right about that, I reckon. But an emergency came up that calls me away before daylight. Might I have a few moments of your time?"

She brushed her red wavy hair behind her ear. "Certainly, Mr. Merced. Shall we go look over your hides now?"

"It is dark," Don Ronaldo protested. "What business can you do in the dark?"

"As I said before," Don Fernando sneered, "he is very young and immature."

"We will take a lantern," she insisted. "That's all right with you, isn't it, Mr. Merced?"

"Yes, ma'am," Merced mumbled. "Are you sure this isn't too much of a bother?"

"It is *Lunes*, and I have a business to run," she insisted as she pointed toward a yellow paper lantern hanging from a post. "Perhaps we can take that one."

"I will go with you," Don Fernando insisted.

She pulled her black lace shawl tightly around her neck. "What on earth for?"

"It is the middle of the night. It may be dangerous."

"In San Juan? With the likes of Wilson Merced at my side? Unless there is a creature more ferocious than a grizzly bear, I believe I am safe."

"And who will protect you from El Americano del Norte?" Don Ronaldo blurted out.

Wilson Merced's right hand went up to the grip of the Paterson Colt tucked in his belt. *Relax, Merced. Don't let him provoke you. He's just jealous. Sort of like how you felt when he was dancing with her.*

Alena slipped her arm into Wilson's.

It felt good.

Very good.

"Mr. Merced, am I safe to go look at hides with you?"

He wanted to squeeze her hand.

He wanted to slip his arm around her waist.

He wanted to pick her up in his arms and carry her off.

What he did was mumble, "Yes, ma'am, you'll be safe."

"You will excuse my sons, Señor Merced," Doña María Martina offered. "They are immature in their manners. We know Alena is perfectly safe with you."

"Thank you, Señora Cabrillo. I will deliver her back to you in a few minutes."

"Yes, *gracias*. Now go on." She waved a fleshy hand that even in the shadows flashed gold and silver rings. "I will wait here for *mi conchita* to come back."

Merced strolled away from the dance floor, a yellow paper lantern in his left hand, Alena Tipton on his right arm. He suddenly wished the hike to the livery was longer.

Ten miles like this would be nice.

"She calls you *conchita*?"

Her grip on his arm never weakened. "*Conchita . . . dulcita . . . mi corazón.* She really does treat me like a daughter."

The jingle from his spurs signaled each step. "I want to apologize for interrupting your fandango like this."

"Are you teasing me?" There was a deep playfulness in her voice. "I've been waiting for hours for you to come over and talk to me."

He stopped and turned to face her. "You have?"

"I danced one dance with you, and you disappeared to the other side of the floor never to be seen again. How do you think that made me feel? Like an old shoe," she pouted. "I'm not used to being rejected so quickly."

"Rejected? Now it is you who is teasing, Señorita Tipton. You were much too busy to think of me."

She pulled her arm from his and strutted on ahead of him in the light of a half-moon. "Yes, Señor Wilson Judd Merced. I am merely a coquette playing for your attention, and I intend to continue to do so unless . . ."

He could feel his rowels drag dirt as he scurried to catch up. "Unless what?"

She stopped quickly and turned around. He almost ran into her. "Unless you start calling me Alena!"

"What?"

"You heard me."

"Let's start this again. Did you really want me to come over and talk to you earlier this evening . . . Alena?"

"Yes, Wilson, I did." She slipped her arm back into his. "What took you so long?"

"I, eh . . . I'm sort of . . . well, I guess I'm kind of timorous about such things." They continued to plow through the night air toward the livery.

"And a lousy dancer, too," she giggled. "But that's no reason to ignore me all night."

"My dancing was pitiful, wasn't it?"

"There is lots of competition, I'm afraid. But I did want to talk to you."

"What about?"

"Anything," she said.

"I don't understand."

"Wilson, you are the only person in California that I can talk to and not have to play the Californio game."

"I thought you like being a Californian."

"I absolutely love it. But now and then I like being real, too. So thank you for rescuing me just now. I envy you."

"You envy me? La Paloma Roja de Monterey is the envy of every person at the fandango. How do you envy me?"

"You seem to be able to enjoy California without needing to succumb to the castes and customs. I like that. How do you do it?"

"Maybe it comes from isolation."

"Your rancho?"

"We are so remote we sort of set our own customs and traditions."

"I like that. It would be the most exciting challenge I can think of."

"Challenge?"

"Oh yes. To build everything fresh and new, yet be obedient to the Lord's leading. You are obedient to the Lord's leading, aren't you?"

"I try real hard, Alena. But sometimes I reckon I don't do so well. How about you?"

"I have a lot of fights between my heart, my mind, and my spirit. They seem to gang up on each other. Does that make sense?"

"Are you sure you are only nineteen?"

"Actually I'm sixty-three. It's the California air," she snickered.

"It makes women look younger?"

"No," she laughed, "it makes men's eyes go bad! You know, I could teach you how to dance."

"Why? I don't aim to ever do it again."

"I think I should come out to your rancho and organize a fandango. What would you do then?"

"I reckon I'd have to dance."

"There you have it. Now, Wilson, do you really want to talk business, or is that just an excuse to walk me out into the dark?"

"Oh no, it's not that. I—I re—really wanted to talk business."

"Why am I not surprised? All right, Mr. Hide Rancher, what is so urgent?"

"I just found out that María Alejandra and Echo Jack took off for Monterey tonight."

"What on earth for?"

"I was hoping you could answer that for me."

"I have no idea. It seems like everyone along the coast is over here in San Juan."

"Anyway," Merced continued, "I want to ride to Monterey and try to find them before her father and brothers do. But that means leaving at daylight, and I'd still like to sell you my hides."

"Shall we take a look at them?"

"The Cabrillo brothers were right. It's a little hard to judge them in the dark, even with a lantern. You just take a look in the mornin'. Whatever you figure is a fair price I'll accept."

"I believe it was less than twenty-four hours ago that you were demanding $4.50 apiece."

"That was a long time ago. I've learned a lot since then. Time is a funny thing, isn't it?"

"Just what do you mean?"

"Sometimes we can go through days, weeks, months, even years with nothin' ever changin'. It could all be condensed into twenty-four hours, and you wouldn't have missed anything. But at other times one day holds a whole lifetime of thoughts, actions, feelings. You've made this into one of those days. I feel like I've known you for years." He took a deep breath and sighed. "Anyway, enough philosophy. Just take a look at those hides come daylight."

"I promise an equitable price."

"Thanks." They stopped strolling, and he patted her hand, much like a man pats the head of his favorite dog. "I, eh, guess that's all I needed to say to you. I'll get you back to the Cabrillos."

She laid her hand softly on top of his, as a mother strokes her baby. "There's no hurry . . . really. I need to back away from the intensity they put me under."

"Oh?"

"The Cabrillo brothers almost killed each other roping the bear and the bull and almost killed some others as well—all because of me. Wilson, I am truly ashamed of that. I don't want anyone to do something dangerous and reckless on my account again. I don't exactly know how to tell them that. Despite their many acts of kindness, I could never really be interested in marrying either of them. And I have no idea why I'm telling you this. You are right. It does seem like a lifetime ago that we ambled through the orchard. It is just as I said. I feel like I can talk about real things to you. Why do you suppose that is?"

"I reckon I overwhelmed you with my dancing."

Alena began to laugh. "Well . . . it is true. Your dancing did overwhelm me."

"See? And if you think that was potent, you should hear me sing."

"Do you sing, Wilson Merced?"

"Ever'body sings. It's just some folks can sing on tune. I can't."

Instead of walking back toward the noise and lights of the fandango, Alena led them to the darkness of the doorway into the livery stable. The small lantern gave enough light for them to see about five feet ahead. "How long will you be in Monterey?"

"Just long enough to find Echo Jack."

"Have you been to Monterey often?"

"Just once or twice. Enough to get lost."

She led them past the wide open door of the livery. A soft aroma of hay, horseflesh, and manure drifted through the night. "How ironic."

He stopped and gazed at the back end of a buckskin horse asleep on its feet. "Why's that?"

In the shadows her face looked sculptured by a highly skilled artist. "I have spent most of the past three years in Monterey. I know every home, every street, every hiding place for miles around it. If I were there now, I could have helped you search for them."

Merced leaned against a shadowy post, then pulled back and brushed straw off his pant legs. "Next time I bring hides in, I'll have to come visit you in Monterey. I mean, if that's all right with you."

"After what you did today with the bull and the bear, I would think you could appeal to the governor for a land grant closer to the coast. He might even give you a rancho in this area." Alena fingered the silver conchos on a bridle hanging from the post.

"I already have a rancho."

"Oh, I know. I was just thinking if you lived a little closer, you could come to Monterey more than once a year."

He dragged the toe of his boot across the dirt floor to the livery. "Now I'm the one who can't believe you are talking to me like this."

Alena slipped her arm from his and stepped back. "Did I say something improper?"

"No, of course not. But you're talking to me like you would like me to visit you from time to time."

"Well, I would. You wouldn't mind, would you?"

"Of course not." Merced's voice dropped to almost a whisper. "But it wouldn't work."

"What wouldn't work?"

"Me and you, you know . . . visitin' all the time."

"And why not?"

"Well, Alena, you know why!"

"Wilson, are you this timid and obscure with everyone or just me?"

"Does it matter?"

"No, I don't suppose it does. But I don't understand why visiting with me more often than once a year is a bad thing."

"I didn't say it was a bad thing. It's a dangerous thing."

"Dangerous?"

"If I talked to you all the time, Alena Louise Tipton, I'd start thinkin' thoughts the Lord doesn't want me thinkin'. I'd have a lot more self-control if you were 200 miles away. Now forgive me for talkin' like this. You're probably wishin' the Cabrillo boys would have chaperoned you. Let me get you back before your mama gets worried."

"Señora Cabrillo understands. And I'm glad we are alone. Why don't you believe me when I say that?"

"I want to believe, Alena. But some news is too good to be true. Will you still be here when I come back from Monterey?"

"When will that be?"

"In a couple days."

"It takes two days just to get to Monterey."

"Not if you're riding horseback and take a spare horse to relay with."

"It sounds like a tiring trip."

"I'll have a whole year to rest up. And I would like to talk to you one more time before I head home."

"Yes, Wilson Merced, I would like that also."

"Now if I don't get you out of this dark barn, two Cabrillo brothers will be hunting my scalp with their shining Toledo swords."

The pound of hooves at the front of the livery caused them to scoot back into an empty stall. Merced turned down the wick of the tallow-fueled lantern. "It might be Echo Jack coming back."

"By himself?"

"Either that or someone looking for him. You stay back here in one of these stalls. I'll check it out."

Merced left the dim lantern in her hand and walked slowly to the moonlight at the front of the livery. A lathered horse was tied to the hitching post. In the shadows a Californio loosened the cinch and pulled the saddle.

"You had a hard ride, partner," Merced called out.

Startled by the sound of a voice, the man in the wide-brimmed round hat spun around. In the reflection of a partial moon, Merced noticed the large knife in the man's hand.

"Whoa, *compadre*, I'm no threat to you. You look in a hurry. Go on. I'll rub down this pony for you."

The man slipped the knife back into the leather sheath under his sash. "I need to find Doña Alena Louisa Tipton. I presume she is at the fandango."

A woman's soft voice rolled out of the darkness of the barn. "Don Manuel?"

The startled man stepped toward the wide-open doorway and peered into the darkness. "Doña Alena?"

She sauntered out of the darkness and stood beside Merced.

"Doña Alena Louisa, what are you doing in the barn?"

"She is with me." Merced took the lantern from her hand and adjusted the wick.

"Oh?" He concentrated on Merced. "Are you Sutter's Americano del Norte?"

"That's me." Merced set the lantern down and began to rub the horse with a rolled-up saddle blanket.

"You are shorter than I thought. I was told you were nine feet tall."

"That was my brother Goliath!"

"What is the matter, Don Manuel?" Alena pressed.

"Well, well . . . it is horrible, Doña Alena . . . just horrible."

"What happened, Don Manuel?"

She noticed he looked thin and exhausted. His partially gray mustache drooped under sad eyes. "A fire . . . a horrible fire."

"Where?"

"At our warehouse on the dock."

"What did we lose?" she asked.

"Everything! All the hides are gone!"

Merced watched in the flickering light as Alena Tipton took a deep breath. For a moment he thought she looked twenty-nine rather than nineteen. He tossed the sweat-soaked saddle blanket to the hitching post and stepped up beside her. She clutched his jacketed arm.

"Did the office burn up?"

"Yes."

"The records, the money box—everything?"

"No, no. I had the records and money box at my house."

"That's good. How did the fire start?"

Don Manuel pulled off his big round sombrero and held it in his hands. "*Solamente Dios sabe.* But if you ask me, I think it was that man."

"What man?"

"The one with the stolen hides."

"What do you mean, stolen hides?"

"Friday afternoon there was a man . . ." He glanced again at Merced. "An Americano . . . I'd never seen him before. No one had ever seen him. He came to town with a cart of hides. He said he bought them from the Indians, and he wanted to resell them."

"Did he have papers?"

Don Manuel rubbed the back of his neck. "No bill of sale and no residence papers from the governor. Of course, the governor is up at the *presidio* at Yerba Buena, so I couldn't check with him. Anyway, the hides were carrying the 2A brand."

"From Real de las Aguilas?" Merced asked.

"Yes. They were not Indian hides. So naturally I refused to buy them."

Merced glanced down at her eyes. They showed concern but not despair.

"What did he do then?" she asked.

Don Manuel was almost Alena's height. He flailed his arms as he spoke. "He made threats on my life."

"What was this Americano's name?" Merced pressed.

"I thought he said it was something like Parker, but his first name was confusing. At the time I did not think I would have any need to remember it."

Merced felt his blood race. "Was it Parkins? Was he gaunt and gangly, with a tan shirt and carrying a flintlock?"

"That's him!"

Alena turned to Merced. Her lips were only a few inches below his. "Who is he?"

"His name is Carty Parkins. He's from Arkansas. He came over the summit a couple weeks ago. I fed him at the ranch and sent him down to Capt. Sutter at New Helvetia. I thought he wanted to come to see the governor at Monterey to get residence papers."

The three huddled around the grounded lantern as if it were a fire. "Why did you take the cash box and journals home?" she asked.

"He frightened me," Don Manuel admitted. "I thought he might be the type to come back at night and break in."

"Your caution was justified, Don Manuel. I am glad you are not hurt."

"What would he do with money?" Merced shook his head, and his hat brim brushed against Alena's hair. "You can't buy anything in California without everyone knowing it."

Alena placed her hand on Don Manuel's shoulder. "How do you know it was Parkins who burned down the warehouse?"

"I don't . . . but he is the only one mad enough to do something like that. Why would anyone else burn us out? What are we going to do? What are we going to do, Doña Alena?"

Merced watched as she tugged at her earrings, then held her hand to her chin. "Is everything lost?"

"Yes, all the hides burned. The whole town smells worse than bone-burning day."

"Did you bring the ledger and cash box with you?" Alena asked.

"Yes, of course. They are here in my saddlebags. I rode all day and all night to get here."

Alena turned to Merced. "Wilson, may I ride to Monterey with you?"

"Certainly."

"Don Manuel, you will stay here and spend tomorrow buying hides. Make your best deals. I will go back to Monterey and see what can be discovered there."

"Señorita, what do you want me to do now?"

She gave orders like a general. "Get some sleep. You will have a busy day tomorrow."

"Are you sure you don't want me to go back with you?"

"If you go back, who will buy the hides? If we don't buy hides now, we will not have a business left."

"Then I think I will sleep in the barn." Don Manuel, toting his tooled-leather saddlebags, disappeared into the dark livery stable.

Merced felt her smooth, soft hand slip into his. "I will go tell Señora Cabrillo and then change my clothes. If you'll saddle the horses and bring them to the Castros', we can leave within the hour."

He gently squeezed her hand. "Both of us need rest. We should leave at daylight."

"But I must return immediately." She squeezed his rough callused hand tightly.

"Riding without sleep does not save time." He loosened his grip. "Your building can do no more than burn to the ground. I will have the horses ready at daylight. That is only a few hours from now."

She refused to loosen her grip. "Are you always this stubborn, Mr. Merced?"

"Yes." He rubbed the back of his neck with his free hand. "Are you always this demanding, Miss Tipton?"

"Yes." Her eyes seemed to be peeking out from the shadows of her face. "The Cabrillo brothers will want to come along, I suppose."

Merced fetched the lantern and began to lead Alena back toward the plaza. "Tell them you need them to search the road from Monterey to San José for the Americano Carty Parkins."

She had to skip to keep up with his long stride. "Yes, that will be good. But what if this man Parkins heads south?"

"Why would he do that?" Now it was Merced's voice that sounded like an officer instructing his troops. "The deeper into Mexico he goes, the more difficult it will be to escape. I think he will ride toward Oregon and try to steal along the way."

"Did he steal from your rancho?"

"I don't think so, but I have nothing of value and too many armed men."

"Why would someone risk his life coming all the way to California from Arkansas and then steal things? A thief would do much better in some Eastern city."

"There are some men I can't figure out at all," he admitted.

"And some women you can't figure out?"

Merced laughed. "Shoot, Miss Tipton, I can't figure out any women."

"I will wait until daylight to go with you, but I will not be able to sleep."

"Then rest your limbs at least. We won't get any rest over the next day or so—that's a fact."

Wilson Judd Merced did not sleep either.

He thought about Echo Jack and María Alejandra.

He thought about the stench from a warehouse full of hides going up in flames.

He thought about Carty Parkins and how Echo Jack had wanted to kill him the minute he came hiking out of the Plumas Cañón.

Mostly he thought of a nineteen-year-old red-haired girl from Boston who did not buckle under devastating news.

Some people need adversity to bring out their strength, Lord. She's got more sand than I figured.

She just might be the type that could make it out here.

You know . . . if she marries smart.

But a promise is a promise, Lord. I'm not backing away until You say so. I will live by my vow all my life, if needs be.

The eastern sky was turning a light gray when Merced saddled the second horse. All four mounts stood at the railing in front of the livery stable. Two with saddles and bridles. Two with lead ropes.

In the plaza the fourth orchestra was still playing, although the crowd had dwindled to no more than fifty. Most of the lanterns had run out of tallow, which created a sporadic lighting effect.

How in the world do they keep going? They are from sturdier stock than me. At least, when it comes to dancing.

There was just enough light to look diagonally across the street to the Castro home. Alena's door to the balcony remained closed.

If she's up, she'll see me here and step out on the veranda.

I think.

I'm not going to go banging on the door at this hour.

Merced squatted down on his haunches and leaned his back against the barn and waited. *I surely would like a cup of coffee. Even some of that chocolate mud would be all right.*

He could smell the whiff of smoke from across the plaza where the Indians camped.

They won't have any coffee, and if they did, not enough to share. That wouldn't be fair.

One of the cooks might be stirring around at the Castro house. I could lead the team over there and hang around outside.

Wilson Merced had just walked all four horses to the front of the house when he noticed an Indian man and a young girl walk right up the middle of Calle Segunda.

The girl looked familiar.

The Indian man, a good foot shorter than Merced, stopped when he saw the Americano.

"Howdy!" Merced smiled and tipped his hat.

"El Americano del Norte, my daughter has a present for you," the man blurted out as he walked forward, the girl hiding behind him. He handed Merced a rawhide and bear-claw necklace. In between each of the twenty claws was a small silver bead.

Merced held the heavy necklace in his hands and looked at the round brown eyes of the girl peeking around her father. She wore a woman's yellow flower print blouse that hung past her knees. Though her black hair remained somewhat matted and tangled, her face was scrubbed cleaner, and her eyes were brighter than when the bear had charged at her.

"Tell your daughter thank you very much. Tell her she looks very pretty in her new dress."

The man turned and patted his daughter on the head and

spoke to her tenderly. She said something back, but it was so soft and shy that Merced couldn't hear any of the words.

"My daughter says this dress was given her by the queen."

"The queen?"

"La Paloma Roja del Monterey."

Miss Tipton, when did you have time to send this little girl your blouse? Merced squatted down on his haunches. He tugged at the rawhide lacing on the side of his buckskin shirt. When it was pulled out, it was about two feet long.

"I have a present for your daughter, too," he announced.

He untied the leather lace of the bear-claw necklace and began to slide out the claws and the beads. The little girl came out from behind her father and bent low to watch him.

No one spoke.

When he was through, Merced had two necklaces lying side by side in the dirt. Both sported ten bear claws.

He pulled off his hat and slipped the one the girl gave him around his neck. Then he pushed his hat back on and picked up the other necklace. He reached toward the girl, but she backed up to her father. He said something to her and pushed her forward.

Merced put the new ten-claw necklace around the little girl's neck. "Tell your daughter this is for her. There were two brave people near the corral yesterday. This way when she grows up to be a beautiful woman, I will be able to recognize her because of the necklace."

The man bent down and spoke gently in the girl's ear.

Suddenly there was a wide smile revealing a missing upper front tooth. Then she leaped forward and threw her arms around Merced's neck and squeezed tight. He hugged back.

Instantly, she dropped her hands and ran back behind her father, this time fingering the bear-claw necklace.

"My daughter says thank you."

Merced took his callused thumbs and brushed the corners of his eyes. "That much I understood."

The two Indians, obviously wishing to avoid the lingering fandango, hiked back down Calle Segunda and turned down the adobe arcade in front of the mission.

"Wilson, may I ask you a question?"

Doña Alena Louise Tipton stood at the railing of the Castro balcony. He pulled off his hat. "Yes, ma'am?"

"How did you ever learn to be so gentle and kind with children?"

"I, eh . . . it was a very painful lesson. I'd rather not talk about it."

"We will have twenty hours on the road to Monterey. We'll have to talk about something."

"Maybe we could talk about Boston."

"That would be horribly boring. We will talk about your rancho."

"We will?"

"Yes. I am ready to go. Doña María Martina packed us some food. Would you like to come in and have a cup of something hot before we leave?"

"I'm sorry, Alena, I really can't enter a—"

"Oh yes. Forgive me. I will bring a cup out to you. What would you like—coffee or chocolate?"

"Coffee if possible, chocolate if there's nothin' else."

Wilson Merced's single-breasted brown wool frock coat was rolled up and tied behind the high cantle of his saddle. Along with most of his other possessions.

The buckskin shirt was soft with age and felt comfortable as they galloped out of San Juan. In one hand were his braided rawhide reins. In the other was a lead rope that guided his two spare buckskin-colored horses. Bouncing on his neck were bear claws that had the day before still belonged to Oso Grande.

Beside him, on the horse she had ridden from Monterey, Alena Tipton dashed along as gracefully as a seasoned Californio señorita. She wore a light wool skirt dyed black. Her blouse was off-white linen, loosely fitting, with sleeves that hung just below her elbows. It had a high neckline covered by a black lace collar. She wore boots very similar to his. It was her favorite riding attire.

Merced set the pattern of the trip. They raced along for four or five miles, then slowed to a trot for the same distance. After that, they repeated the regimen. After the third season of gallops, they stopped and rested a few minutes while he switched saddles to the spare horses.

During the gallop prolonged discussion was next to impossible. It was during the trot cycle that conversation flourished.

"Wilson, you look younger after you have shaved."

"Thank you, ma'am. I feel mostly skinned."

He seemed to be staring at her.

"Is there something wrong?"

He turned away and looked ahead over his horse's ears. "Nope. I just realized that I can't quite figure you out."

"Oh, is this the what-in-the-world-is-a-young-lady-from-Boston-doing-in-a-wild-country-like-this question?"

"Nope. No one has to explain to me why they want to live in California. If folks back in the States had any idea about this land, they'd be flocking out here in droves."

"Many Californios think that will happen someday. They say that the Americanos will want this land for their own. But tell me, what is it about me you can't figure out?"

"I thought I had pegged you the night we rode into town."

"How's that?"

"Oh, I'd rather not say."

"Well, then I'll tell you what I thought about you. When you first rode into town, I pegged you for a foul-smelling, foul-mouthed, uncouth hide rancher who wanted no more out of life than to get drunk and chase women."

His square jaw slackened. "You did?"

Even with her head slightly down, her nose seemed to be turned up. "Yes, and I was very wrong. Now you have to be honest. What did you think about me?"

"I figured you were just one of those beautiful women who's caught up in yourself, with little strength of caring or character."

"You did? Oh, my! Is that how I come across? How horrid!"

"I was wrong," he admitted.

"I'm thrilled to hear that. What made you change your mind?"

"First, I found out you have a strong faith in God. That's something that's important to me. Second, you are very easy, even for an old hermit like me, to talk to. Third, at the fandango I learned you had a mind of your own and didn't just go along with the crowd. Fourth, I knew you had sand when you didn't break down and bawl when you heard about the fire in the warehouse. But fifth, and most of all, I found out you have a heart when I saw your good blouse on that little Indian girl."

"Thank you for your list of attributes. I take it you've been thinking about this."

"I couldn't sleep, so I had to think of something."

"Well, you, of course, shamed me into being generous with the little girl. Both your first opinion and your second were partially correct. But I can't explain why I am not completely depressed over the fire. This business gives me a reason for staying in California, and it gives me an income. Maybe more important to my ego, it gives me status. Saturday I would have been devastated by such news. Now I'm not. Can you explain that, Wilson?"

"Me? I can't even explain myself, let alone someone else."

"I wonder if it has something to do with you."

He brushed his hat back until it dropped off his head and settled on his back. "What did I do?"

"I don't know. Yet. Perhaps the reality of it all will sink in when I stand beside the burnt ruins of a warehouse. Maybe then I will break down and bawl. I don't know. But for now, it's like riding over that big hill up there." She pointed straight ahead to a brown grassy hill crested with scattered oak tress. "I have no idea what's on the other side, but I'm looking forward to seeing it nonetheless."

"Is this the way you always respond to adversity?"

"I suppose." Alena tried to readjust her position on the sidesaddle. "The night my father died, I cried until midnight. Then I stopped crying, washed my face, and started planning my life without him. I decided life does go on. God is still on the throne. Our Lord and Savior has promised never to leave or forsake us, so whatever happens next is under His watchful eye and tender care."

"That doesn't sound like a nineteen-year-old."

"I'm really much older, just well kept."

Wilson caught the spark in her eyes and the suppressed smile.

"Actually," Alena admitted, "some days I act thirty, and some days I act twelve. You must have met me on a mature day."

"I know what you mean. There are times I feel like an old man with barely the strength to run a ranch . . . and others when I feel twenty, ready to bust the wildest horse."

"Well, that means, Mr. Wilson Judd Merced, that on certain days when I act mature and days when you act youthful, we are about the same age."

"I reckon you're right about that. But it don't . . . anyway, why talk about that?"

"What?"

"Are you ready to race up that hill?"

"Is it that time already?"

"Yep."

"Aren't you going to finish your sentence?"

"Not if I can help it." Merced touched his spurs to the horse's flanks and galloped on up ahead of her, leading the spare horses behind him.

By the time they stopped to rest and eat around noon, Alena was stiff, sore, and extremely warm from the bright sunlight and the dry, still air. But Merced never seemed to tire. He was never out of breath. Never slump-shouldered. Never a word of complaint.

She found some shade under an oak where the grass was still green and motioned for him to join her. "Wilson, it's more pleasant back under here."

He sat cross-legged on his saddle in the sunlight beyond the tree's shadow. "I'm sure it is, but I don't sit under oak trees in the heat of a summer day."

She unfolded a small quilt one yard square, spread it out on the grass, and then sat down. "You certainly have a lot of things you won't do," she called out.

"I wouldn't sit back there, Alena," he urged. "You know how oak trees can split up in the summertime."

"What are you talking about? I've lived in California for three years, and I've never heard of anything like that."

"That's because you've lived at the coast. Here where it's hot, these old trees become real brittle in the summer heat. Then on a day like this with hardly a breeze stirring, a whole limb will break off. People have gotten hurt by them falling."

"That's preposterous. You really don't think I'd believe that, do you?"

"Whether you believe it or not, I'd feel a whole lot more comfortable if you moved out here next to me."

"Mister, is that just a wild story to talk me into sitting next to you?"

"No, but did it work?"

"I'll come sit next to you, Mr. Merced, on one condition. You have to finish that sentence you started before the last gallop."

He dug through the food sack and pulled out a large corn tortilla. "I've not told that to anyone before."

"Not even Echo Jack?"

"No one."

She stood, gathered her quilt, and hiked through the short wild grass toward him. "I won't tell another soul."

"I don't know why I started to tell it to you. It's awful personal," he admitted.

She unfolded the little blanket and tucked her booted feet back under her as she sat down. "If it's concerning an inappropriate topic for conversation, I will certainly press you no further. I am a bit young, but I assure you, I am not naive." She fanned herself with her hand, then glanced back at the shade. "Were you serious about oak limbs falling off?"

"Yep. The first summer I was here, I tied a good brood mare to an oak while I went down the creek to wash up. All of a sudden in the middle of a still, hot day, a limb as big around as your . . ."

"My what, Mr. Merced?"

"As big around as your waist snapped off the tree and hit the horse. It broke her neck."

"No! How dreadful!"

"Folks tell me it happens quite often, so I just avoid 'em on days like this."

"Are you avoiding the subject, too, Mr. Merced?"

"What subject is that?"

"Although you keep refusing to finish a sentence, I believe the subject is why our age difference and something in your past keep us at a distance."

"You're a blunt young woman."

"I've been told it's an American characteristic."

"Since I've never told this to anyone, I'm not sure where to begin. Anyway, here goes. I have one brother."

"I have three."

"My mama died right after I was born, so that ended the family. Just my older brother Raft and me."

"Where does he live?"

"I'm getting to that. You see, I was down in Texas with Sam Houston."

"You fought for independence?"

"Yep. I even stayed down there a few years. I was going to go into the cattle business, but like here, there's just no market down there. I freighted down to Santa Fe for a couple seasons. Then I sold out and went back to winter at my brother's place in St. Louis."

"So he lives in St. Louis?"

"Let me tell this while I have a mind to."

"I'm sorry," she said.

"Anyway, my brother Raft, his wife, Tina, and his two kids were livin' in St. Louis, and I was determined to make it to their place before Christmas. I pushed it pretty good for a week, but I didn't get there until the day after Christmas, bone-tired and wet from a cold rain."

"I've never been to St. Louis. I thought it was mild there."

"Not in the middle of winter. Anyway, I gave them some fruit and gifts I brought. Then I drank a hot cider and crawled into a cot in the pantry just off the kitchen. Raft and the family had rooms upstairs."

"Well, Raft, he worked for the Rocky Mountain Fur Company at the time. He gets up in the middle of the night and comes down and stirs up the fire in the kitchen. I sort of remember him nudging me and saying he had to go down to the docks on emergency and that I should tell Tina not to worry, that he'd be back by breakfast."

"Don't tell me something happened to him and he never returned," Alena gasped.

Merced stopped talking.

"Oh . . . I'm sorry," she said. "I'm running ahead of the story. Please continue, without interruptions."

"Sometime later I woke up real warm. It was like the first time in two weeks that I'd been warm and dry. So I crawled out of the covers and lay there trying to remember where I was. I don't know if you have traveled day after day, sleeping out in the open, but after a while you wake up in the morning and can't remember where you are. Well, I'm laying there for just a second when I realize the room is full of smoke. I start coughin' and hackin', tryin' to catch a breath. That's when I see the kitchen is in flames."

"Oh no! No wonder you were warm."

"I staggered to the back of the pantry and found a door that opened to the back porch and out into the yard. Outside, it was total confusion. Neighbors yellin', some runnin' around with buckets of water, and I'm crawling across the frosty yard on my hands and knees wearin' nothin' but my long johns. I couldn't get the smoke out of my lungs and was about to cough my guts out when this lady wrapped in a big fur coat tossed a pail of freezin' cold water all over me."

"What on earth for? Were you on fire?"

"Nope. I guess she panicked. Now I'm staggering around in the yard wearin' soakin' wet long johns and freezin' to death, still trying to remember where I am. The house is totally consumed, and there's nothin' to do but try to keep the neighbors' houses from burnin', too. Well, about then someone grabbed me by the shoulders and shook me back and forth."

"Your brother?"

"Yeah. He had run all the way home. He kept yellin', 'Where's Tina and the kids? Where are they? Are they safe?'"

"Oh . . . no," Alena moaned.

Wilson Merced just stared across the rolling hills. She reached over and put her hand on his arm. "You don't have to continue. I had no right to press you in this."

Tears trickled down his cheek. He didn't bother to wipe them.

"Anyway . . . when Raft realized that his family hadn't made it out and I didn't even remember to try to save them, he got mad. Mad at the fire. Mad at God for letting it happen. And mostly mad at me."

"What did he do?"

"He tried to bust my head open with his fists."

"You two got into a fight?"

"It wasn't much of a fight. I didn't throw a punch. How could I? He'd just lost his wife and kids, and I didn't do anything about it."

"But if the house was on fire before you woke up, what could you have done?"

"I could have died trying to save them. There are worse things than dying heroically."

"But he can't blame you."

"He did. Still does, I reckon."

"What happened after that? Did you two reconcile?"

"Not hardly. I haven't seen him since that night. I borrowed some clothes from a neighbor and pulled out of town. I had left my poke in saddlebags down at the livery. So I sent him all the money I had and a note of apology. Told him I'd wait out the winter at Uncle Burtrum's. He could reach me there. After that I'd go west and stay out of his sight like he wanted."

"Didn't he contact you at your uncle's?"

"He's not really my uncle. It's just what we called him. But Raft never sent word. So I left in the spring and came to California. Told Uncle Burtrum he could reach me in Monterey."

"Did he ever write?"

"Raft didn't. But I get a letter from Uncle Burtrum about once a year."

"That's a frightfully sad story. Is that why you don't enter two-story buildings?"

"I told myself if I just stayed out of big buildings, then I couldn't fail someone. And then I made the vow."

"What vow?"

"I told the Lord that if Raft had to go through life without a wife and children, I should have to go through life without them, too. It wouldn't be fair for me to have all of that when Raft lost his."

"You promised the Lord you wouldn't get married?"

"Yep."

"But . . . but the Lord's forgiveness covers all our sins. And you didn't sin. A pledge like that is penance. It's like trying to do something to prove yourself worthy of forgiveness. None of us is worthy of the Lord's forgiveness," Alena protested.

"It's not penance. I know the Lord forgives me. I don't think my brother forgives me. And I know I can't forgive myself. It has nothing to do with forgiveness or salvation. It's justice. I failed. And it should cost me."

The crack of a limb breaking sounded like a rifle shot. Wilson Merced pulled his Paterson Colt from his belt. Alena Louise Tipton dropped her tortilla. Both spun around toward the oak tree. A huge limb sprawled in a cloud of dust.

"It really happened!" she cried out.

"That's why I don't take chances. With trees . . . or with buildings."

"But the fire . . . Tragedies happen all the time. It's the world we live in. You can't take the blame for what happened in St. Louis."

"I don't take blame for the fire. They figure Raft stuffed the firebox, and it overheated and exploded. I don't even take the blame for an innocent woman and two beautiful children dyin'. What I blame myself for is not doin' what I should have done."

"That's why you went chargin' right at that bear yesterday, wasn't it?" Alena pressed. "You were going to save that girl or die trying."

"I reckon that's sort of it. Anyway, now you know the complete story of Wilson Judd Merced."

"Not the complete story. There are still chapters to write," she challenged.

Merced glanced up at the deep blue eyes, then let his sight wander to her hands folded in her lap. *I should have met her five years ago, Lord. Maybe things could have turned out different. Good grief! Five years ago she would have been fourteen.*

This is crazy.

This whole relationship is crazy.

And hopeless.

Six

When Alena Louise Tipton was eight years old, she stood with her entire family in the front yard and watched her grandmother's rural Massachusetts home burn to the ground. She had carefully studied her Granny Bracken's reaction.

There were no tears.

No regrets.

"Well," the white-haired lady announced, "I never did like that old house anyways. I'll just have to build me a new one."

But she didn't.

She moved to Boston instead.

Now it was Alena's turn to view the ruins that were once her only titled possession in Alta California. A block away from the docks, the Tipton Warehouse had been in the perfect location for storing hides and loading them on ships. She was determined, like Granny Bracken, not to cry.

But the scene was different.

She was not surrounded by loving family.

She had no one.

Even Mr. Wilson Judd Merced had gone his way to search the streets for Echo Jack.

I never liked that old building anyway.

I will build a new one. A better one. But I'll need money for that. I

*will write back to Boston and secure a loan. . . . Of course, that could take
six months—or more. In the meantime I'll rent . . . I'll construct . . .*

She strolled along the dirt street viewing the piles of burned
hides and rubble. Only a little ways from the ruins small yellow
birds fluttered around huge pink, white, and blue hydrangea
blossoms.

*Life goes on. The birds hardly notice the change. And the flowers?
They sing their sweet praise no matter what the stench.*

*Don Manuel was right. It does smell worse than horn-burning day.
Alena, you are not thinking very clearly. You have just lost your business; you are going to be short of funds. You should trade what hides Don
Manuel manages to buy in San Juan for a ticket back to Boston. What
choice do I have?*

Lord, I don't want to go back to Boston in defeat.

I do not want to go back to Boston at all.

*I can't go back and spend the rest of my life wishing I had stayed.
My life is here—whatever that life is to be.*

Alena hiked up the pine-crested hill that rose 100 feet above
the rubble of the warehouse and sat down on a log worn smooth as
a park bench by the backside of countless other visitors. She stared
northwest at the blue-green waters of the Pacific. The morning fog
had long since burned off, leaving only the purity of a sparsely
inhabited coastal community.

She studied the curvature of the earth on the water's horizon.
The cloudless bright blue sky reflected the yellow rays of the summer sun. A slight breeze drifted off the water, bringing an aroma of
saltwater mixed with pine trees and a tinge of burnt hides. The
town of Monterey sprawled around the harbor. Most homes were
separated from the neighbors by gardens, pastures, and open fields,
giving the entire area a wide-open pastoral feel.

Lord, I don't understand many things.

*I don't know why my father had to die. For nineteen years I didn't
have a worry. Father made all the decisions. He provided for me.
Protected me. Told me that one day my husband would do the same.*

*I don't know why my business had to burn to the ground. It was an
honest business. Built up with hard work and long hours. I know how to
run it even in a foreign land.*

I don't know why I have to be so stubborn about staying in California. I've known for three years that my destiny lies just over the next grass-covered hill and past another sprawling oak. For me to go back to Boston would be to imprison myself in the past. It would be to forfeit the abundant and purposeful life You've promised. But I'm all alone with no business and an unknown future. What do I do now?

I'm going to have to trust in Your leading me.

I suppose that was Your point all along.

You took away Father, and I had to learn to live my own life. You sent a thirty-two-year-old hide rancher to teach me to be more compassionate and caring. Then you sent a fire to teach me to be totally dependent on You.

Well, I'm learning, Lord, but I'd like to catch my breath.

That's enough for now.

Lead me to something noble and true.

Please.

I feel like a young hawk on a precipice, ready to jump. I'll either fly . . . or I'll dash myself to death upon the rocks below. I wonder if the little hawk really knows which will happen.

I sure don't.

Alena pulled a handkerchief out of the sash at her waist and dabbed the tears out of her eyes. Then she stared at the back of her hands. They trembled slightly.

Look at you, Alena! You want to pretend to be so mature. You shake like a schoolgirl.

You're tired.

A person can't get much sleep on a horse.

I should go to the Cabrillos' and rest. Wilson said he would meet me there tonight. After that . . . I have no idea on earth what I shall do. I will fly . . . or fall.

She sat up and brushed down the folds of her skirt.

"Review your options."

That's what Father would say.

All right.

I can sail home and live with Robert and his family until I get settled in Boston.

Never.

I could live with Doña María Martina and Don Francisco . . . for a few years anyway.

But I have to pay my own way.

I could start a different business. You are not thinking clearly, Alena Louise. This is Alta California. Women do not run businesses.

At least, not any that I want to be a part of.

And, oh yes, I could get married.

Don Fernando would be a good choice. Stable. Well mannered. Good family. Connections. A future leader in California. Boring.

Or Don Ronaldo? Flashing, enthusiastic. Foolish. Reckless. Unreliable.

If that hide rancher would move to Monterey and ask me to marry him . . . this is crazy. I've known him for three days.

I'm too tired. My mind is wandering. It's siesta time. I will contemplate the future of Alena Louise Tipton after a nap. I'll see things more clearly then.

Fly or fall.

It's one or the other. The ledge was just burnt out from under me.

Lord, give me some direction . . . because my life is much more complicated than my daydreams about it.

The hacienda of Don Francisco Cabrillo contained a dozen large rooms sprawled over two stories, with the kitchen and dining area in a separate building. When everyone was home, the grounds bustled like a small village in itself.

But everyone was not home.

Besides Alena, only two servants remained at the estate. The rest were either at San Juan Bautista where Padre Estában was being laid to his final rest, or they had been given time off to visit with their own families.

The gardener and one of the cooks were so unobtrusive that Alena felt as if she had the house entirely to herself. Most of Monterey was similarly deserted. The governor and his entourage were still north at Yerba Buena. The remaining California troops were on standby at the *presidio* because of the presence of the well-armed American sailing vessel in the harbor.

When Alena awoke from her very sound nap, the sun was low on the Pacific horizon. A cool breeze drifted in through the open double doors in her second-story room that overlooked the courtyard of the hacienda.

She unfastened several buttons at the high neck of her dress. She could feel the cotton material damp with perspiration. *I shouldn't have slept in my dress. But I was so tired. I am not sure I will ride a horse again for a while.*

She pulled herself out of bed, sauntered barefoot across the cold tile floor to the mirror, and stroked her wavy red hair with the abalone-handled comb.

"All right, Miss Tipton, you took your *siesta*. Now what? Your business is still gone."

She walked out onto the covered balcony, combing her thick hair. The wood floor still retained some of the afternoon heat and felt warmer than the tile.

"You are stranded in Alta California . . . and you are all alone." *Lord, this would be a wonderful time for You to say something . . .*

"Evenin'!"

The strong masculine voice rolled from behind her and gripped her like a surprising hug from a long-lost friend.

She spun around. "Wilson! It's—it's you!"

"You expectin' someone else?"

"Of course not! It's just that . . . I was . . ."

"Talkin' to yourself?"

"How long have you been here?"

He sat on the bench outside her bedroom, hat pushed back, boots resting on the rowels of his spurs, arms folded across his chest, buckskin shirt pushed up to his elbows, and bear-claw necklace circling his neck.

"A couple hours, I reckon."

"But—but—how did you get out here?"

"Up the outside stairs."

"You almost came into a two-story building."

"I almost did. But not quite."

"I was asleep."

"So I noticed. I've been dozing off myself."

"You—you didn't come into my room while I was sleeping, did you?"

"Well, I looked in on you when I first got here."

"You did what?" She began to pace, wringing her fingers.

"I just glanced to see if you were asleep."

"But—you can't . . . it's not right!"

"I couldn't find anyone around this place to bring you a message, so I decided just to wait until you woke up. You were fully dressed, you don't snore, and you had your mouth closed, so I don't reckon there was anything to be embarrassed about. But if it will even the score, you can stare at me while I'm asleep sometime."

Alena continued to stalk in front of the seated hide rancher. "That's not the point!"

"What is the point? I told you I'd stop back this evenin'."

"Well . . . I've never had a man stare at me while I sleep."

"How do you know?"

She fumbled at the neck of her blouse and ended up fingering her gold cross.

"That's a pretty cross," he added.

She turned away from him and stared out at the harbor. "I like wearing it. It reminds me that Jesus died for my sins. . . . And it is empty because He rose from the dead and will return for me someday."

"I like that." He rose and strolled over to the railing and stood beside her. "Are you still mad at me for waiting up here?"

"Maybe," she said.

"Maybe?"

"I'm still a little sleepy. Maybe I'll be more mad at you later. I like to think of my sleep as something private. I mean, what if I'd been in a nightgown instead of my dress?"

"Then I wouldn't have mentioned looking in at you."

"Somehow that is not too comforting." She thought he was going to slip his arm around her and was disappointed when he didn't.

"Well, what's it going to be? What did you decide?" he asked.

She continued to stare out at the ocean. "About what?"

"The warehouse. The future of the hide business."

"The warehouse is totally lost."

"Yeah. I went by and took a look."

"Doesn't it smell horrid?"

"I've smelled worse."

"When?"

"A few years back I rode through a Shoshone village up on the Snake River. Smallpox had taken every person a week or so earlier."

"Were they all dead?"

"Yep."

"What did you do?"

"Held my nose, set fire to the place, and kept riding."

Neither spoke for a moment.

He's been through so much. I've led an extremely sheltered life. She laid her hand on his. "Did you find Echo Jack?"

"Nope. But I know where they went when they were here."

"*Were* here? They aren't in Monterey now?"

"Best report is that they are headed back to San Juan."

"How did we miss them?"

"I imagine they were taking a more scenic route."

"Oh?"

"I reckon lovers don't always want to be seen."

"Oh . . . that route." She thought about putting her arm around him and was disappointed when she didn't. "Well, where did they go when they were here?"

Merced pointed out to the harbor. "Out there, so I hear."

"To the American ship? What for? Were they trying to book passage and run off?"

He reached down and tucked his pant leg into his tall tooled-leather leggings. "Well, if I can believe the Costanoan Indian woman who sells jewelry down in front of the customs house, they went aboard ship to get married."

Alena's hand flew to cover her mouth. "They what?"

"I surmise they had the ship's captain marry them." Merced shrugged. "It's legal for him to do it."

"But it won't be recognized in California. The *padres* won't accept that. And neither will her father. For Californians nonchurch weddings are like living in sin. That's ridiculous anyway. They can't get married. They've only known each other a few days."

"When a person makes up his mind to marry, I reckon days don't have much to do with it. But it does seem strange that Echo Jack would think this is the time for marriage. She must be quite a girl. Maybe he's got a new job lined up I don't know about. Rancho Alázan is a mighty rustic place to bring a bride home to."

"What do you mean, days don't have much to do with it?" She knew her face was now flushed the same color as her hair. "They just can't go off and get married three days after they meet. Why . . . why that's no longer than you and I have known each other!"

"Yep."

"What do you mean, yep?" she demanded.

"I'm just agreeing with you."

"Agreeing about what?"

"That they've only known each other about the same length of time we've known each other."

"Oh. Well . . . now that we have that straight, what are you going to do about it?"

"About what?" He flashed a silly, awkward grin.

"About getting the marriage annulled and warning Echo Jack before someone gets killed. What did you think I was talking about?"

"I think I'll go out there." He pointed to the ship lying at anchor in Monterey Bay.

The sun was almost down, the breeze cool, and yet she felt perspiration on her forehead. Her pulse raced. "What for?"

"I want to know for sure what they went aboard ship for. Maybe my information is wrong. Perhaps the captain knows where Echo Jack and María Alejandra are now. The Indian lady said she saw them ride off after they returned to land. If he's married her, I can't do anything about it. But I could have the facts right, just in case they are called into question."

"When will you be going to the ship?"

"I think I'll see if there is a dory down at the docks that can row me out."

Alena suddenly remembered how she had stood in the very same place on the veranda and listened to Don Ronaldo serenade her only a few days before. "Are you going by yourself?"

"Did you want to go with me?"

"Why on earth would I want to do that?"

He stretched his arm out behind her back, then relaxed it on his hip. "To see if the ship is sailing back to the East."

She folded her arms tight against her chest. "I'm not leaving California." *I don't believe Wilson ever serenaded a woman in his life.*

"I thought you might like to know what the passage would cost. You know, just as an option."

"I'm not leaving," she snapped.

"Would you like for me to ask them?"

"Please don't bother."

"It's not a bother."

Alena turned to face him with her arms still folded in front of her. "Mr. Merced, are you trying to get rid of me?"

"No, ma'am."

"Good. Then I have decided I'll go with you."

"You will? Why?"

"I want to see if they are buying hides. I could have those from San Juan here in a day or so, and I better sell them immediately, since I have no warehouse. When will you be leaving?"

He took her by the arm. "Right now, I reckon."

She stepped away from him. "I reckon we are not going until I comb my hair, brush my dress, and put on my hat, shawl, and shoes."

He stared down at his boots. "That's what I meant."

"Wilson, I will feel a whole lot more comfortable if you'd wait for me down at the bench by the almond tree." She pointed to the courtyard below.

"Me, too. This is about as close to entering a two-story building as I want to come."

The *Pride of Baltimore* lay anchored like an island in the calm waters of Monterey Bay. The four-man crew rowed the dinghy out carrying two crates of silver-adorned leather saddles along with two passengers. The light breeze seemed almost tropical as it rolled over the water and rustled the feathers on Alena's hat.

She wore what she called her Boston best. It was her least favorite outfit in California, but she believed that the charcoal-gray light wool dress with simple lace collar would give her an air of authority before the New England seamen.

At least, she hoped it would.

One of the sailors led Tipton and Merced to the captain's quarters.

Capt. Archibald Malynton greeted them with a wide smile and a firm handshake. "We are headed around the Horn and straight for Baltimore. And, yes, we do have a little cabin space left. Will it be for both of you or just your daughter?" he blustered, rubbing a full gray mustache as he examined Alena. His full lips seemed to be pursed in a permanent smile.

Merced pulled off his hat and scratched his head. "My wh-what?"

"Oh, excuse me," the captain quickly apologized. "The boatman said you wanted passage for your daughter."

"We are very good friends, but he is not my father." Alena strutted across the cabin. "And neither of us seeks passage."

"Well, you don't say." He began to laugh deeply. "My apologies." He motioned for them to be seated on a bench next to his desk, but he continued to pace the cabin. "That's what I get for running ahead of myself. My wife says I'm too quick to draw assumptions. Quite so. Now what can I do for you?"

Merced awkwardly fidgeted with his fingers and began to crack his knuckles. "Captain, I'm looking for a friend of mine who came out to your ship yesterday. I've been trying to locate him. I thought perhaps you could assist me."

"What is his name?"

"Echo Jack."

The captain spun around. "You are a friend of Echo Jack and María Alejandra?"

"Yes, he works for me."

Capt. Malynton toyed with a polished brass spyglass, then laid it down on the cherrywood desk. "They came out here to get married."

Alena shook her head in disbelief.

Wilson Merced scooted to the front edge of the bench and rested his elbows on his knees. "You performed the ceremony?"

"No, I let the preacher do that."

"Preacher?" Merced questioned.

"The reverend is returning home from the Sandwich Islands. Says they're going to start a mission work out there, and he's heading back to New England to raise the funds. He's a Congregationalist, you know."

"A Congregationalist clergyman is on board?" Alena realized she had her palms on her cheeks. She lowered her hands to her lap.

"Well, he's not exactly on board at the moment. He took some mail into Monterey. Said he knew one of the folks the letter was for and thought he'd pay a visit. Isn't that a coincidence?"

Alena stared past the captain toward a porthole on the wall. *I promised Grandmother I'd have a Congregationalist clergyman perform my wedding. Lord, are You teasing me or testing me?*

"So Echo Jack and María Alejandra got officially married?" Merced pressed.

"Right out there on the deck. Most of the whole crew witnessed it."

"Do you know where they went after that?"

"Nope. But they were mighty cautious. Said they planned to avoid the authorities."

"Because of the marriage?"

"I suppose so. It's official in most parts of the world. Don't reckon it will sit well with these California *padres*. But I figure it's about time they open things up. With more and more Americans hearing about this land, I don't suppose they can keep the infidels out. Now keep this under your hat, but there's a lot of talk in the East about war with Mexico coming soon. If the *generales* attack the Texicans again, it could start the whole crusade. In fact, some of my men have been urging me to run up the stars and stripes right away."

"What's the reverend's name?" Alena hadn't heard a word of the captain's political commentary.

"The Reverend Jeremiah Traxter."

The words shot out of her mouth like rocks from a slingshot. "The Reverend Jeremiah B. Traxter from Middleborough?"

The only thing wider than the captain's smile was his bushy gray mustache. "Yep. You know him?"

"Know him? Why—why, he's my grandmother's minister! I can't believe this!"

The captain glanced at some papers on the table. "Are you Miss Alena Louise Tipton?"

"Yes. How did you know my name?"

"Rev. Traxter has mail for you and your father. That's why he went into town."

"My father died two months ago." Alena felt her shoulders slump. Two strong but tender hands suddenly held her up.

"Are you all right? Is this preacher some sort of a renegade?" Merced asked. She thought for a moment he was going to hug her. But he didn't.

"Oh, no, Wilson . . . no, the reverend is a wonderful man. . . . It's just . . . Here in California? I—I can't believe it."

The captain scooped up an invoice from the top of his desk. "You wouldn't happen to be Wilson J. Merced, would you?"

"Eh, yes."

"That's the other person he has a letter for."

"For me? Who was it from?"

"I couldn't tell you that."

"Could we get a lift back to Monterey now?" Merced queried. "Perhaps we can find the reverend. I don't know how I missed him earlier."

"He had to go check in at the *presidio* first," the captain said.

"That's the one place I didn't look."

"I'm afraid I already sent the dory in to pick up the reverend. You'll have to wait aboard ship a little while." He waved his arm around the room. "Please make yourself at home in my cabin. I have some work to do on the bridge."

Alena walked over behind the captain's desk to a porthole

that formed a frame for the setting sun. Wilson stood a few feet behind her.

"Are you feeling all right, Alena?"

"Other than my head spinning around, I suppose I'm fine."

"That's quite a coincidence, you and me both having a letter at the same time."

Alena turned back and glanced at his trusting light blue eyes. "You think it's a letter from your brother?" she asked.

"Nope. It must be from Uncle Burtrum. It must be his Christmas letter."

"In June?"

"It takes awhile to get here. So this Rev. Traxter is a square fella?"

"Yes, he's a very devout man. My grandmother claims he's the best preacher she's ever heard. But this is very, very strange."

"You mean, of all people to run across?"

"Yes, this afternoon down at the warehouse, or what's left of the warehouse, I prayed for some guidance about the future. I want to do the right thing. All my plans seem to be crumbling—or burning down—so I asked the Lord to lead me."

"You wanted Him to show you a sign?"

"I didn't use those words, but that was what I was thinking."

"And here's a clergyman you know who could escort you back to Boston."

Her hands dropped to her sides. "He could do what?"

Merced searched for agreement. "You know, so you wouldn't have to sail by yourself."

Alena forced herself to take short, quick breaths. She could feel her neck beginning to heat. *Is that the sign the Lord sent?* "Wilson, why are you in such a hurry to send me off?"

He turned away, hat in hand. "I'm not . . . I can't . . . It's too . . ."

She poked a finger into his back. "You will get to the point soon, won't you?"

He whipped around, his face only inches from hers. "Can we go for a walk?"

"We're on a ship, remember?" She thought for just a moment that he was going to kiss her.

"I mean, a walk around the deck."

"Certainly." She took his arm. "Maybe it will help to keep my head from spinning."

They hiked up the stairs and out onto the main deck. In a few minutes they found themselves at the railing, watching a slow bright orange summer sun sink below the horizon.

She held tightly to his coat-clad arm. "Now, Mr. Wilson Judd Merced, are you going to explain why you keep insisting on my leaving California?"

He stared out at sea. "Alena, I'm going to say some presumptuous, even foolish things. Please hear me out. When I get all through, we'll both have a good laugh and go about our business."

Lord, help me keep my mouth shut and listen to him. "Yes, Mr. Merced?"

"Well, you . . . you . . . you . . ."

My word, say something!

"I'm sorry," he mumbled. "What I'm about to say is so foolish I can't believe I'm going to say it."

She bit her lip and held her breath.

"I know I'm goin' to regret tellin' you this, but I'm goin' to regret not tellin' you even more. So here goes. . . . You have extremely complicated my life, Alena Louise Tipton."

That's it? I'm a complication.

"I had things figured out. I would live on the frontier alone. Or maybe with a *vaquero* or two. I would not marry. I would not have a family. I would live under my self-imposed banishment for the rest of my life. For the past several years that philosophy has worked just fine. But now . . . in just three days you have confounded my life."

Alena refused to look at him. *Don't say it. Keep quiet. Lord, seal my mouth!*

"I have spent most of the last three days wonderin' what it would be like if things were different."

"Different?" The word popped out like an escaped whisper.

"I keep thinking, what if my brother's family had survived the fire? What if I hadn't made that kind of vow? What if you and I were closer in age? What if I had a ranch closer to Monterey? And ever' one of those 'what ifs' makes me dissatisfied with the way things are. I've been happy with things for years, and now I'm dissatisfied."

Alena had a sudden urge to unfasten the buttons at the neck of her dress and let the sea breeze cool her chest.

She didn't.

"So you want me to go back to Boston so that your life will return to normal?"

"I never said I wanted you to go to Boston."

"Well, what do you want, Mr. Merced?" She started to slip her arm away from his.

"What I want is . . ." He clamped her arm tight.

"Yes?"

"What I want is what I can't have." He sighed. "I have no right to even think of it."

"Wilson, I would like very much to know what you are thinking. My life, too, has taken a chaotic twist this week. I am searching desperately for direction from the Lord. Perhaps I will understand better after hearing what you have to say. So what is it you have no right to think of?"

"Alena, it is probably a sign of ingratitude to the Almighty to want what a man cannot have. But I thought about this all the time I sat on your balcony this afternoon."

Does this man ever get to the point?

"Anyway, here's what I was thinking. If I hadn't made that vow to the Lord . . . and if I was three or four years younger and you were three or four years older . . . well, it would be nice to come call on you once a month or so. Then perhaps after a year or two . . . if you and me were still on speakin' terms—I mean, if we proved agreeable to each other . . . and if . . . you know, a Congregationalist or Presbyterian minister just happened to sail into the bay, we could, you know . . . and all that."

"We could what?"

He mumbled something so softly she couldn't hear.

"Excuse me?" she said.

"Oh . . . nothin'."

"Wilson!" she barked, sticking her face in front of his. "Would you please speak up!"

Startled, he almost shouted, "Then we could get married!"

She sensed several sailors staring at them. She turned back and leaned on the railing, slipping her arm back into his.

"Alena, I apologize for my words. I'm just making things complicated for both of us. All of that was only a daydream."

The gentle rhythm of the ship on the placid waters of the bay rocked them into silence. It was not until the sun was completely below the Pacific horizon that she slipped her soft, thin fingers into his callused, strong ones. "It was a pleasant daydream."

He looked sincerely surprised. "It was?"

"I must admit I've had similar thoughts." She traced her finger across the back of his hand.

"Now you're teasing me."

Alena brushed a hank of red hair that had escaped her ill-fitting hat away from her eyes. "No, I'm not teasing. It's just like we met at the wrong time and the wrong place and under the wrong circumstances."

His arm circled her waist and hugged her gently. "I wish it could have been different."

"What are we going to do?" she asked.

He stood straight and announced, "We're going to do whatever is right and proper in the Lord's sight."

"How will we know what that is?"

"That's what I've been trying to figure out."

"Does the Lord ever lead us to the wrong place?" she asked.

He leaned back over the railing next to her. "What do you mean?"

"I said earlier perhaps we met at the wrong time and the wrong place in our lives. But when I think about it, does the Lord lead us to the wrong time and place?"

"I don't think so, but . . ."

"What if this is the right time and place? For, you know . . . what you said."

"For coming to see you once a month . . . and getting to know each other and . . ."

"Yes. What if it's the right time for all of that?"

"But my ranch is too far away to come visit more than a couple times a year."

"And I no longer have a business in Monterey."

"And I'm still thirteen years older than you."

"And you still have that vow to the Lord."

Wilson brushed the back of his hand across her smooth, pale cheek. "I've been working hard for years to make my life simple, and it's as if all those plans exploded in my face."

She reached up and pressed his hand tight against her cheek. "Life is never simple, is it?"

"I reckon not. Thanks for not laughing at me and my daydreams." He tugged her hand to his face and kissed her fingers. "I needed to tell you. It would have haunted me for years if I hadn't."

She sighed and leaned her head on his shoulder. "You know what would haunt me, Wilson Judd Merced?"

"What?"

"If I never knew how this felt." She stood on her tiptoes and quickly pressed her lips against his. They felt rough, chapped, startled, cold, warm, soft, and enthusiastic all at the same time.

He did not quickly pull away.

Nor did she.

"You're not making this any easier, Miss Alena," he finally muttered.

"Sure I am."

"How's that?"

"If you hadn't made that vow, if you lived closer to Monterey . . ."

"If we were closer in age?" he added.

"That doesn't make any difference to me."

"It doesn't?"

"No. Does it to you?"

"Well . . . I reckon not."

She reached up and kissed his cheek. "So if those things were different, I'd say yes to this awkward proposal of yours."

"Proposal?"

"You did say that you dreamed of marrying me, didn't you?"

"Well, yes, but I meant . . ."

"At the Lord's timing?"

"Yeah, something like that," he said.

"So do I. I mean, if other things were different."

"And we had time to get to know each other better."

"Yes." Still holding his arm, she glanced up at him. "Wilson, do you love the Lord?"

"Yes, ma'am."

"Do you believe that a marriage is supposed to last forever?"

"Yep."

"I can tell by your compassion you love children."

"You're right about that."

"Are you honest and open with your feelings?"

"I believe you could say that."

"Could you treat me gently even when I'm horrid?"

"I suppose I could learn."

"You might want to think carefully about this one. . . . Do you love me more than anything else on this earth?"

"Yep."

"You didn't take much time to decide."

"I already know the answer. Now what's this all about?" he asked.

"I'm getting to know you better." Alena smiled. "Sometimes it takes months, even years, to find all of that out about another person. Now do you want to get to know me better?"

"Eh, yeah." He raised his full dark brown eyebrows. "What did you have in mind?"

"I had in mind that you ask me some questions."

"Oh . . . yeah . . . well . . . Miss Tipton, are you trusting Jesus as your Lord and Savior?"

"Yes, I am."

"Could you live on the edge of the wilderness?"

"I could learn."

"Could you shoot a gun in order to protect your family?"

"I believe so."

"Could you grow in faith even if there wasn't a church nearby for a long time?"

"Yes, I know I could."

"Could you raise children and school them on your own and still have time for a husband?"

"I would like to spend my health and my days trying."

"Could you put up for a lifetime with a man who's liable to do some foolish things?"

"If he were absolutely crazy about me, I could."

"Could you learn to love a man thirteen years older than you?"

"I already do."

He paused for a minute.

"Did I pass?" she asked.

"Yep. Did I?"

"Yes."

"Now what?" he asked.

"Now we get back to the real world," she said.

"It must be the salt air," he mused. "I don't get into this kind of trouble back on the ranch."

"There aren't any women back on the ranch."

"That's a good point."

"I think it's California. Doña María Martina says California is made for lovers."

"In that case, we're in a hopeless situation."

"Yes," she added. "I still don't know if I'm flying or falling."

"What?"

"Look! The dory's coming back." She pointed toward the dock at Monterey.

The Reverend Jeremiah B. Traxter, D.D., never walked. His five-foot-two, 150-pound frame, with his neatly trimmed gray beard, seemed to march to a silent tune wherever he went. Even when it was merely crossing the deck of a ship to meet an old friend.

"Miss Alena Tipton! My heavens, look at you! How long has it been—two, three years?"

"Just over four years, Rev. Traxter. I just can't believe you are here in California."

The reverend strutted on the deck. "Actually I'm on my way home to raise funds for mission work, but I suppose the captain told you that. Imagine, I went ashore to find you, and you came out here.

I trust that was humorous to the Lord. I'm so sorry to hear about your father. I knew nothing about it until I inquired in town. My, the village is deserted. They told me there was some big dance going on inland in honor of La Paloma Roja. I never did understand Catholic festivals. I trust it isn't some pagan ritual. I just couldn't face your wonderful grandmother and tell her I was in California but didn't visit with little Alena. Not that you are little anymore, of course. I suppose your grandmother will always call you 'Little Alena.' How is that dear lady?"

"I haven't received a letter in quite a—"

"Letter? Oh my. That was the whole reason I went ashore. There was a letter for you." He fumbled through the pockets of his two-button light wool coat and vest. He glanced up at Merced. "I trust you are Wilson J. Merced?"

"Yes, sir."

"Well, I have a letter for you, too. When I was visiting with one dark-skinned lady selling jewelry, she said there was an older gentleman chaperoning Miss Tipton, and she saw them come out to the ship. Frankly, I was looking for a more fatherly type. Now I feel quite impetuous for going ashore. If I had stayed here, I could have just handed you the letters. Yes, here they are." Rev. Traxter marched over to thrust one into Alena's hands and the other into Wilson Merced's.

"Isn't God's providence wonderful? I had no idea Robert had died, but the Lord brought me here to escort you home to your charming grandmother. That's just the sort of thing He does for His children."

"Actually I'm not planning on—"

Wilson Merced reached out and grabbed the reverend's arm as he strolled by. "Reverend, I wanted to ask you about my friend Echo Jack."

"You know the Jacks? Oh, how delightful. They were in such a hurry to leave the ship, I didn't have a chance to give them this." He held up a folded piece of paper.

"What is it?"

"Their marriage license."

"So they really got married?"

"Oh yes. Surely the captain told you that."

"I sort of wanted to hear it from you."

"Will you be seeing them soon?"

"I hope so. Do you know where they went?"

"I believe back to his rancho. Well, this is convenient. The Lord provides!" He handed Merced the paper.

"You carry marriage certificates with you all the time?"

"Oh my, yes. In mission work one never knows when he has an opportunity to deliver a couple from living in sin. I have much to tell you about the work in the Sandwich Islands. King Kamehameha, III, has agreed to let some missionary work begin. It is quite exciting. You will be joining the captain for supper, I presume."

Merced glanced over at Alena, who still held her letter in her hand. She nodded.

"Yes, we'll stay."

"Oh, fine. I'll go to the galley and tell the cook. Oh, perhaps I should tell Capt. Malynton first. Would you two excuse me?" He took two hurried steps, then spun back around. "Little Alena! This is so incredible!" Then he tramped off across the deck.

"Is he always that exuberant?" Merced quizzed.

"Yes. You should see him when he preaches. He absolutely stalks all over the chancel area."

"You are being escorted by an 'older' gentleman? Did he really say that?"

"You are not that old."

"The more we stand next to each other, the older I feel."

"Well, in that case, I'm going to sit. I have a letter to read. This is my brother Bob's handwriting."

"Well, mine is definitely from Uncle Burtrum. He's the only one on earth who spells my name with two l's."

"Is your name supposed to be spelled with two l's?"

"Nope."

Merced leaned against the ship's rail as he read his letter. Alena plopped down on a barrel and read hers.

She wiped tears from her eyes and glanced over at Wilson Merced as he stared out to sea. "Sad news?" she asked.

He spun around quickly as if he had forgotten she was there. "Oh! No, actually it's . . . I, eh, didn't . . . Tell me about yours first."

"It's from my brother, Robert, Jr. He sent this before he got my letter about Father."

"What does he say?"

"He says that we should stop sending hides."

"Why?"

"Says there's another revolution going on in Argentina, and they are selling off all their cowhides at prices half the price of ours. He says they can't sell a California hide for any price. He wants me to hold off buying any for at least six months and says I should come home and look over the situation for myself."

"Are you going back?" Merced challenged.

She slipped the note back into the envelope. "What's in your letter?"

"Do you want to go back to Boston?"

"I want to know what is in your letter, Mr. Wilson Judd Merced."

"I can't tell you until you tell me if you're going back to Boston."

"This is a ridiculous conversation," she seethed. "What does it matter?"

He stepped up beside her as she continued to sit on the barrel. "Alena, it's important to me. With what you know now, are you going back?"

Her shoulders slumped. Her chin drooped to her chest. She stared down at the letter she held in her hand. "I can't."

"Stubborn pride?"

"Stubborn love."

"Oh?"

She stared down at the ship's deck. "There's an older gentleman hide rancher that I just don't think I can leave right at the moment."

He reached over and put his hand on her shoulder. "Now I'll tell you about my letter."

"How's your Uncle Burtrum?"

"He's fine. At the end he says, 'Raft and his new family seem to be doing well. I hear she has three girls of her own, and they are expecting their first in May. Perhaps this would be a good time to write to him again. I'll see that the letter is delivered.'"

"Your brother's remarried?"

"That's what it says," he replied.

"And he has children?"

"I reckon that's what it means."

"Then he doesn't have to go through life without a wife and children?"

"Apparently not."

"What about his handsome younger brother?" she prodded.

"The one that took off for California?"

"Yes, whatever happened to him?" she asked.

"He went into hide ranching, I heard."

Alena held his hand tight. "Did he ever marry?"

"I doubt it. Life's too tough out there. Adobe houses. Dirt floors. Indian raids. Going to town once a year. A woman wouldn't want to put up with all that."

"I think you're right."

His shoulders sagged. "I am?"

"Yes. I hear he's getting up in years now. Certainly no woman his age would be able to stand those rigors."

He stood tall and pushed his hat back. "That's true."

"Of course," she posed, "if he found a young wife, one who was strong and adventuresome . . ."

"You might be right about that." He slipped his arm around her waist and pulled her up to her feet. "I wonder where in the world I could find one?"

Her curled fist struck him with a thud right below the rib cage. "Is that strong enough for you, mister?" She faked a snarl. "I can do it harder."

"Oh, no, that's strong. But are you adventuresome?"

"I'm living on my own in California thousands of miles from home."

"Yes, and I think it's going to your head. You are sounding totally irrational."

"Me? What about you?"

"I've never been accused of being too reasonable anyway," he stated.

"What are we going to do about it?"

"I think we should talk to Rev. Traxter before either of us comes to our senses."

She brushed a quick kiss across his cheek. "Is this really happening?"

With one arm around her waist, he lifted her off the deck. "No, it's just a dream."

She threw both arms around his neck. "Well, it certainly is a pleasant one!" She pressed her lips against his.

Seven

❦

It didn't seem right to stay at the Cabrillos' sprawling, almost empty hacienda. And Monterey boasted of nothing that would be considered a hotel in New England.

So the honeymoon suite turned out to be a canopy of stars in an oak grove. The mattress was buckskin grass on deep brown dirt. But there were no noisy people in an adjoining room, no liquor fumes, and no brawls or fighting out in the street.

Alena awoke to the snap and crackle of a small fire next to the two-wheeled cart that contained two wardrobe trunks and four small wooden crates—the sum total of her possessions that had escaped the warehouse fire.

She peeked out from under a red and gray wool blanket. "Don't look at me!"

Wilson pushed his hat back and smiled. "Why? Did you change overnight?"

"As a matter of fact, Mr. Merced, I did change." She ran her hand through her hair and pulled out a small, dry oak leaf. "But I don't like anyone to look at me until I clean up a little and brush my hair."

"You look as beautiful as the legendary La Paloma Roja de Monterey."

"It sounds really ostentatious, doesn't it? I should have never allowed them to call me that."

"I like it. It wears well on you," he insisted.

She sat up, letting the blanket drop to her waist. The morning breeze already felt warm on her flannel nightgown. "Mr. Merced, I don't mean to sound personal, but did we get married aboard a ship out in Monterey harbor last evening, or did I just have some wild dreams after eating bad abalone?"

Wilson squatted on his heels next to the fire with a book in his hand. A coffeepot hung on an iron hook over the flames. "Contrary to all logic and good sense, we really did get married, Mrs. Alena Louise Tipton Merced. And then we giggled our way back to the Cabrillos', borrowed this cart, packed up all your things, and drove into these hills until midnight. Although I can't remember why we thought we had to drive so far."

"I think we were both too nervous to stop."

"I'm still nervous," he admitted.

"Why?"

"Because good things don't usually come my way."

"Is that what I am? A good thing?"

"You're the best thing that's ever happened in my life. That's why I get nervous. I keep looking over my shoulder thinking someone is going to come along and tell me there's been a big mistake. You were really supposed to marry some rich, handsome young prince or something."

"I did marry a prince. Everyone knows El Americano del Norte rules a vast estate."

"Well, it is vast," he chuckled. "How about that rich, young, and handsome part?"

"Three out of four isn't too bad," she teased.

He tossed an acorn at her, and she caught it in her left hand. Her toes felt cold. Alena noticed they were peeking out from under the wool blanket. "Do you have any idea of the ramifications of what we did yesterday?"

"Me? I thought you were the one who had this figured out."

She glanced down at her fingers. *I don't think I've ever had dirt under my fingernails before in my life!* "I don't know anything. I'm only a nineteen-year-old girl."

"You might be nineteen, but you are not a girl, Mrs. Merced."

"No . . . I'm not, am I?" Alena could tell she was blushing.

"I put a basin of clean spring water over there by those rocks. And I think you said that satchel holds your personals. That area's the designated dressing room."

"How charming. Thank you, Mr. Merced."

"You're welcome, Mrs. Merced."

"I really, really like that name."

"I'm glad, because you're going to be stuck with it for a long, long time."

She reached out and patted the ground next to the bedroll. "I like this quaint dirt floor."

"That's good. Because that's all we have at Rancho Alázan."

"Yes, I . . . eh . . . my, this is going to be a grand adventure."

"I'm glad you see it that way. It scares me to death," he said.

"Living in a remote place like Rancho Alázan?"

"No, living with a wife at Rancho Alázan."

Alena struggled to her feet and tiptoed to the basin of water, the blanket still wrapped around her waist. She could feel every pebble, twig, and leaf poke into her bare feet. "Now you can't look until I'm fully dressed," she insisted.

"I don't think so." He grinned. "I believe I have the right to look anytime I want."

"Oh, well . . . yes, that's true. It's just . . . it's going to take some getting used to. Be patient with me."

"I've got a lifetime. But I'm afraid if I take my eyes off you, you'll disappear."

"Well, turn around for a few minutes anyway. I promise I'll be right here. There are some things I just can't learn overnight."

He scooted around, his back toward her. "You like your eggs scrambled?"

Alena struggled to pull on her yellow dress with the blanket still wrapped around her. "I'll do the cooking. That's a wife's job."

Wilson banged around, pulling a pan out of a wooden crate. "You ever cooked over an oakwood fire?"

"No." She plopped down on a boulder and brushed off her feet before pulling on her stockings.

"Have you ever cooked at all?"

"Of course, but not since I came to California."

"That's what I thought. I'll tell you what. Whenever we're camping out in the open, I'll cook. When we get to the ranch, Piedra will cook until we build our own place. Then it's your job."

"Perhaps Señor Muerto will teach me some of his techniques."

"Maybe, providing you don't call him Señor Muerto. He's just Piedra. Now do you like your eggs scrambled?"

"Yes, that will be fine."

"Good, because the yokes already broke."

Alena glanced in the small hand-held mirror. *I can't believe I slept in these dangling earrings. I can't believe I slept at all!* She checked to see if he was watching her.

He wasn't.

"What were you reading when I woke up?" she asked.

"Your Bible."

"Wilson, do you have a Bible?"

"Yep, but I left it at the ranch. I figured now that I'm a husband, I'd better learn what I'm supposed to do."

"What did you read this morning?"

"The passage I was reading was where the Lord told Abraham, 'Get thee out of thy country, and from thy kindred, and from thy father's house, unto a land that I will show thee.' It seems like that's the way He led me to California."

Alena tugged on her black riding boots. "Well, I was thinking about a Bible story also."

"Which one?"

"The one where the servant of Abraham shows up and asks Rebekah to leave her home and go to a distant land and marry Isaac, whom she had never met."

He stood as she approached the campfire. "It that the way you feel? Like Rebekah?"

"Yes, but I have a great advantage. I got to meet my husband several days before I said yes." She slipped her arm around his waist, and he returned a strong hug.

He lifted her chin with callused fingers until their eyes met. "Say, is Rebekah the one who had twelve sons?"

"No!" She pushed herself up on her toes and brushed a kiss across his lips. "That was Rachel. Rebekah just had Esau and Jacob, the twins. At least, that's all I remember."

He interlaced his fingers into hers. "Are you ready to go to that distant land of Rancho Alázan?"

"Yes, I am."

"It won't be easy."

"Good. The easy life doesn't seem to bring out the best in me. But I do have one question. What does *Alázan* mean?"

"Sorrel."

"Like the color of a horse?"

"Yep."

"I thought all of your horses were buckskin."

"About a dozen of 'em are, I suppose."

"How many horses do you have?"

"They belong to you and me now, Mrs. Merced."

"Well, how many horses do we have?"

"I reckon upwards of 120."

"And how many cows do *we* have?"

"I don't know. I've never counted them," he admitted.

"I am truly going to be a stranger in a foreign land."

"You'll do fine. Now what are you going to tell Doña María Martina?"

"She'll understand. I'll just ride up and say, 'Oh, by the way, while we were in Monterey looking at the destruction of the warehouse, we decided to get married. I'll be moving to the edge of the earth and be fortunate to see you once a year. Don't think of it as losing a daughter but gaining a guest room.'"

"I'd like to watch you tell her that." He squatted down and shoved several dry sticks into the fire.

"You doubt my ability?"

He pulled the iron skillet with the eggs off the fire. "At this particular moment, Mrs. Merced, I believe you can do anything on the face of this earth—including walking on water."

"Good. Hold that thought. At least, until after breakfast."

It was midafternoon on the second day out from Monterey when they caught sight of the white adobe of Mission San Juan Bautista. He reached over and patted her dress-covered knee. "Do you have your speech ready?"

"I hope so." She spun her small yellow parasol in her hand. "How about you?"

"I need a speech?"

"The Cabrillo brothers will not be pleased with you. They were quite jealous that you danced with me at the fandango."

"Yeah, I suppose marrying you will put a damper on their pursuit. Maybe we should just say our piece and then keep right on going for Rancho Alázan."

"Yes, if we can." Alena tried to brush the road dust off her dress, but it all fogged up in her face. She folded her hands and replaced them in her lap. "What about Echo Jack and María Alejandra?"

Merced noticed several small brown-skinned children run out of an adobe house and point at Alena. "Perhaps that will all be settled by now."

Alena waved at the smiling children. "Do you believe that?"

"Nope."

She pointed down Calle Cuarta. "Let's swing around behind the Castros' and park in the alley behind the livery. That will give me a chance to explain before they see me drive up with all my possessions in your cart. If Doña María Martina sees us ride up like this, she'll figure it out."

"You go talk to Señora Cabrillo. I'll scout around and see what I can learn about Echo Jack. Maybe they got word to someone. I really don't think they would come back here. Surely they know her father will be on the prowl."

"Where else would they go?"

"Like the reverend said, maybe they left for the rancho already."

"Echo Jack abandon his responsibilities without telling you? Is that the way he is?"

"No, you're right. He must be skirtin' around here somewhere."

Wilson parked the cart in the ally behind the corrals and gave a boy instructions concerning the care of the horses.

Alena pulled her cowhide purse off the cart. "I'll have to talk to Don Manuel. I'm going to give him the hides that he purchased. He's been a very loyal manager."

Wilson fastened the top button on his collarless white linen shirt, "I'll be over to the Castros' in a few minutes. I'm sure it will all work out. Perhaps we've been too worried about this."

Alena blocked the bright summer sun with her yellow parasol as she strolled across the nearly empty plaza. She could hear her long cotton dress swish as she walked. Its hem skimmed only inches above the dirt. *I wonder if I look married? Some people say they can tell if a woman's married by merely looking at her eyes. I don't think that's true, is it, Lord? Of course, I do feel married.*

I feel giddy . . . scared . . . thrilled . . . bewildered . . . a little guilty . . . and extremely nervous . . . but I do definitely feel married. I meant it, Lord. We both meant it. You're our witness. You, Rev. Traxter, and the sailors. "Till death do us part!"

Just as Alena reached the edge of the plaza, Señora Cabrillo's wail from across Calle Segunda caused her feet to lock tight and her chin to drop.

"Doña Alena! It is so terrible, so terrible!" Most of Señora Cabrillo's body bounced in rhythm as she jogged across the street toward Alena Merced.

"Doña María Martina, what happened?" *Has she heard that we're married? Did someone in Monterey beat us here?*

"It is horrible. Most terrible. I did not believe it when I first heard it. Nothing like this has ever happened before."

It's not all that serious. We are Americanos. Protestants. Adults. Calm down, Alena Louise Merced. Be calm. Be gracious. Be understanding. Give her a reasonable explanation.

If you have one.

Señora Cabrillo wrapped her strong arms around Alena and hugged her tight. She could hear the older woman's gold necklaces tinkle against her own gold cross. "How can this happen in our

California? Perhaps in your Boston or in Vera Cruz, *sí*, but not here! I am so sorry for you!"

Okay, so she is not taking this well. Wilson is right. We must leave immediately. Perhaps he should not have unhitched the horses.

"*Pobre* Don Manuel. . . . He was such a fine man," Doña María Martina sobbed.

Alena stepped back. Her hand and parasol dropped to her side. "Don Manuel? What do you mean, poor Don Manuel?"

"You have not heard? *Conchita . . . mi dulcita . . .* how I wish not to have to tell you this. Don Manuel has been murdered!"

Alena could feel the blood rush down out of her face. Only the strong arms of Señora Cabrillo kept her from collapsing. She tried to suck in great gulps of air. "Don Manuel? Murdered! When? How? Why?"

"Let me help you to the bench." Arm in arm, the two women hurried across the street and plopped down on the bench in front of the Castros' house.

With an arm around Alena's shoulder, Señora Cabrillo rocked her back and forth. "We sent a rider back to Monterey to tell you."

"We took a back road. We must have missed him."

"El Americano del Norte is with you?"

"Yes, he's . . ." Alena took a big, deep breath of air. "You see, we decided—"

"That is good. That way we know he was not also a part of it. Not that I ever believed the rumors." She patted Alena on the knee.

"What rumors?"

Doña María Martina stared at the climbing rosebush by the front door. "It was that man, Echo Jack. He killed Don Manuel and stole your money."

"Echo Jack? The one who works for Wilson?"

"Wilson?"

"Eh, Señor Merced."

"Yes, that is the man. María Alejandra's father caught him in the act."

"I—I don't believe it."

"Oh, I know, *mi dulcita*. I told you nothing like it has ever taken place in California."

Alena leaned her head only inches from Señora Cabrillo's. "Tell me what happened."

"Right after you left for Monterey, Padre Rudolpho arrived from San Luis Obispo. He was appointed by the mission president to conduct the service for Padre Estában. He declared a day of mourning, and no business was to be done."

"So Don Manuel did not buy any hides?"

"No, and I might say, it was a beautiful service. You know how everyone liked Padre Estában."

"Yes, yes, but what about poor Don Manuel?"

"May the Blessed Virgin have mercy on his soul," Señora Cabrillo lamented. "The next day, about daylight, María Alejandra's father and brothers were camped in the plaza when they heard shouts and gunfire from the olive grove beyond the corrals. When they arrived, Don Manuel lay dead. Echo Jack was there with his rifle in one hand and your ledger in the other."

"And the money?"

"He must have hidden it. He will not tell anyone where it is. He didn't even resist. They knocked him unconscious and hauled him over to Generale Castro. The people in town wanted to kill him immediately, but the *generale* said there would be a proper inquiry, and then he would be executed. But no matter what they do, he will not tell them where the money is."

"What about María Alejandra? Was she harmed?"

"No, she had nothing to do with the robbery. She said Echo Jack is a mean man who deserves to die."

"You heard María Alejandra say that?"

"No, that is what her father reported that she said."

"When is the inquiry?"

"Yesterday."

"What? Did María Alejandra testify?"

"Oh no. Her father has taken her off somewhere so she doesn't have to suffer anymore."

"Have they murdered Echo Jack yet?"

"Murder? *Conchita*, an execution in this case is justice, not murder. He will be shot by firing squad tonight at sundown."

"Did he admit to killing Don Manuel?"

"No, he claims there was a man—kind of a phantom killer—who shot Don Manuel. He says he arrived just in time to fire a couple of bullets, but the man escaped."

"With the money."

"*Mi dulcita*, that is what he says. But no one saw any stranger in town."

"Not at daybreak, of course. Could he be telling the truth?"

"Oh, of course not, *conchita*. He is lying to save his life. We buried Don Manuel today. Padre Rudolpho conducted the service before he left to return to San Luis Obispo. He declared it a week of mourning. It is so sad. So horrible."

"It's difficult to believe."

"*Sí, sí, conchita*. And to have it thrust on you all at once. I nearly forgot. How is it in Monterey? Is your warehouse truly gone?"

"I'm afraid so."

"Don Francisco insists that you stay with us for as long as you wish. We will help you build a new warehouse."

"Doña María Martina, I must talk to you—"

"Not now, *mi conchita*. You go upstairs and rest. This is a horrible thing. We will talk later."

"No, I really must—"

"Hush, *mi niña*. You rest; then we talk. You must be worn out from such a quick trip to Monterey. You look like you had very little sleep last night."

That much she can see. Alena sighed and brushed her hand through her hair.

Señora Cabrillo struggled to her feet. "Come, I will help you go up to your room." She held out her gold-ring-covered hand.

"No . . . let me just sit here a moment. I am overwhelmed." Alena slumped back against the wall of the house. She could feel the texture of the adobe press through her light yellow dress.

"I will be in the backyard helping with the ovens. We have many people to feed. No one has left town. They came for the fandango, stayed to bury Padre Estában, and now want to watch the execution."

"Where are they keeping Echo Jack?"

"In the cellar at the mission. Why do you ask?"

"Perhaps Señor Merced can talk to him."

"Yes, yes . . . perhaps he will tell the Americano del Norte where your money is. This is so horrible. Why does this happen in our beloved California?" Señora Cabrillo started through the door, then stepped back outside. "Can I bring you something, *conchita*? You look very worn out."

"*No me falta nada. Gracias.*"

"My poor little one."

"I'll be all right. I just need to sit here and catch my breath."

Alena could hear the jingle of spurs long before the running man came into view. By the time the familiar hat and profile appeared in the doorway of the livery stable, she had stood and crossed the street.

"Did you hear about Echo Jack?" Wilson panted as he reached her side.

"Yes . . . it is incredible."

"He didn't kill Don Manuel. And he is not a thief," Merced insisted.

"I believe you." Alena glanced back at the Castro house to see if anyone was watching her, then reached over and took his hand. "But they all are convinced of it."

"Didn't María Alejandra come to his defense?"

"I heard that her father whisked her off and refused to tell any-one where she is. I was told Echo Jack is at the mission and that some have tried to persuade him to confess to the crime."

"Persuade? You mean they have beaten him?"

"That is my assumption."

"I tried to go see him, but they refused to let me," Wilson reported.

"Who is in charge there?"

"I don't know. I believe María Alejandra's brothers, plus Don Fernando, Don Ronaldo, and others are there."

Alena gazed across the plaza at the mission. "Let's go together and see if they will reconsider."

He held out his arm, and she laced hers in his. "Did you tell Señora Cabrillo about our marriage?"

Alena's words came out softly, almost weakly. "No, she did not give me a chance."

"This whole thing is bizarre."

"It is not the answer to my prayer for this day. I asked that it be a peaceful and beautiful day."

"This day is surely not an answer to anyone's prayers," he added. "But the day is not over."

Several armed men lounged in the arcade that stretched along the front of the mission buildings. Don Francisco stood in the doorway, his sword hung at his side. A pistol was shoved into the red sash at his waist. His drooping mustache made his mouth look like it was in a permanent frown. "La Paloma Roja, you heard about poor Don Manuel?"

"Yes, I am still in shock," she replied, releasing Merced's arm.

"You are partially responsible." Don Fernando marched forward and addressed his words to Wilson Merced. "You brought this renegade into our village. He has been banned throughout other towns. You knew that. He should have been shot like a rabid dog."

"I want to talk to Echo Jack," Merced replied.

"I told you before, we will—"

"Don Fernando." Alena's voice was soft yet insistent. "At sundown Echo Jack is to be shot. If that happens, I will never know where my money is. Would you allow Señor Merced to talk to him? Perhaps he will reveal something to us."

"He won't talk!" One of the other lounging men spoke up. "We beat him black and blue, and he won't talk."

"Let me try," Merced insisted.

"Please . . . Don Fernando," Alena pleaded, laying her hand on his jacket-covered arm. "I know you are a kind, gentle, and fair man. I need the money badly. The warehouse and hides are gone. Please let him try."

Don Fernando looked at the others, then sighed. "All right.

Just for La Paloma Roja de Monterey." Then he turned to Merced. "You will leave your weapons here."

Merced laid down his rifle and his Paterson Colt revolver. He pulled a large hunting knife out of his boot and laid it beside the others. All the men in the arcade stared at his revolver.

Alena stepped over and snatched up a small loaf of half-eaten bread and jug of water from in front of one of the men.

"What are you doing?" the man protested.

"Even a condemned man should have bread and water," she said.

The man brushed crumbs off his thick mustache. "Says who?"

"Jesus. It is a cup of cold water given in His name."

"I'll take it to him," Don Fernando offered.

"No, I will go. We will go alone."

"That is impossible," Don Fernando replied.

"Why? It might be the only way I learn the place of my money," she argued.

"He might try to escape."

"What? A man you have beaten black and blue, who has no weapon, is going to break his chains, throw open a locked door, jump up, and defeat all of you strong men?" she challenged.

Wilson Merced reached down and picked up his revolver, handing it grip-first to Don Fernando. "Train this revolver on the doorway. If Echo Jack comes out, you can put five shots in him before he ever gets out of the arcade."

Don Fernando nodded. "I will do it."

"Yes, well . . . be careful," Merced cautioned. "Don't put five shots through me."

The storeroom of the mission was stacked with dust-covered crates and barrels. There was no light except what filtered through the cracks of the shuttered windows and from a small tallow lantern burning in an arched alcove carved into the adobe wall. Wilson took the lantern and led Alena to the iron grate flat on the floor, covering the steps to the cellar. The holes in the grating were about six-inch squares. A heavy padlock fastened it down.

"Echo Jack? It's me . . . Wilson."

A man in a tattered shirt crawled up the stairs.

"Oh my . . . no!" Alena moaned as she viewed the black eye and bruises about his face. *Lord, is this what you meant by Your word that I would be a "light to those that sit in darkness?"*

"I am sorry for my appearance, señorita!" Echo Jack mumbled.

"We have some water and bread for you," she replied in a monotone, trying not to stare at his wounds.

"To keep me alive until they shoot me?"

"To keep you alive until we figure how to get you out," Merced insisted.

"They are not with you up there in the storeroom?"

"Not at the moment." Wilson Merced bent down on his hands and knees and shoved the bread through the grate. "Here is the water also. Now tell us what really happened."

"The best day of my life was followed by the worst day of my life," Echo Jack mumbled between bites.

"We know about you and María Alejandra getting married on the ship in the harbor," Merced announced.

"You do?"

"Yes, we, eh . . . talked to the captain and to Rev. Traxter."

"I tried to do it right, Wilson. I love her. I wanted to marry her just like you always told me I should." He stared up at Alena. "For three years he has said it is not right to chase the women, that I should settle on one and get married. That would please God. *El Patrón*, you and I both know the *padres* and her father would never approve a half-breed marrying a Californian. So I went to your Americano reverend."

Merced squatted on his haunches and rocked back and forth on his heels. "But why did you come back here?"

"She wanted us to slip into town and tell Señora Castro and you. She said that was the right thing to do. Then we planned to leave for Rancho Alázan. They would not follow us there. None of them dares go that far into Indian country. You know that. We didn't know her father and brothers were here. We camped in the olive grove last night. Then at daylight María Alejandra went over to talk to the Castros. I headed to the livery to look for you, and then I heard a ruckus down near the road. A little man in a round hat was being robbed."

"Carty Parkins? Was it Parkins who shot Don Manuel?" Merced interrupted.

"How did you know?"

"He's been a busy man. He burned down my warehouse in Monterey," Alena announced. "We just returned from there."

"We? You went to Monterey together?" Suddenly she saw a sparkle in Echo Jack's battered brown eyes. "Say, are you two . . . eh, *compadres*? I heard you got *El Patrón* to dance at the fandango."

Wilson Merced cleared his throat. "Let's just say you aren't the only couple Rev. Traxter married on deck of the *Spirit of Baltimore*."

"No!" Echo Jack shouted.

Immediately Don Fernando burst through the door. "Doña Alena Louise, is everything all right?"

"Yes. Just give us a few more minutes alone with him."

Don Fernando returned to the arcade.

"It is true," she leaned down and whispered to Echo Jack.

"That brings a ray of light into a very dark soul."

Alena stood and rested her hands on Wilson's shoulders.

"What direction did Parkins head when he left?" Merced asked.

"Straight east. But that could have been just a decoy."

"Parkins doesn't seem all that brilliant," Merced added.

"Well, if he keeps going east, he'll run into Miwok returning to Plano Tulare. I saw them pull out right before daylight."

"I'm going to go try to catch up with him and bring him back by sundown."

Echo Jack shook his head. "He's got too big a head start."

"Maybe the Miwok will slow him down. Besides, he doesn't know anyone's chasing him. I'll be back before dark. If I don't find him, I'll try something else."

"What?"

"I have no idea."

"I've got a favor to ask La Paloma Roja." Echo Jack poured some of the water over his bruised face and then looked straight at Alena. "You must go see María Alejandra and tell her that even though my body dies, my heart remains full of love for her. She must hear these words."

Alena wiped the tears from her eyes. "You tell her that."

"They won't let me see her."

"Do they know you are married?"

"Oh no. You must not tell them that. If I die, she is better off that no one knew of our marriage."

"Then I will go get her and bring her here," Alena promised.

"They will never agree."

"Sure they will. I will tell them you insist on telling only María Alejandra where my money is hidden."

"I don't think her father and brothers care about you or your money."

"The Cabrillo brothers do. They will see that it is done."

"How can you be so sure?"

"I am very good at whimpering and crying. It is my specialty."

Wilson Merced stood up. "It is worth a try, partner."

"Yes," Echo Jack replied. "I am grateful for you two trying to help. You have warned me for years that chasing women would ruin me. I will say hello to Jesus for you when I see Him face to face."

"Go ahead and settle up with the Lord, but don't count us out just yet," Wilson Merced insisted. "We will be back."

Echo Jack collapsed down on the adobe stairs leading to the cellar. "I think I will just wait here."

It took words, tears, batting eyelids, and clinging to Don Fernando's arm before Alena was allowed to go and talk to María Alejandra. By the time she arrived at the little farmhouse north of San Juan, Wilson Merced had crossed the San Benito Valley on horseback and was climbing into the brown grass foothills of the Coast Range.

For two hours María Alejandra's father forbade Alena from even speaking to the girl. When she finally was allowed to speak, he insisted on being in the room and monitoring the conversation. María Alejandra, dressed in a long black dress, sat in a straight wooden chair on the far side of the sparse adobe room. Alena sat against a distant wall next to a large window. Don Fernando, who accompanied her, stood in the doorway while María Alejandra's father paced the room, acting as a human barricade between the two women.

"María Alejandra, I do not wish to make your life more difficult. But that money is all I have left. My father has died. My warehouse and hides have burned to the ground. I need my money. I've just been to visit Echo Jack."

For the first time, María Alejandra lifted her eyes off her hands that lay folded in her lap.

"He told me that he would tell only you where my money is. Would you please come and visit with him just once so that I might not suffer complete poverty?"

María Alejandra's dark eyes stared blankly across the room at Alena. *She knows he didn't take the money. She knows I am lying. Why should she come with me?*

"I told you I would not let my daughter go and see that man," her father huffed. "If that is the only reason you came, you might as well leave. I will not allow her to go."

Don Fernando stepped into the room. "I beg of you to reconsider. La Paloma Roja de Monterey is one of the most trusted young women in all of Alta California. If the rumor were to circulate that you refused to help her find her money . . . well, who would buy your crops? Who would sell you goods? Who would invite you to a fandango?"

"You cannot threaten me," her father fumed.

"It is not a mere threat," Don Fernando insisted. "It is a fact. In your heart you know it is true. It is the way things are done in California. Do you wish to die a hermit, living in a cave like Don Pedro Acuna? That is no life. I can guarantee you we will not allow this man to harm your daughter in any way."

"She does not want to go with you."

Alena leaped to her feet and sprinted across the room. She stuck her face only inches from María Alejandra's. "Please come help me recover my money from that despicable Echo Jack." It was Alena's wink that softened the girl's hostile stare.

"Yes, I will go."

"You can't!" her father shouted. "I forbid it!"

María Alejandra jumped up and brushed her red skirt. "It is my Christian duty to help another person, especially one who is without family of her own, like Doña Alena. You would not prevent me from fulfilling my Christian responsibility?"

He waved his fist in her face. "Was it your Christian duty to run off with this renegade in the first place?"

María Alejandra turned and walked away from him. "I explained that to you."

"Then I will go with you," he fumed.

"By all means," Don Fernando insisted.

"But," Alena cautioned, "we must give her some private time to talk to Echo Jack. That is the only way I will find my money."

"I don't trust him alone with my daughter."

"Oh, I didn't mean completely alone. I will be there, of course, to find out about my money." Without looking back at the men, Alena mouthed out the words, *"He said to tell you he loves you!"* A sparkle burst forth from the girl's sad eyes.

Alena pulled back and retreated toward the door. *And it's obvious that you love him.*

It was well past noon when they returned to San Juan. After a frantic, quick meal at the Castros', they paid a visit to the imprisoned Echo Jack. His bruises almost seemed to heal at the sight of María Alejandra.

At first her father insisted on being in the storeroom, even though the prisoner was still locked in the cellar. After an hour of indirect conversation, he and Don Fernando were persuaded to leave, but only after Alena was given a pistola and had promised to shoot Echo Jack if he made any attempt to escape.

She closed the door behind the men, then turned back and sat down on the floor, barricading the entry.

"What are you doing?" María Alejandra asked.

"I'm blocking the door. If your father wants to come in, he must shove me aside first. Now go on over and visit. I don't know how long they will allow us to stay in here."

"We need two lamps," María Alejandra asserted.

"No, leave this one here. You don't need a lamp to whisper and touch, do you?"

Even in the shadows, Alena felt the girl blush.

"No."

"Besides, if someone does burst in here, we don't want them to see what you are doing. Now go on."

"I can't thank you enough," María Alejandra wept.

"Go on. You're wasting time. We will try to stall off the execution until Wilson returns."

"Do you really think he will find the murderer?"

"If it's humanly possible, he will do it."

"Do you love him, Doña Alena?"

"Yes."

"Will you marry him?"

"I already have. Now get over there before I let your father back into the room."

Alena calculated it was about five o'clock when Doña María Martina brought two baskets of food to the arcade at the mission—one basket for the men who stood guard, another for Alena and María Alejandra.

Alena met her at the door.

"*Conchita*, has the blackguard told you about your money yet?"

"No, but he has promised to do so sometime before he is shot."

"Why does he wait?"

"I suppose he hopes for a pardon."

"There is no pardon for murderers, not even from *El Señor*."

"I'm afraid we disagree there. God can forgive us for anything."

"Yes, He will forgive us. We would repent. But him? I don't think so. Why do you stay?"

Alena pointed to the gun that rested on the dirty tile floor next to the open door. "To protect María Alejandra. Thank you for the food."

"You hardly know her, and you hover about her like a sister."

"You taught me that, Señora Cabrillo. It's the Californio way, right?"

"*Sí. . . sí.* You are right. We must look after each other. When will you come back to the Castros'?"

"Whenever I find out about my money."

Señora Cabrillo leaned close. "Does María Alejandra love him?"

Alena peeked out to see if any of the men in the arcade were listening. They were occupied with the food basket. "Yes, she does."

"I didn't believe that story of her father's either. That's why you are doing this. You want to give them a little time together before he dies."

Alena nodded her head. "Yes, that is part of it."

"That, too, is the Californio way. I have told you many times, *conchita*, it is a land for lovers."

Alena closed the door behind her and toted the basket to the cellar door. "I don't suppose either of you is hungry."

"Have you heard from Señor Merced?" Echo Jack asked.

"Not yet."

"How much time do I have left?"

"Two hours perhaps. It depends on how they interpret sundown."

"It is," María Alejandra reported, "when the evening shade completely covers the plaza."

"Where is the sun now?" Echo Jack asked.

Alena retreated to the window and stared out past the men in the arcade. "It's still near the street where the dance floor was."

"Already?" María Alejandra began to sob. "It will only be an hour."

"Don't cry, *mi corazón*," Echo Jack encouraged from beneath the iron grate. "Let us eat and rejoice. That means *El Patrón* will be riding up any moment now."

Half an hour flashed quickly by, and there was no sign of Merced. Alena paced the musty, stuffy storeroom. Both she and María Alejandra, who knelt in the shadows by the iron grate to the cellar, had streaks of sweat rolling down their faces. When the shadow of the western mountains reached the sundial only a few feet from the eastern edge of the plaza, the big, heavy oak door swung open. Don Fernando and Don Ronaldo led the procession of rifle-toting men.

Don Fernando put his hand on her shoulder. "It is time, Doña Alena Louisa."

"But . . . the shadow isn't . . ."

"It will be by the time we have him tied to a post."

"But," Alena protested, "Señor Merced has not returned. He is going to find the real killer."

"Maybe he just went home to Rancho Alázan," Don Ronaldo suggested.

"He did not go home!"

"Perhaps you two women should go to the Castro home and wait."

"No!" María Alejandra shouted from the shadows.

"We will stand up front and watch you shoot an innocent man," Alena announced.

"Innocent?" Don Ronaldo exhorted. "Has he bewitched you both?"

María Alejandra's father, who had been listening from the arcade, now burst into the room. "She is beside herself. She doesn't know what she is saying. Come with me!" He stormed to the back of the room, grabbed his daughter's arm, yanked her to her feet, and began to drag her across the room.

Suddenly Alena reached down and picked up the pistol that lay on the floor. She pointed it at María Alejandra's father. "Let her go!" she demanded.

"What? You tell me what I can do with my daughter?"

"In California a woman has a right to make up her own mind." Alena forced herself to speak slowly. "Doña María Feliciana Arballo de Gutierrez established that precedent when she traveled here with Capt. de Anza and his expedition in 1775."

"La Paloma Roja is right," Don Fernando concurred.

"My daughter has no such privileges. She is not a woman. She is a girl!"

Alena kept the pistol pointed at the man. "Don Fernando, Don Ronaldo, I ask you to be the judges. Look closely. Is María Alejandra a girl or a woman?" *Don't let me down, boys.*

"Definitely a woman," Don Ronaldo pronounced.

Thank you. I knew I could count on you. "Let her go. She can make up her own mind."

He released her and then pushed his face into hers. "You want to go with me, don't you, *mi niña?*"

María Alejandra backed away from her father and slipped her arm into Alena's. "I will stand with La Paloma Roja de Monterey at the front. That way every time you see me, my eyes will reflect the fact that you shot an innocent man."

"You mestizo! You have corrupted my daughter," the man screamed in the general direction of the cellar and Echo Jack. "I will be the first to pull the trigger."

The multitude that hovered in the plaza was almost the same size as that which had attended the fandango. Only the inland Indians had departed.

But this time the crowd was nearly silent. They stood so still, as if merely a painted backdrop to a stage performance, that it was difficult for Alena to tell which ones supported Echo Jack and which condemned him.

She led the procession out of the arcade of the mission. The shorter, dark-skinned, black-haired María Alejandra was at her side. Arm in arm, they marched to the middle of the plaza where Generale Don José Tiburcio Castro in military uniform waited for them. Standing with him were several leading citizens of San Juan and Monterey, including Don Francisco Cabrillo.

His sons and the other guards led a battered, chained, yet defiant Echo Jack. He was barefoot. He wore buckskin trousers and a tattered shirt. Even at twilight, his cuts and bruises could be seen. Alena thought she heard some of the women sob when they saw him.

"Are you quite certain you have chosen the correct side in this matter, Doña Alena Louisa?" Don Ronaldo cautioned.

"I am most certain that I have," she replied. "Can you men say the same?"

"The inquiry found this man guilty of murder," Generale Castro insisted.

"Then the inquiry is wrong. What kind of land is it that condemns a man when there are no witnesses?"

"There was evidence. He was at the scene. His gun had been fired. He held your ledger. He has a reputation for violence."

"He has a reputation for chasing beautiful women, not violence. You have no motive."

"Robbery."

"Then where is the money?"

"You said he would tell you."

"That was only a stall. But tell me, General Castro, if Echo Jack stole my money and yet was still standing next to the body with my ledger in his hand when they found him, when did he have time to hide the money?"

"He is a very tricky *hombre*," Don Ronaldo insisted.

"Tricky?" Alena thundered. "If he made the money disappear, he is a magician. You know in your heart there is not enough evidence yet."

"I know in my heart he must die," María Alejandra's father cried out.

"I do not know if you even have a heart," María Alejandra replied.

"It is sundown. It is time for justice, *alcalde*!" her father raged.

Alena released María Alejandra's arm and paced alone in front of the officials. "I do not understand why you all are in such a hurry to slay a man. There have been two funerals this week already. At this rate San Juan will be populated by only jack rabbits and coyotes by Christmas. Why don't you wait until Señor Merced comes back? Perhaps he has found the real killer."

"Perhaps he has your money and will never be back," a short man wearing a silk top hat shouted.

"Or maybe he will come back with a legion of Americanos to loot, rob, and kill," another called out.

"Why do you say that? Last Sunday you were ready to proclaim Señor Merced a saint, and now you call him a traitor and a thief without any evidence whatever."

No one replied.

Finally, Señora Cabrillo shouted from the crowd on the south side of the plaza, "*Conchita* is right. Señor Merced has acted as a friend to all of us."

The crowd broke into uncertain applause.

It was General Castro who now paced the dirt plaza. "I stand corrected. El Americano del Norte is a good man, but he is not here. The fact remains—it is the appointed time for the execution."

"Since when does a few minutes here or there matter in California?" Doña María Martina screamed from the crowd of well-dressed women at the south edge of the plaza. "Our clock is not the minutes in an hour but the seasons in a year."

"Enough!" María Alejandra's father shouted. "Carry out the sentence!"

Alena could feel María Alejandra's hands clutch her arm. "We must do something," she whimpered.

"Take him to the post," General Castro ordered.

"Wait!" Alena called above the sobs of the woman beside her. "Doesn't a condemned man get a chance to say something before he is shot?"

"Do you have something to say?" Don José Castro asked Echo Jack.

The chained prisoner looked straight at the weeping María Alejandra but shouted in such a way that everyone in the plaza could hear, "I love you, *mi corazón*! It is a love that death cannot sever!"

Alena could hear other women in the crowd begin to wail.

"How dare you insult my daughter!" María Alejandra's father drew his sword and rushed toward the prisoner. Stunned, the other guards drew back, but Alena dashed in front of Echo Jack.

"Get out of my way!"

"I ask all of you," Alena shouted through her own tears, "is it an act of heroics or cowardice to strike down a battered, unarmed, chained man? Such a man would probably run a sword through innocent women, would he not?"

In unison the Cabrillo brothers grabbed María Alejandra's father and jerked him back.

"Do not play the villain, *compadre*," General Castro cautioned him. "Now tie the prisoner to the post. Let us finish these unpleasantries. May the Lord have mercy on your soul, Echo Jack."

"I am sure he has mercy on innocent men wrongly condemned," Echo Jack replied. "But I am not sure he has mercy on those who know they murder an innocent man."

"Enough of this!" General Castro silenced him with the wave of his glove-clad hand.

Alena held the weeping María Alejandra as Echo Jack was tied to a post, similar to the one that had held a bull and a bear only a few days before. The horseshoe-shaped crowd of several hundred huddled a little closer. Ten men with rifles formed a line ten *varas* west of the prisoner.

They had not yet lifted their weapons when five rapid shots came from somewhere beyond the peach orchard along El Camino Reál.

"It's Wilson!" Alena shouted. "It is El Americano del Norte, General Castro. It is a signal. No other man can fire that many shots so rapidly."

"Doña Alena Louisa is right about that," Don Francisco concurred.

"We must wait for his report," Alena insisted.

"I will not wait!" María Alejandra's father shouted as he put his gun to his shoulder.

Alena held her breath and could feel her heart pound in her chest. *No! Lord, no! This can't happen!*

The barrel of Don Fernando's rifle was instantly jammed into María Alejandra's father's temple. "We will wait for Señor Merced."

They waited.

Those with rifles waited in the middle of the plaza.

Echo Jack waited chained to a post.

Alena and María Alejandra waited in each other's arms.

But the crowd rushed to the roadway to observe Wilson Judd Merced riding through the orchard, leading a horse behind him. The buzz of the crowd turned to a roar as he rode right out into the middle of the plaza.

Most everyone stared at the body of a man draped over the saddle of the second horse.

Alena stared at the bloody bandage wrapped around Wilson Merced's left forearm.

He's been wounded!

Merced slid down out of the saddle and walked back to the second horse. With his hunting knife, which he pulled from his leather leggings, he cut the saddle strings, and the dead man dropped to the dirt.

"This is the murderer. His name is Carty Parkins. I tried to convince him to come in without a fight. He disagreed. I took a little knife wound in the arm. He took a bullet in the head."

Then he walked over to Alena and handed her a large leather envelope. "And here are your funds, Doña Alena Louisa."

"How do we know this man is the murderer?" María Alejandra's father shouted. "Perhaps Señor Merced killed this man just to get his *compadre* off the hook. Americanos can be treacherous."

"Are you saying he killed another Americano to save a half-breed's life?" Don Francisco challenged. "Don't be absurd."

Wilson Merced held up his hand to quiet the crowd. "This is the man who burned down La Paloma Roja's warehouse in Monterey. He knew Don Manuel, and he knew there was no money left there. The money has been recovered. The guilty man is dead. Justice has triumphed. Turn Echo Jack loose, and we will go our way to Rancho Alázan."

"And I will personally escort you two out of town," Don José Castro insisted.

"We will all escort you out of town," Don Ronaldo added.

"I will not go without my wife!" Echo Jack shouted, still chained to the post.

"Your wife?" the general quizzed.

"María Alejandra and I were married three days ago," Echo Jack cried out, silencing even the town dogs who now seemed to be aware of the gravity of the scene.

"That is impossible," her father screamed. "I did not give my approval to a *padre*."

"We were not married by a *padre*."

"Then the marriage is not a California marriage."

"We were not married in California. We were married at sea. On the ship in Monterey harbor," Echo Jack explained.

"By some Americano ship captain? That is blasphemy!" her father insisted.

"No," Echo Jack cried out, "by a minister of the Gospel from Boston!"

"It is not recognized in California. Besides, you are a known liar," María Alejandra's father yelled.

"It is true," María Alejandra sobbed.

"I do not believe you got married at all."

"You do not believe your own daughter?" Alena challenged.

Wilson Merced stomped out into the clearing between the bound man and the armed men. "Listen to me! Listen, everyone." He reached into his coat with his right hand and pulled out two documents. He glanced at the first one, then shoved it back in his coat. He unfolded the other and waved it at the crowd. "Here is the proof. It is the marriage certificate. It is signed by the reverend. It contains María Alejandra's signature and Echo Jack's mark. It is witnessed by the ship's captain and first mate. You can look for yourself."

"It is not valid in Alta California," General Castro proclaimed. "We all know that. They must be married by a *padre*."

"But no *padre* would marry us because I am a half-breed."

"Then you admit you defiled my daughter?"

"I admit only that I love her and that she is now in the eyes of God my wife."

María Alejandra's father pushed his hat to the back of his head and wiped the dusty sweat from his forehead. "She is not your wife in the eyes of California! Her brothers and I will kill him. The guilt will be on our heads alone."

María Alejandra stalked up to her father. "Then you will be the one who can explain to your grandchild why you murdered his father."

"Grandchild?"

She looked down at the red skirt that covered her stomach. "Perhaps already in my womb."

Her father's eyes flashed a wild trapped-animal look. "He has defiled my daughter. I demand revenge immediately!" he screamed.

"He has made love to his wife," Merced hollered back, his right hand reaching for the Paterson Colt at his belt. "That is not a crime in California, is it?"

"You will not threaten me. We heard you shoot all five shots. Your gun is empty," her father snarled.

Merced stepped back and stood alongside Echo Jack. "Then you can shoot me also."

"Why?" Don Francisco gasped.

Wilson Merced pulled the other paper out of his coat pocket. "Because this is my own marriage certificate. Two days ago Doña Alena Louisa and I were also married by the Americano reverend. If it is a sin, I stand condemned with Echo Jack."

A muted cheer went out from some in the crowd.

"No, *conchita!* Is it true?" Don Francisco gasped.

Alena stood straight and stepped away from María Alejandra. "Yes, I am now the wife of El Americano del Norte. And if these men deserve to die for what they have done, so do I." She marched over and stood next to Wilson in the evening shadows of the plaza. "I will not leave my husband's side," she said as she waved her arm at the crowd. "Surely women of California understand that a wife cannot leave her husband."

María Alejandra, still sobbing, ran to the side of Echo Jack. All four stood on the plaza next to the Mission San Juan Bautista and faced the gunmen and the crowd.

"Do you have another plan in case this fails?" Alena whispered to Wilson, whose arm she held.

"I have five shots in my Colt."

"But I thought . . ."

"I put in my spare cylinder. But it's not a desirable option."

General Castro stormed in circles, waving his sword as if to keep the immobile crowd at bay. "What are we to do?"

"We need Padre Estában to tell us what is right," Don Ronaldo commiserated.

"We will tell him what you have done when we see him," María Alejandra cried out.

"Wait!" Doña María Martina Cabrillo shouted. She held up her long black dress and trotted out between the crowd and the two couples. "Wait! Who has brought this demon of insanity among us? This is absurd. What are we talking about? Will we actually kill them all because they loved each other enough to get married?"

"He defiled my daughter, and I demand my rights."

"You have no rights. She may marry whom she chooses."

"She should marry someone of a higher class."

"That's exactly what my husband's mother said about him marrying me. She thought I wasn't good enough. Hah! I fooled her. I outlived her!"

Suddenly, as if on signal, the tension melted into laughter.

"I want everyone here to listen to me. In the history of Alta California, there are many important stories. Some of them involve you . . . and your ancestors. But if *El Diablo* gets his way today, and these four are slain, it will be known as the day love died in California! How proud you will be to tell your grandchildren that you were there when love was slaughtered, and you did nothing."

"Get out of my way, Doña María Martina," María Alejandra's father called out. "I will shoot them all myself and rid us of this blight."

Don Francisco Cabrillo stepped over and hammered the back of the man's head with the barrel of his rifle. María Alejandra's father crumpled to the dirt. "He will be able to think more clearly after he has had a nap."

The crowd again roared with laughter.

María Alejandra's three brothers ran to their father's side.

"Would you, too, like naps?" Don Fernando and Don Ronaldo threatened.

All three brothers tossed their weapons to the dirt.

"Let us declare that love did not die in California today," Doña María Martina called out. "May honest lovers always rule this land! It is too beautiful for anything less!"

The crowd began to cheer so loudly that Alena could no longer hear what Señora Cabrillo was saying. The officials in the middle of the plaza seemed to be huddled in discussion. Finally General Castro fired a shot in the air to silence the crowd.

"Doña María Martina is correct. California is for lovers. There will be no shooting here today. However, there must be justice.

Failing to have your marriage sanctioned by the church is a violation of law. I banish Echo Jack, María Alejandra, Señor Wilson Merced, and La Paloma Roja, Doña Alena Louisa, from entering any California village for one year."

A chorus of moans swept through the crowd.

"And one year from this date, they must appear before me right here in this plaza." Then he looked at Alena and winked. "Because we will have the biggest and most lavish fandango Alta California has ever known!"

The roar of approval had a deafening effect as the crowd swirled around the four. Don Francisco began to unfasten Echo Jack's chains.

Señora Cabrillo tugged at Alena and Wilson. "You are stealing our joy and our delight, Señor Merced."

"I love her dearly, *suegra*."

Doña María Martina's brown eyes flashed. "You had better." She grabbed Merced's coat collar and yanked his face down next to hers. "Do you see all of these strong, well-armed men?" She waved at the crowd. "I will tell you something. What they could do to you is nothing—nothing!—compared to what I will personally do to you if you ever mistreat *mi dulcita*! Do you understand?"

Merced threw his arms around the older woman and hugged her tight, kissing her on one cheek and then the other.

A startled Señora Cabrillo glanced over at Alena and raised her eyebrows. "He understands," she laughed.

"We should have a wedding dance tonight and celebrate these marriages," Don Francisco announced. "You can leave for Rancho Alázan in the morning."

"Oh, no!" Echo Jack protested. "I am not waiting for María Alejandra's father to finish his nap."

"Echo Jack's right. We will load the bull in the hide cart and leave immediately," Wilson Merced insisted.

"But it will be dark soon. Where will you sleep?" Señora Cabrillo challenged.

"We will sleep on California dirt under God's own gaze," Alena reported. "You have slept under the stars, haven't you?"

Doña María Martina looked at Don Francisco and shook her head. "It has been a very, very long time, *mi conchita*."

It took a frantic, confusing hour to get an angry El Toro Diablo loaded in the cart and both rigs loaded and ready to roll. It was already dark when a couple dozen people crowded alongside El Camino Reál next to the peach orchard, holding lanterns and waiting to send them off.

Señora Cabrillo hugged Alena and kissed her lightly on the lips. "My heart will be broken until next year, Doña Alena."

"And mine will be very full," Alena assured her.

"Yes, yes . . . well, I do envy you in one way."

"How is that?"

"Being newlyweds and having no in-laws. That is as close to heaven as one gets."

"California is as close to heaven as one gets," Alena laughed.

"*Sí, sí, es verdad, es verdad*." Doña María Martina pulled back. "But you will be dwelling on the very edge of heaven."

"I look forward to living in the shadow of the Sierra Nevadas," Alena admitted.

"When you are that remote, you are living in the shadow of death, *conchita*."

"In the shadow of what?"

"In the shadow of death. Oh, I didn't mean to frighten you."

A smile broke across Alena's face. "That's the most wonderful thing I've ever heard!"

Señora Cabrillo tugged on Wilson Merced's arm. "She is so bewildered she does not know what she is saying."

"No, no," Alena protested. "Just this moment it is clear to me. It's the fulfillment of my verse. 'To give light to them that sit in darkness and in the shadow of death.'"

Doña María Martina shook her head and smiled. "Now you are sounding like a *padre*."

"Good."

Alena settled onto the hard wooden bench seat on the lead cart and watched as Wilson swung up next to her.

Don Fernando and Don Ronaldo rode their tall black horses up beside them.

"Are you sure you don't need us to escort you to Paso Pacheco?" Don Fernando asked.

"I appreciate the offer, but we will get along all right," Wilson replied.

"Well, in that case . . . *adios*, La Paloma Roja." Don Ronaldo tipped his hat. "We are on our way to San José."

"Oh?" Alena laughed. "What's her name?"

"Doña Alena! How could you imagine we could think of someone other than you?"

"You didn't answer my question."

"Her name is Doña María Paula Escríbar y Montana from San Diego," Don Fernando admitted.

"And she also has a beautiful younger sister who has been away at school in *Ciudad* Mexico," Don Ronaldo added.

"Well, that does sound promising. Will there be a big fandango?" Alena asked.

"Most certainly." Don Ronaldo grinned.

As the Cabrillo brothers rode off into the darkness, Doña María Martina approached the cart. "Señor Merced, you must promise to bring *mi dulcita* home next summer."

"You have my word, Mama."

"I will be anxious to see the baby."

"Baby?" Alena blushed. "We don't know if . . . We haven't talked . . . It might not . . ."

"Hah! This is California! I know better. There will be a baby." Señora Cabrillo stepped back and blew a kiss from her ring-covered hand. "Perhaps it will be a girl. Martina is a very lovely name, don't you think?"

Look for Book Two in the

Old California Series

by Stephen Bly

THE LAST SWAN
IN SACRAMENTO

Follow the struggles of Martina Merced
as she battles the business barons
of Sacramento in 1865.

For a list of other books by
Stephen Bly
or information
regarding speaking engagements
write:

Stephen Bly
Winchester, Idaho 83555